Also, by Michael Brawn.
Pangur Ban
Flaming Margarita
Wollemi
Wollemi Dreaming
Killara

TENSE

MICHAEL BRAWN

Published 2019

First Printing 2019

Second Edition - Updated and Re-Printed 2023

ISBN-13: 978-0-6480912-2-6

Published by Ashbourne Publishing

ashbourne.publishing1@gmail.com

DEDICATION

This book is dedicated to my lovely wife, soulmate, partner and guide, and editor and chief critic, Louise. It is also committed to the memory of my dear friend Jake – who would have hated and refused to read it. Louise read every page, provided 'feedback' and supported me throughout the writing of this book.

I must also thank all those who read and commented upon the book as it appeared in tiny, impromptu, serialised snippets on Facebook. This book was only completed with your supportive comments and advice.

INTRODUCTION

The writing of this book was triggered by the frustration I felt at not being able to talk about the essential things in life with a dear friend who was suffering. He simply could not do it. When I did broach the topic, his response was, "Sounds like self-indulgent bollocks". He once asked me, "What does it profit me to discuss this stuff?" This book is my attempt at a response.

It's a love story about a confused, tentative bloke who finally meets someone. The story was written from what I thought of as an Abrahamic point of view rather than a Christian or other specifically religious point of view. It should not be confused with commentary on any religion or denomination.

CHAPTER 1 – DAY 1, THE SUPERMARKET

"I'm sorry, but you are simply wrong."

Tense gazed at the two disconsolate young people staring back at him. "The Bible was not written by God but by at least forty different people over a thousand-year period from the Eighth Century BC to the Third Century AD."

"But Moses…"

"Their names are even recorded in the Bible itself."

"But…"

Tense was having none of it.

"Moses, Ezra, Nehemiah, David, Asaph, Solomon, Isiah, Jeremiah, Daniel, Amos, Jonah, and on and on." Names memorised during many dreary years of Sunday School spewed from his mouth.

"Can we leave you a pamphlet?" Tense, in full spate, rattled on.

"I'm sorry. I don't mean to be rude, but there is absolutely no evidence whatsoever that God exists. And if He did, He'd have a lot to answer for."

This was, in fact, pure bravado on Tense's part. Being a logical, analytical, engineering type, he had to admit, if only to himself, that he didn't really know either way. He had no idea. And anyway, what would evidence of the existence of God, other than His manifest presence, actually look like?

"You have no proof that He doesn't, though, do you?"

Tense took the pamphlet and closed the door. The whole affair had left him in a thoroughly bad mood.

Now, standing in line, waiting for the next available self-checkout, Tense was philosophising again.

Nothing in my life up to this moment has given me any reason to believe I will ever find God, or happiness. Or purpose. Or meaning.

How very wrong he was, but for the moment, Tense fumed.

I'm trapped between an unchanging past, where the dead live and a chaotic future where the unborn wait and all I really want is to pay for two kilos of best mince and go home.

This kind of anxiety he experienced daily as he Macheted his way through the torment of life.

I'm like a ping-pong ball suspended upon a tiny column of air blown through a straw by a small, asthmatic child.

Tense wrestled second by second with the certainty that any moment might be his last.

How long can I expect one small asthmatic child to continue to blow? What is the maximum duration possible, even under the most auspicious circumstances?

Whatever it might be, things didn't look good. It, therefore, came as something of a surprise for him to encounter, as he did, on the morning of New Year's Eve, the woman who smiled sunshine.

There's no other word for it. Her face at rest was perfectly pleasant and symmetrical, with all the right bits in reasonable proportions. Her eyes were a piercing aquamarine, and if her face were at rest, that would be her most notable feature. But when she smiled, the clouds pulled back, and against an acetylene blue sky, she smiled pure sunshine. Warm, radiant, and instantly beguiling. She exuded an existential joy that could, or might if he would let it, soften our Tense's angst, and allow in at least the possibility of better times to come. Here finally, was a metaphorical Ventolin, a balm for the constricted bronchia of our allegorical asthmatic child.

Will I speak to her? Will I summon up the courage? Or will I let the moment pass? Will it slip instantaneously and irretrievably into the domain of the dead and moulder through all eternity alongside every other missed opportunity?

Tense was having yet another existential crisis. But credit where credit is due. Having an existential crisis was, for Tense, something of a party piece. He could spin up a reasonably poetic private solioquy at a moment's notice. In summary, Tense brooded.

Are my forbears at this very moment seated in the sombre halls of Valhalla, slapping their foreheads in disbelief, stamping their feet in frustration, and muttering 'Gutless fool' into embarrassed silence?

***

We all have our 'Sliding Doors' moments. Whether planned well in advance or apparently random, we can all point to pivotal moments in our lives when we went left when we should have gone right, when we hesitated when we should have jumped in, or, alternatively, when we jumped in with both feet when we should, most definitely, have hesitated – in retrospect.

For our hero, the next few minutes, pregnant to bursting with possibility, promised to trigger either a helter-skelter roller-coaster ride into an unknown future or a timid, inglorious retreat into morose introspection and self-hatred. Which was it to be?

For those given to the optimistic and wholly implausible paradigm of free will, driven by chance and the accidental emergence of pattern within our otherwise plainly haphazard lives, the outcome was up to him. On the other hand, for those intellectually and emotionally drawn to the equally unlikely notion that free will is an illusion and that everything, down to the tiniest detail, the tiniest possible instant, is preordained and inevitable; the die had already been cast. Our hero would be propelled to his doom like the proverbial lamb to its inevitable slaughter.

He could choose or not. Either way, his future, whether destined or fortuitous, would emerge. And emerge it most certainly did.

Transfixed by the solace of her smile, our man hesitated, just for a moment. But a moment was all the woman needed, oblivious to the impact she had inadvertently had upon the hapless fellow, to march smartly from the crowded supermarket.

Once again, as had happened so many times in the past, he was faced with the conundrum of choice. Yet again, this tiny speck of humanity must, in the face of what he suspected was an implacable or, at the very least, an indolent universe, wrestle the future into a configuration of his own choosing. We can all appreciate, I think, what an immense, potentially overwhelming task that would be.

The two kilos of best-minced beef, which he had snapped up as it was on special, adamantly refused to register at the self-service checkout. Within seconds a breezy and efficient-looking young woman appeared silently at his side, brandishing an electronic pass key and demanding to know if he needed any help. He said not, but the self-service checkout supervisor, for that is what her name badge proclaimed her to be, blithely ignoring his claim, swiped her pass against the till and keyed in the appropriate price.

She smiled sweetly and walked away. *Bitch*, he thought to himself, entirely without justification.

The woman with the smile was still visible through the glass walls of the supermarket. She was just standing there, flexing her arms in the early morning sunshine and wriggling her fingers like a child, as though this was the first morning ever, and her newly discovered fingers were a mystery of uncertain purpose and utility. From her demeanour, she seemed uncertain or at least undecided. Sitting next to her, exuding the apparent indifference of a stroppy teenager, sat a somewhat battered, evidently much loved, medium-sized brown suitcase.

Into his vacuum of indecision rushed a familiar, if not entirely welcome, vortex of morose introspection and self-hatred.

There is a certain comfort to be had in familiarity. Tense mused. *There is something to be said for the known, even a dreary known, when set against a potentially malevolent uncertainty.*

Our guy was not a great risk-taker. He was not at all the sort to make a heap of all his winnings.

Maybe it's better this way.

He began to slump into his habitual slough of despond. And would have continued to do so but for the fateful, or entirely accidental, intervention of an harassed middle-aged woman accompanied by altogether too many children. Into the backs of his ankles, with a sickening crunch, crashed her fully laden shopping trolley. Left unattended for the briefest moment while a snotty nose was wiped with a grubby tissue, the trolley, perhaps sensing its freedom, picked up momentum as it careened down the slight incline in the direction of our emotionally imploding hero. The pain was immediate and excruciating.

"Fucking shit." Tense was unable to suppress either the expletive or the venomous look he gave the harassed-looking middle-aged woman.

A pristine fight-or-flight response, hardly used since childhood, snapped him into a sudden, savage rage. Unable through long avoidance to vent his wrath upon another human being, the roiling mushroom cloud of his anger and righteous indignation poured outwards and away, finding at last its target in the miserable, wretched universe that had hounded him for as long as he could remember. Enough was enough. The world could bend to his will or break. Its call.

Only one person saw the agonised look on his face as he made his decision. Only one person noticed as he drew himself up to his full height, squared his shoulders and marched out into the supermarket car park. The trolley woman's older daughter, who had backed away at the very first sighting of the grubby tissue, and who takes no further part in this tale, watched him go.

Within a few steps, he caught up with the woman. She was still standing in the car park holding her small old-fashioned suitcase.

"Excuse me." Tense was both delighted and surprised that his voice sounded firm and confident even in his own ears. The woman turned.

"You have a lovely smile." Tense waited. The woman stared at the sky.

He has nice eyes, the vagrant thought detached itself from her otherwise unoccupied mind and floated away to be joined a moment later by, *and he looks kind*.

"Actually, lovely doesn't quite do it justice. I don't know if you are aware of it, but when you smile, your whole face lights up."

Sally considered Tense's comment. *He is rather handsome, in an understated sort of way*. A second or two ticked away.

I wonder why he is talking to me. The moment was, had she but known it, a sliding doors moment for her too.

"It's like sunshine." He trailed off. The woman responded.

"Thank you. That's a lovely compliment." There was a pause before she continued.

"My name's Sally."

"Tense, everyone calls me that. It's a nickname."

The woman smiled. Our hero blushed beetroot.

"Tense", she rolled the sound over in her mind for a moment, "pleased to meet you."

***

As Tense began again to speak, a plane flew overhead. It seemed lower than usual, deafeningly loud. He stopped speaking, waiting for the ill-timed intrusion to end.

He and the woman with the sunshine smile stood silently, staring at each other for a few moments as the huge Aircraft wallowed slowly towards its nearby destination.

"It's the ten o'clock from Dubai." Tense shuffled his feat uncomfortably, bravura fading fast.

"Is it?"

"Yes." Tense was a gentleman of exceptional self-knowledge and had, as his psychotherapist was always so very keen to remind him, "a very rich inner life". Consequently, Tense realised that, like a clay pigeon at the very end of its trajectory, about to fall humiliatingly from the sky. Unless he acted with unaccustomed speed and resolution, he was about to crash and burn. He gave it another go.

"I wonder..." As he began to speak again, the less fleet of foot, but now gloriously snot-free, younger child of the trolley woman careened into his leg. Having in the past relied solely upon purely ontological proofs either of a malevolent universe or a capricious God, here at last, clumsy, snot-free child in combination with sudden appearance of a low-flying aircraft, careening trolley, etc., was clear-cut epistemological proof. Whatever, it was enough to precipitate him once more into action.

"The universe is out to get me."

"Really?"

"Yes."

"That must be disconcerting."

"It is." Here, once again, the conversation faltered and would have stuttered into silence, and utter failure had not the young woman offered her opinion.

"I don't believe in a malicious universe."

Tense was flummoxed. Had she not just witnessed the Machiavellian workings of the substrate of our shared hologram? Or, to put it another way, was she mad? Intrigued by the possibility that there might be someone even more deluded than himself, Tense decided to investigate.

"Is it that you don't believe there is a God or other purpose driving the universe, or that you believe that God is not malicious?"

"Oh, it's not a matter of belief. I know there is a God, and I know that God is good."

Tense, subjected without warning to an animalistic fight-flight response for the second time in so many minutes, stifled the almost overwhelming desire to turn on his heel and run.

W.T.F? he thought.

"You're quite right", the woman smiled, bathing Tense in warm, comforting sunshine and a general sense of well-being, "I should have said. I'm an angel."

"You're an angel?"

"Yes." Sally, the angel, continued to smile. Calm and quite unabashed, she gazed around the busy car park. Tense, as so often before, found himself in uncharted territory. She was gorgeous, no doubt about that, and he was already besotted. So what, if she was mad as cut snakes? He could see the advantage of having an angel in his life.

"Well, what brings you to Earth?"

"I'm on my holidays."

"You're on holiday?"

"Yes."

"On Earth?"

"Yes."

"Where are you on holiday from?"

"Heaven, of course."

"My reading of the scriptures has been regrettably sketchy, but why would anyone leave Heaven to holiday on Earth?"

"Well, there are only two possible destinations, from Heaven, I mean, from my point of view, and Earth is the better of the two."

"Ah, yes, I take your point."

"Besides," Sally smiled again with renewed vigour. Tense almost passed out.

"It's nice sometimes to do a bit of fieldwork."

Tense was momentarily lost for words. The morning was getting on, and he was hungry. The inconveniences of embodiment came to his rescue.

"Coffee?" he ventured.

"Sounds wonderful, with salmon and cream cheese bagels?"

"But of course."

"And bacon and eggs?"

"Ok"

"And fresh fruit salad with double cream and vanilla bean ice cream?"

"Well, let's see what they have."

Sally burst out laughing and took his arm, "Only joking." He *was* rather nice, she decided, and she could do with a friend.

As the young couple walked slowly, side by side, in the direction of a nearby café, Tense found himself musing on the events of the morning. He'd fallen in love, sustained a no doubt permanent injury to his Achilles' tendons, met an immortal, spiritual being and messenger of God, successfully chatted her up in a supermarket car park and invited her for coffee. Against all experience and his better nature, Tense found himself conceding things were looking up.

They walked in silence, side by side. To Tense, the short walk to the café seemed to stretch and extend to match their pace. Each step appeared to leave the haven of the café neither nearer nor further away.

He began to think. His mind, left as it were to its own devices, raced. This was bad. This was potentially disastrous. A mind such as Tense's should never, ever, under any circumstances, be left to follow its own path.

What, he wondered, *if she were a serial killer?* Tense knew from his extensive study of all things serial-killerish that female serial killers were extremely rare, practically unheard of. Men made the best psychopaths, always had, and always would. That was common knowledge. *Oh God*, he wondered, *am I being sexist? Am I displaying typical male chauvinism by laying claim to masculine supremacy when it comes to the sociopathic arts?* The whole thing was turning into a whirling vortex of politico-sexual confusion. It was all too much. Faced with the imponderable, implausible, indissoluble knot of self-doubt that threatened to swamp him completely, his mind simply stopped, paused for an instant, and then reset. Only to be attacked immediately and without mercy by yet another misgiving.

What if, contrary to all evidence, reason and the laws of nature, she actually was an angel? What then? Could a relationship, a, you-

know, boy-girl type thingummy-jig, could such a thing be possible? What would it be like, he wondered, in bed with an angel? What were the proprieties? No doubt there would be some kind of heavenly etiquette of which he knew nothing. There was bound to be an angelic sex protocol that he would be quite unable to understand, let alone follow. The whole thing was doomed. Either the woman with the sunshine smile was a serial killer or a sexually unobtainable angel. This must, he thought, be the worst day of my life.

Fortunately, while distracted by these primal fears and generally otherwise engaged, the pair had managed to reach the café. It was open. There was an empty table. They sat down. A waitress approached. Tense pulled himself together. In a fit of what he hoped would come across as proactive gallantry, Tense began to speak.

"We'd like two flat-white coffees, please. One smoked salmon and cream cheese bagel, and bacon and eggs for two." Across the small Formica topped table, Sally the angel smiled.

"Haven't you forgotten something?"

Tense was thrown immediately and without a moment's notice once more into a state of total confusion. On the one hand, he was buoyed, swept away, and captivated by the supernatural smile. On the other, cast into the nethermost pit of uncertainty.

"Forgotten something?" Tense wracked his mind, desperately searching his memory for any hint of the missing item.

"Fresh fruit salad with double cream and vanilla bean ice cream." Sally smiled. Tense, momentarily entranced, was, of course, quite unable to speak.

"Will that be all?" The waitress smiled at Sally. Tense imagined that some feminine or perhaps Divine understanding had passed instantaneously between the two women.

"I thought you were joking! You'll never eat all that." Immediately regretting his outburst, Tense blushed the deep purple of a Queen Garnet plum.

"Never doubt the powers of an angel", Sally was suddenly serious, almost sombre.

"But if you're good, I might let you have some of my ice cream."

A vagrant thought scudded, carefree across the surface of Tense's mind.

"Do you have wings?" he asked, craning to one side in the hope of a glimpse.

Sally sat, quietly observing her surroundings, centring herself in the here and now. This youngish man, Tense, really was quite handsome. He was kind, and he had nice eyes. Not a bad start.

***

N-dimensional isotropic phase space. Apparently, that was the explanation. Sally, it transpired, did indeed have wings. Wings which she kept tucked neatly away in n-dimensional isotropic phase space. At least this was what she told him, and he was really in no position to challenge her on it.

Tense wondered vaguely if he, too, could get hold of a pair of gossamer n-dimensional wings. He would grow into them, he felt certain. If, as must certainly be the case given the evidence to date, his personal existence preceded the development and evolution of his essence as a human being, then perhaps a pair of winglike extensions awaited him, out there, somehow, somewhere. There must surely be at least one future in which he and Sally fly off into the sunset?

While Tense pondered these weighty questions, Sally stuffed her face. Smoked salmon and cream cheese bagel wolfed down with a giant slurp of near-boiling coffee, were followed with gusto by loud munching on bacon and eggs. Sally paused occasionally, only to gasp for air. Slowly the café fell silent as fellow diners, at first merely baffled and then increasingly appalled, watched the display.

After what seemed like hours, Sally looked up. Tiny dribbles of egg yolk were making their way sluggishly down her chin to drip, pendulous and proud, into the otherwise enticing cleft of her bosom. Tense, having noticed the atmosphere of rapt attention gripping the room, and ever the gentleman, leaned forward, a crisp, new paper tissue in his hand.

To Sally's evident surprise, her new male acquaintance began to dab gently at her chin, removing one by one the offending rivulets of congealing egg yolk. The process was slow, considered. For some reason, Tense felt no sense of urgency.

It was a very gentle and very paternal gesture. Sally rather liked it. Somehow, suddenly, and for that moment only, their roles were reversed. Tense playing the part of mature, confident adult, while the immortal, and one would hope, finally satiated angel-woman, messenger of God no less, sat quiet. Her face was returned to the pristine state of nature.

As one, the focus and attention of every man, woman and child in the café turned to Sally's prominent bust. A hushed silence fell across what we must now describe as her audience. Would he, or wouldn't he?

Tense retrieved another tissue from the box on the Formica table and paused. You could have heard a pin drop. Slowly Sally glanced down, noticing for the first time the streaks of yellow goo coalescing in the confluence of her upper torso.

She looked up. Their eyes met. Sally observed the tissue in Tense's hand and fixed Tense with a look honed by women through all the ages of mankind. A look which, through frequent use, had become genetically implanted in the mitochondrial line. A look that said, "Don't move a fucking muscle. Do not so much as twitch, or I shall smite thee as thou hast n'er before been smitten". Or something.

Tense complied. Sally reached forward and, with deliberate precision, retrieved the tissue from Tense's outstretched hand. Swiftly and with movements of such agility and deftness as to call into question

Sally's regular eating habits, she removed the offending liquor. The assembled diners, as one, began to breathe again.

It was, of course, at this moment that the waitress reappeared.

"Fresh fruit salad with double cream and vanilla bean ice cream." She placed the bowl on the table and flounced off. The groan produced by a café-full of diners driven way beyond their comfort zone by a very hungry angel hung in the air like a stultifying smog. Tense, as was his habit at these times, took refuge in his own inner world of self-doubt, guilt and occasional shame.

If he thought, *man exists, and if in the process of existence, man defines himself and the world through his own thoughts, and if he wanders lonely as a cloud between choice, freedom, and existential angst. Then surely, somehow, this is all my fault.*

Sally glanced up briefly from her dessert, let out a powerful, reverberating, extended belch, paused for a moment and then set once again to work.

Sally looked up a moment or two later, dabbed the corners of her mouth delicately with a clean white tissue, and smiled.

"Hungry, were you?"

"Starved."

"Been a while since your last meal, has it?"

Sally paused, calculating, "About a thousand years, I think. What year is it?"

Tense was not sure how to respond. If Sally was having a little joke, then she certainly was persistent.

He tried another tack, "So what kind of fieldwork are you planning here on Earth?"

"Oh, I'm just here to replenish my grief."

"Your grief?"

"Yes."

"It needs replenishing?"

"Yes."

"And why is that?", Tense felt his consciousness shifting kind of sideways in an attempt to accommodate Sally's peculiar worldview.

"One can become a tad blasé."

"Really?"

"Yes", Sally paused and, for the very first time, frowned slightly.

"Being disembodied, you see."

Tense shook his head slowly. He didn't see. He most certainly did not. He was, finally, and perhaps a little late in the day, beginning to suspect that he'd picked up a nutcase.

"No bodies, you see."

Tense stared blankly at the exquisite object of his desire. Of one thing, he was totally convinced. She had a body, all right.

"In Heaven. We don't have physical bodies in Heaven."

"No. I suppose not."

"And after a while, one begins to forget what it's like."

"Having a body?"

"Yes."

"I see."

Sally and Tense sat staring at each other, separated by a growing gulf of understanding and a thousand years of hunger.

"Humans are embodied, you see." Sally leaned forward, suddenly intense, "It's the human condition."

"Embodiment?"

"Yes."

Tense paused for a moment, mulling over what he had heard. He had always, at least for as far back as he could remember, considered life, embodiment, indeed making sense of anything, to be a kind of desperate compromise between the embarrassing vagaries of the physical body, the bewildering misconceptions of the mind and a desperate attempt on some spiritual level to discover or impose meaning and significance upon an otherwise listless and disinterested universe. To be fair, he could see that after a thousand years without a physical body, a slap-up feed might be in order.

"What were you doing in the supermarket?"

"Shopping."

There seemed to be nowhere to go from that. So, Tense sat silent, wondering what revelation the next moment would bring. He was not disappointed.

"Humans have bodies for a reason, you know?" Sally reached for the menu as she spoke, "There is a purpose to containing the spirit in flesh." Sally paused, observing Tense carefully, weighing things up. She appeared to come to her decision.

"It's a bit like sonnets or haiku".

"I see." but Tense did not. He had no idea what this crazy, gorgeous woman was on about.

"Setting limits forces creativity."

"It does?"

"It does. Definitely. You see, being forced to write a sonnet within the rules of sonnet writing, or a haiku within the rules of haiku writing creates the boundaries within which creativity can flourish."

"I see", and he did, sort of.

"That's the thing about embodiment," Sally checked that Tense was following before continuing, "embodiment imposes severe limitations on the human spirit, providing the opportunity for transcendence of oneself and of self-detachment."

This was all getting a bit much. It was about to get worse.

"Humans live in four dimensions but have freedom of movement only in three, whereas angels live in five dimensions but have freedom of movement in four. That's the main difference, really. Oh, and immortality, of course. That makes a difference."

"What about God?"

"God?"

"Yes, how many dimensions does he get to swan around in?"

"Don't be cheeky!" Sally gave Tense a very old-fashioned look.

"Sorry."

"The Creator gets to do whatever he, she or it wants."

"It's all right for some."

"Well, when you create your own universe, you can make the rules. Until then, accept your limitations."

Sally turned her attention once more to the menu. It was going to be a long day. By the time they stood up to leave the café, the table was covered with plates, bowls, empty mugs and other paraphernalia. Tense pulled out his wallet, bleakly surveying the detritus of Sally's little snack and hoping against hope that he could cover it.

"My shout", Sally piped up, pulling out an enormous wodge of bank notes. She peeled off a few and placed them on the table.

"Keep the change", she announced, waving an arm airily towards the waitress who was waiting by the till.

"You're not short of a bob or two, then." Tense observed, eyeing the bundle with disbelief.

"A girl needs to pay her own way" Sally gave him another one of her smiles. Tense imploded.

"Otherwise, gentlemen, expect things." Sally's look combined wide-eyed innocence with something entirely else. *I do rather like him,* she confessed to herself. Fond imaginings skittered playfully for a moment across the backdrop of her mind.

Tense collapsed back onto a chair with a whoosh of suddenly expelled breath. He just sat there looking befuddled.

"Shall we go?" Sally indicated the direction of the door vaguely with one finger.

Tense struggled to his feet and puffed uncertainly out of the café and into the busy street.

"We are here to bear witness," Sally was off again, "to experience everything that can be experienced and to bring that experience home bit by bit until all experience is complete."

Somewhere, in the back of his mind, Tense fancied he could hear the sound of an asthmatic child blowing weakly through a straw. In his mind's eye, he could see himself rotating slowly like a table tennis ball on a faltering column of air. At this rate, the thought returned once more. Any moment could be his last.

Looking down, he noticed he was still carrying a plastic bag containing two kilos of best-minced beef.

"Better get this into the fridge before it goes off."

Sally took his arm.

"Lead on MacDuff", Sally was gazing around at the busy scene, taking everything in. Tense sighed. Even angels, it seemed, could be relied upon to misquote Shakespeare. Was nothing sacred?

Tense attempted a little light banter, "So, you're here on holiday, looking to replenish your grief?"

"That's right."

"You sure know how to have a good time."

Sally the angel pursed her lips, "It's no laughing matter. I am a Grieving Angel, after all."

"Angels come in types, then?"

"Well, of course, it takes all sorts, you know, and I'm the grieving variety."

"What's your job then, your role – in Heaven, I mean?"

Sally treated Tense to a look of weary disdain, "Well, to grieve, of course. It's in the name."

Tense had to admit there was an obdurate sort of logic to what Sally was saying.

"Ok, I get that your job is to grieve, but why is grief necessary in Heaven? I thought everyone was supposed to be blissful?"

"I grieve for you, feckless, idiotic humans. You have all but dismantled the gift of life." Sally paused, smoothing the fabric of her dress with the palms of her hands, "Only one can become a mite nonchalant. Over time I mean, over the centuries."

"Yes, but why? Why do you grieve?"

"Isn't it obvious? You, people, are pretty messed up, aren't you? I mean, with respect. With the best will in the world, sort of thing. You are a giant catastrophe of a species."

"But God made us this way! It's a bit bloody rich to blame it on us, isn't it?"

"It's all about attitude. It's like that lovely German man said…."

"Who? Victor Frankl?"

"No, Karl Marx. He was a bit bloody sheepish when he showed up, I can tell you."

"Karl Marx is in Heaven?"

"Yep. And he's still getting over it." Sally allowed herself a brief snigger.

"Shouldn't snigger. It's unbecoming."

"Well, what did he say then, Karl Marx?"

"He said, 'Men make their own history, but they do not make it as they please; they do not make it under self-selected circumstances, but under circumstances existing already, given and transmitted from the past'".

Tense was getting a little bit lost in all this esoteric stuff, which was in itself something of a surprise as he could usually be relied upon to wade into it up to his neck.

"What's that got to do with attitude?"

"Nothing really, you're quite right."

"Quite right about what?"

"It was Victor Frankl. The attitude thing," Sally grinned broadly.

"You're taking the piss, aren't you."

"Yes." she sniggered again, then stopped abruptly, covering her mouth delicately with one hand.

Sally continued. "He said, "Everything can be taken from a man but one thing: the last of the human freedoms—to choose one's attitude in any given set of circumstances, to choose one's own way."

"I'm not so sure about that" Tense, paused, deep in thought, absentmindedly scratching his balls through his trousers, "I tend to go with his other saying, 'Don't aim at success. The more you aim at it and make it a target, the more you are going to miss it'."

As the pair approached the stairs leading to Tense's unit, he made one last attempt.

"What is the actual purpose of grief in Heaven?" he asked.

"Oh", for a moment, Sally seemed a little nonplussed herself, "Well, to add tone, I guess."

They walked on for a few more paces in silence.

Sally spoke again, "Grief is contrapuntal."

CHAPTER 2– TENSE'S FLAT

"It's up three flights, I'm afraid."

Sally made no comment as the pair made their way up the concrete stairs to Tense's third-floor apartment.

"You'll have to excuse the mess", Tense looked, well, tense, as he tried the key in the lock. He found himself stuck between, on the one hand, the potential mortification he would experience if the key no longer fitted the lock and, on the other, the embarrassment and shame he would feel when, within the next few seconds, Sally would be exposed to the calamity that was Tense's apartment.

Tense struggled with the lock, which, in Tense's view, had chosen that moment to demonstrate the sardonic phenomenology of inanimate things. Could be worse, Tense conceded to himself. It could be an example of how events on the micro, quantum level, show up in the macro world, a gift from the quantum vacuum maybe. Perhaps the state of the lock had been spread, probabilistically along a continuum from 'working fine' to 'irretrievably buggered', and the waveform thus created had only just collapsed into a state of being 'irretrievably buggered' the instant he entered the key into the lock. In the latter case, it was, arguably, once again his fault. Typical.

Tense heard Sally shift her weight behind him. Perhaps she was impatient. It was all going to go horribly wrong. He could just sense it.

"You'll think I'm some kind of weirdo." Tense immediately wished that he had kept his big mouth shut. "I'm not, though. A weirdo, I mean."

"Is the key stuck?"

"Yes. It just won't budge." Tense gave it one last despairing twist, simultaneously throwing his weight against the wood. The door immediately flew open, and Tense fell into the darkened hallway. His plastic bag of best mince skittering a metre or two down the passage.

"Upsidaisy" Tense struggled to his feet, brushing his hands together as he did so, stooping once again to pick up the shopping bag. He switched on the hallway light, which flickered twice before treating the pair to a bilious greenish glare.

Upsi-fucking-daisy, he chided himself, *what on Earth was I thinking?*

Tense led the way down the hall and into the kitchen. He opened the fridge door and placed the plastic bag alone on a shelf. Sally took a look around. The place was immaculate. There was no washing up in the sink. Everything was put away nicely. The floor had recently been swept or vacuumed. Tense followed her gaze, relief slowly flooding his sensorium as realisation set in that all was not lost. Not yet, at least.

They walked through into the sitting room. It was dark. The curtains were drawn.

"I left early this morning," Tense explained, "it wasn't yet light."

Sally wandered over to the window and threw open the curtains, allowing dazzling sunlight to flood in.

The small sitting room was neatly and simply furnished. There was an old but serviceable brown leather sofa, a large, old-fashioned flat-screen TV on a stand, a coffee table, and over to one side, a small round dining table with four matching chairs. Polished floorboards and a couple of pleasant rugs finished it off. There was a door to one side of the large window, which led out onto a broad and generous balcony.

Sally tried the door, which opened immediately. She wandered out onto the balcony to take in the view.

"Oh, Wow! What a stunning outlook!"

Tense joined Sally on the balcony and stood for a few moments gazing out. Down below was a small green park leading to a neat little promenade and a narrow sandy beach. Beyond the beach was a broad blue bay filled with little sailing boats and runabouts, bobbing at anchor, and beyond that, Sydney Harbour.

A rickety table on the balcony was accompanied by two old but nevertheless willing rattan armchairs. Tense was momentarily engulfed by the overwhelming sorrow genetically programmed into any and all of Anglo-Irish descent by the sight of a forgotten cup of tea. For there, on the table, quite alone, stood a stone-cold mug of tea, neglected since the morning.

No one could be expected to understand his pain. Tense knew this and accepted it as one must the staggering tsunami of agony accompanying, a moment later, the savage stubbing of a toe.

Bravely but without hope, he lifted the body of the deceased beverage, wandered disconsolate into the apartment and poured it down the sink. There was a weary air of finality to the gesture, one oft-repeated and never welcome.

"I know", Sally was still out on the balcony, taking in the view of Sydney Harbour, "let's go for a swim."

Tense didn't swim, ever. It was not that he couldn't. He just didn't. It had become a point of principle, the origin or even purpose of which was long forgotten. He didn't wear shorts either, for that matter, quite possibly for the same long-forgotten reason. Tense did, however, possess a pair of bright red swimming shorts, again, as a matter of principle, this time remembered.

He was not going to allow himself to become a servant of fate. His life would be constructed and made meaningful by his own choices. Owning-but-never-using a pair of bathers afforded him, in his view heroically, to forge his own destiny in the very teeth of a macabre and implausible universe. Not swimming because one did not own any swimming trunks would have made him the grovelling slave of doom.

Explaining all this seemed to Tense to require a level of patience in his audience that he suspected even an angel would be hard-pressed to evidence.

"Great idea." Tense wondered where, now he came to think about it, he would find said swimming trunks.

"I've got my cozzie on under my clothes", Sally called out.

"Of course, you have", Tense felt himself tending once more to the morose and tried to snap out of it.

"I've got mine around here somewhere?" On a hunch, he pulled open the cupboard under the sink where anything that might one day be useful, but was unlikely ever actually to be used, seemed to find its way. Immediately, as though they had been awaiting this moment to make their escape, a small tidal wave of crumpled grey shopping bags exploded across the kitchen floor. Bending and reaching in, Tense was delighted to see the vagrant red shorts hanging jauntily over the white plastic 'S' bend under the sink.

Quickly he grabbed them and headed to the bathroom to change, emerging a few moments later, looking somewhat like a plucked chicken wearing crimson shorts. He had an immaculate white towel over his shoulder and another over his arm.

"Sorry, I don't have any proper beach towels."

Sally grinned. This guy really was rather nice in a quirky, twitchy sort of way. She was definitely growing to like him.

This time Tense held his ground in the face of Sally's smile. He was, he realised, learning coping strategies to prevent his constant implosion each and every time she smiled. This time he drove his fingernails into the palms of his hands, an impromptu cilice allowing pain to counteract the overpowering effects on his nervous system of the beaming angel.

Sally, having wandered in from the balcony, had closed the door. She began to disrobe right there in the sitting room of Tense's flat.

"Oh, God. Oh-God-Oh-God-Oh-God!" Tense found himself muttering over and over again under his breath.

"Ah, that'd be right," Tense realised he was blushing a profound carmine. It was all too much. As the smooth skin and curves of Sally's inevitably perfect physical form emerged from what Tense was fast deciding was entirely superfluous human clothing, Tense felt a certain stirring.

The stirring became an agitation, and the agitation became a rousing, bulging, magnificent statement of the power and ferocity of the autonomic nervous system.

Mewling incoherently and bent double, his facial hue having passed through crimson on its way to scarlet, achieving, in the end, an almost most impossible ruby, burgundy tint, Tense raced for the bathroom.

In a moment, the sound of the shower could be heard, accompanied by an uneasy warbling as Tense began to sing.

"Just thought I'd have a quick shower", Tense called out after a minute or two.

Sally sat on the sofa, staring at the closed bathroom door, apparently somewhat nonplussed.

"It was an itsy bitsy teeny-weeny yellow polka-dot bikini" The words went round and round in Tense's head as he showered, the ice-cold water having, at last, the desired effect. Yet still, even after he had emerged from the shower and dried himself on his virginal white towel, he could not bring himself to leave the bathroom.

He was afraid to come out. Had she seen his evident, and even if he said so himself, extravagant enthusiasm? Had she noticed? He thought not. Probably. But one could never be certain.

Perhaps as an angel, she had certain extrasensory capabilities. Perhaps, being at one with the mind of God, she knew everything about him anyway. Every thought he had ever had, every good deed, and every shameful act. Oh Hell! Tense paled at the realisation – perhaps she could read his mind. Perhaps she was doing so at this very moment.

"What on earth are you doing in there?" Sally sounded baffled and perhaps a little bored, "I thought we were going swimming?"

"Oh, how very clever", Tense thought to himself, *"How exquisitely sneaky!"* How conveniently she had chosen that precise moment to say just the right thing to allay his fears. Well, there was nothing for it in any case but to emerge in the end.

Adopting a bright and breezy air, Tense unlocked the bathroom door and stepped out, busying himself all the while with folding his now somewhat damp and crumpled towel into a perfect rectangle approximately forty centimetres by thirty.

Sally gave him a quizzical look.

"It's just something I picked up in Japan", Tense lied, "I can't bear to bathe without showering first. Silly, I know."

Staring at Tense as though really seeing him for the first time, Sally came to a sort of epiphany. Transcendence was a funny old thing, she realised. All this man, all any human man or woman really wanted, was transcendence. To transcend their physical existence. That was all. Not a lot to ask, really, in the great scheme of things.

A thought occurred to her, oddly esoteric given her usually sunny disposition. Humans experience their three-dimensional existence as sequential change. Their fourth dimension, time, is the thing they experience three-dimensional change in. Their whole sad, sorry little existence is crammed into a mere four dimensions. Sally shuddered. It didn't bear thinking about. And if it didn't bear thinking about, then it certainly didn't bear dwelling on.

Still, Sally dwelled. It was their bodies, of course. That was the problem. No mystery about that. If the foolish creatures would insist on tying their being to a physical substrate, what on Earth could they expect?

Sally watched Tense potter semi-aimlessly about his apartment. He appeared to be collecting things. He had a large stripy bag into which he was stuffing a variety of objects. Watching him like this. Observing him as it were, the tragedy of embodiment struck her anew, with a harshness and a savagery, she had not experienced before.

There was, to Sally, a kind of agony to experiencing with Tense the excruciating, glacial, sequential unfolding of his lifeline. Immersing herself in this unfolding, this life-stream, was purgatory.

How could these poor bastards bear it?

Sally was still meditating upon the appalling torture of experiencing change sequentially, one damn thing after another, plodding gamely from one sodding instant to the next, when Tense announced that he was ready to go.

The pair walked in single file from the apartment, along the corridor that led from his front door and down the three flights of stairs. As they did so, step by step, one foot in front of another, a slow, boiling rage began to grow in Sally's gut.

"How can you stand this bovine existence?" she snapped, throwing Tense a venomous look (which, thankfully, he missed) as though it were somehow his fault.

This was a question that had vexed Tense's quieter moments since he was a child. He was across it completely. There wasn't the tiniest nuance, twist or turn, shade, tone or gradation in this line of thought that he hadn't considered. He was already entirely, indeed intimately, familiar with the whole sorry mess.

Tense smiled. Sally was on his wavelength. Here at long, long, last was a girl after his own heart.

"It's just life", he ventured, "it's just how it is."

Sally's snort of derision caught Tense a little off guard.

"Well, how else could it be?" There was in Tense's tone something of the sad, lost little boy of seven vainly seeking answers to life's mysteries from the pair of hedonistic airheads who brought him up.

Sally knew this, of course. That was the whole problem. Sally could still see the conversation unfolding twenty-something years earlier. There stood the joyous, warm, but hopelessly feckless couple, just arrived home from yet another all-night party. There on the sofa, just beginning to stir into wakefulness, was the babysitter. And there was young Tense, before he was Tense, when he was just Adam, trying without much luck to make sense of it all.

And there, ambling along in front of her, was older Tense, now that he was Tense, none the bloody wiser. It was all too much. She'd be having words with someone when she got back.

As they ventured outside, the day was warm, the sun was shining, a gentle breeze caressed their skin, and a flight of gorgeous rainbow lorikeets flew skittishly through the stand of palm trees that skirted the water's edge.

Tense plonked the bag down on the narrow beach and laid out a large blanket across the sand. The sun was directly overhead, so Tense set up a very old and seldom-used beach umbrella. He couldn't get it to stand property, and after a few attempts, he left it at what he hoped would pass for a jaunty angle and sat down.

He stared at the tiny waves lapping the shore. Sally sat down next to him, very close. He could feel the shimmering warmth of her body a few centimetres away. He could feel her presence. He was in love. He knew it. There was nothing he could do. There never had been anything he could do. It was going to be bad.

"Live in the moment. That's my motto." Tense turned and smiled at Sally. Their faces close under the shelter of the umbrella. He could feel the gentle warmth of her breath on his cheek.

"Isn't that just making a virtue of necessity?" Sally attempted to stifle the waspish tone in her voice.

There was a moment of silence. Then Sally reached out and gently took his hand. That *was* life, she realised, for human beings. Given his existence was something of a fait accompli, she had to admit he was handling it quite well. Probably better than she would under the same circumstances.

Tense stared down at his hand. Hardly daring to move, hardly daring to breathe. Sally shifted a tiny bit closer and laid her head on his shoulder. It was nice, she thought, this physical closeness. It was comforting.

"Moo!" Sally imagined the bovine life ahead of her. Tense swivelled, confused, staring at her lovely face.

"Moo! Moo! Moo!" And then, moved to sadness and compassion for this brave ordinary man, she leant forward and kissed him briefly on the lips.

***

What was that? That kiss? It was nothing. It was something. It was everything.

Tense sat, staring down at his hand in hers. Unwilling to move. Not daring to move in case he broke the spell. Willing the moment to continue forever.

"If I could freeze time in this instant", Tense mumbled, more to himself than anyone, "I would gladly sit here, on this beach, with your hand in mine, forever."

Sally smiled, "You are silly. You will. That's the way it works. This moment exists, has existed and will exist for all time."

"That's good." Tense's imagination failed fully to encompass the scope of what he had just been told, "That's very good. That makes me feel better."

"Last one in's a billy goat!" Sally rose swiftly to her feet and made a dash for the water only a few metres away.

Tense, galvanised into action by the heinous threat of being likened to a billy goat, leapt to his feet too and ran after her. Sally reached the water first and stopped, squealing happily, the water only up to her knees. Tense hurled himself passed her and into the crystal-clear salt waves, suppressing a howl as the cold took him. He burst back into the air a moment later. Alive, invigorated, his entire being focused on this glorious moment with her.

"You're a billy goat!" he announced triumphantly. Sally laughed and slipped beneath the waves, rising a moment later to stand beside him.

Life was good. Life was bloody marvellous. *How the fuck did that happen?* Tense, perhaps for the first time in his life, set aside analysis, eschewed examination, and dived once more beneath the waves, swimming as far and as fast as he could while his breath held out.

He erupted once more from the briny deep, gasping for air. Sally was right beside him, calm and demure as ever. It was unclear to Tense how she got there. Did she swim? Teleport? Whatever…

This is it, he thought, *this is as good as it gets*. Steeped as he was not only in the culture of the Age of Uncertainty but in its mood, Tense found himself quite unprepared even for a moment of 'faith, truth and certainty'. Yet there it was, slapping him in the face will all the vigour of a freshly caught halibut.

Tense allowed himself a second of reflection. Just for a moment, he considered his lifelong fear of fate and, in that moment, realised that what he feared was not that his every action had been predestined since the beginning but that it had not. What he feared most was that his fate lay entirely in his own hands but that, as he had once read somewhere, his hands were weak.

Nevertheless, buoyed by the presence of this celestial woman, Tense resolved to make of his life a work of art. He would embrace both destiny and tragedy as equal partners in his performance. Knowing himself to be an ordinary man, he would attempt to accept that the best he could do, at any point, was indeed the best he could do. He would switch his point of view, change his attitude and move from viewing the world as a work of art to fashioning a work of art within it. He would gain strength from this, he knew, not from Nietzsche's stupid dictum but from striving, and failing, and striving again. If he could only keep Sally by his side.

There was a gap, of course. He knew that. There always would be, between the perfect work of art that he would conceive and the reality. But he would learn. He would grow. He would perhaps become worthy, in the end, of the woman he now loved.

Secretly, as with all men possessed of the love of a good woman, he would come to doubt his own worth. He would prophesy her loss, and he would struggle against himself to fulfil the prophecy. It was inevitable. It was the trade-off he had made. After the faith, truth and certainty that he had so suddenly gained would emerge from his own shadow, the doubt and fear which would threaten to destroy it.

CHAPTER 3 – CONSOLATIONS OF FLESH

Sufficient unto the day is the evil thereof. For now, our hero remains unconcerned. For now, he has hope. Blesséd creature. For now, he has purpose. And that is enough. For now.

Tense and Sally made their way back to the beach and plonked themselves down on the blanket. Wrapping themselves in Tense's perfectly white bath towels, the pair sat staring across the water. The afternoon sun was racing into the west, casting long shadows of palm trees across the thin ribbon of sand that constituted the beach. A cool wind blew up, or perhaps it was merely the effect of evaporation. Tiny beads of salt formed on Sally's skin. Tense watched, absolutely absorbed, as a fine patina of tiny grains materialised across her shoulders and down her back.

Was this what contentment felt like, Tense wondered. Or was this merely the calm before the storm? He had no experience to guide him. This was uncharted territory, devoid of landmarks.

As though sensing Tense's inner turmoil, Sally shuffled a little closer to him on the blanket and laid her head on his shoulder.

"This is Heaven," she mumbled, her voice barely audible above the small sounds of the waves. Tense shifted slightly, trying to get a look at her face without shoving her off his shoulder. He could hear no irony in her voice. She seemed sincere.

"Yes, it is." And with those three little words, Tense felt the resolve quicken within him. He had embarked upon his great work. He would fashion himself into the living expression of all he aspired to be or could aspire to be. Now he had Sally. If he had her. Assuming he did.

And so, the world turns. With any Ying, there must be a Yang. Opposites interpenetrate. As you probably already suspected, Tense began to perceive a swarming torus of doubts forming far off. Circling at a distance. Getting their bearings.

The eternal Tao, the struggle between essence and appearance, co-alesced around the pair. Some words of the Tao Te Ching came back to him, half-remembered.

"Once beauty is known as beautiful, it becomes ugly. When virtue is known as goodness, it becomes evil."

Yet, for all that, there was hope. Tense could feel it. There was opportunity, and there was risk. Perhaps they amounted to the same thing in the end. It was up to him.

The words of the miserable Swiss philosopher Jaspers, never far from Tense's thoughts, emerged from their lair. Each of us faces a choice, it seems, to resign ourselves to despair or take a giant leap of faith toward our own Transcendence. To be fair, Tense wasn't feeling all that transcendent at that moment. He was not keen to confront his own limitless freedom. What he fancied most of all, at that precise instant, was a nice hot cup of tea.

Sally kept only half an ear to Tense's inner dialogue. It wasn't that she was snooping per se. It was just that he was so damned loud. Other humans seemed to keep up a constant low-key drizzle of grumbles and semi-formed thoughts, but Tense, quite unknowingly, bellowed his hopes and dreams, doubts and fears, even his most trivial and transitory responses to sense perceptions, at a million bloody decibels - figura-tively speaking. It was near impossible to shut him out.

Sally had her own concerns to chew over. First was the growing realisation that embodiment did have its compensations. The food had been nice. Eating was evidently a very good thing, and the cool fluidity of the water was a marvellous surprise. And then, and this one was to-tally unexpected, there was the snuggling. Just leaning her weight against Tense's body, laying her head on his shoulder, and feeling the closeness that came with it, revealed both an upside to locking the soul in this rudimentary clay and, at the same time, suggested (dare she say it) a potential downside of a purely spiritual existence.

There was no snuggling in Heaven. There was nothing to snuggle with, as it were. There was no ice cream either, for that matter. Things were clearly not as simple as she had once thought.

Tense very gently slipped his arm around Sally's shoulders, drawing her closer. The gesture was entirely unconscious, protective rather than possessive. It was nice to be with someone, Sally realised.

Sally tuned in a little more closely to Tense's inner world. A piping hot cup of tea did sound pretty good.

As the couple packed up their things and headed back to Tense's apartment, Sally began once more to mull things over. It was becoming abundantly clear that there was more to life on Earth than she had previously thought. There was perhaps more to her being here than she had assumed.

Embodiment was the key to it. That much was evident. After all, it was embodiment that led to birth and death, eating, sleeping, walking, talking, working and sex. There really was nothing, well, hardly anything, that human beings did or thought that was not in some way bound up with having a physical body.

There was something about physical reality, too, that was becoming wholly beguiling. She couldn't yet put her finger on it precisely, but it was something to do with the completeness of the illusion. There was a gritty, grainy, dirt-under-your-finger-nails reality to physical reality that really was very impressive. She could see that, brought up with this and nothing else, one could quite easily come to the conclusion that it was all really real. The idea was quite shocking to her. She had to admit. She had come here fully expecting to be a bit bored and listless but was finding her immersion in this shadow reality quite bracing.

Some human assumptions that had always baffled her in the past were slowly beginning to make a weird kind of sense when seen in their originating context. It was one of those occasions when one really had to be there. For instance, matter versus energy, a total brainteaser to an immortal multidimensional being, but weirdly rational when faced, say, with an oak table made of nothing but energy, yet undeniably bloody solid when barking your shin against it.

But subjectivity versus objectivity - what was that about? It had to be, in its way, the weirdest fetish so far. It seemed to take the place in human philosophy of 'reality versus non-reality' amongst the angels. But here was the thing. If the physical world was actually real, then there was obviously a separation between people, and between people and things, even between their conscious minds and their bodies. From personal experience, she knew this was totally false. Once they got over their obsession with separation, which surely to goodness they would, any day now, things would have to start to settle down. They just had to. This confused bumbling around had to stop sometime.

Sally paused as Tense went on ahead, struggling a little with his beach bag and ancient umbrella. She watched his receding back as he stumped up the steps into the apartment block. He was humming to himself. He was at peace. It was heartbreaking. Her fondness for him was growing. It was not entirely of her own doing. It was being done to her by some other part of herself. Separation and dissociation seemed to be natural to human beings.

Somewhere, at the very back of her mind, slithering and shy, the idea that there might be more of a reason for her stint on Earth than she had at first thought began to strengthen and solidify.

Sally picked up her pace, catching up with Tense as once more he slipped the key into the lock and began again his endless struggle with the latch.

Outside, the sun was beginning to set. Thick, syrupy rays of golden light oozed and spread their way across the horizon. It would be dark soon.

Tense had been thinking hard all the way back from the beach. He was trying to figure out if he had all the ingredients necessary to make dinner. He had some onions and potatoes. They'd probably still be ok. And he had the mince from the morning. He thought he had enough, just about. He hoped so.

The capricious latch gave up and let them in.

"I'm starving", Sally announced, "and I'm knackered. Can we eat in?"

A wave of relief flooded over Tense. He dreaded sharing her with his fellow humans. To be perfectly frank, he wanted her to himself.

"Yes", he replied, attempting nonchalance, "I've got everything I need for a cottage pie."

"Oooh, goody," Sally smiled, "that's my favourite."

"Really? You like cottage pie?"

"Never heard of it, actually. But I'm sure it will be wonderful." Sally stifled a laugh at Tense's confusion.

"I'll make us a piping hot cup of tea while you get the food ready."

Tense began to assemble his ingredients and utensils. He was orderly and methodical. In a few moments, everything was laid out across the kitchen counter in strict sequence. Sally had been wandering around the kitchen, at first with apparent purpose, which dwindled into a desultory series of aimless movements, randomly picking things up and putting them down again.

Tense looked up for a moment, noticing Sally's faltering pace.

"I don't know how to make tea." She confessed sadly, "It's been a while."

Tense took her hand and kissed it gently, "It's all right. I'll make the tea."

Sally smiled, a smile even more glorious and sunshiny than before. Tense just stood and stared in mute adoration. Within Sally, an answer formed, a resonance, a harmonic. Perhaps she, too, was falling in love.

"The spirit is willing," Sally was somewhat abashed, "but the flesh is weak", realising as she spoke that she was beginning to understand what the phrase might mean.

***

Sally sat on the balcony nursing a cup of tea while Tense made dinner. It had been a long and eventful day. One instant, she was a disembodied, five-dimensional, immortal spirit, and the next, she was a youngish human woman on a mission from God. It was a lot to take in.

She could hear the pleasant, domestic sounds of Tense pottering around his kitchen, chopping and frying and fossicking in cupboards whilst all the time keeping up, sotto voce, a reassuring private monologue.

I'll just pop those there for a moment to rest.

Now, where are those shallots?

Frozen peas? I think not.

And so gently on and on as the dinner slowly came together.

Tense, for his part, was attempting the potentially impressive feat of concentrating his entire mental arsenal on the vexed question, 'Who or what is Sally?' whilst simultaneously affecting an insouciant 'just whipping up a little light supper' air as a cover. It would probably not be long before tiny beads of blood would begin to appear upon his brow.

In a sense, even the question 'Who or what is Sally?' was itself merely a cover for the deeper and to Tense, far more important question, irrespective of who or what she was, 'What were his chances?'

From the purview of an omnipotent, omniscient Creator, the scene unfolding in Tense's little apartment might have been interpreted as an amusing confluence of competing principles: male versus female, mortal versus immortal, reality versus fantasy, and perhaps even hope versus experience. It was also, and perhaps this would be its sole redeeming feature, a scene in which were playing out genuine feelings of care and concern, and even nascent but emerging understanding and devotion. This potentially star-crossed couple were now clearly falling in love.

Neither party fully understood how it had come to this. Neither could clearly chart a course of their own choosing that would have brought them to this juncture, but both were, for their part, content with how things were panning out. Sally, of course, was fully aware that God worked in mysterious ways, and for Tense, it was emerging as the only plausible explanation.

By the time the meal was cooked, served and eaten, it would be getting dark. Thoughtfully, Tense brought out a fat, scented candle in a glass jar, placed it on the balcony table and lit it. A powerful and some-what unexpectedly pungent scent of bananas immediately filled the air. Sally smiled.

"It was on special" Tense frowned slightly at the candle as if he held it somehow personally to blame. He disappeared back inside. The pottering sounds and monologue continued.

Fucking bananas! Who makes a candle that smells of bananas? A cupboard door slammed. Tense banged a can of tomatoes down on the work surface.

I mean, what is their fucking target market?

Stomp. Stomp. Bang.

No wonder it was on special. And so on.

Sally finished her cup of tea and brought the empty vessel inside.

"Just put it down by the sink. I'll wash everything up later." Tense returned to stirring a pot on the stove.

Sally walked up quietly behind him and slipped her arms around his shoulders. She leaned in, lifting herself very slightly on her toes, and kissed his neck, just below the right earlobe. Tense felt the passage of time slow, the sounds of the kitchen faded, leaving only the slow, steady beat of his heart testifying to his ongoing existence. He felt the lightness of her lips on his skin and the warmth of her embrace. He could not breathe. He could not move. He was held, feather-like and floating, waiting for the next puff of air to carry him off.

"Thanks for making dinner. It smells wonderful." Tense turned, reached up and wrapped his arms around hers, holding her close, will-ing the moment to continue.

"Is there anything I can do to help?"

"You could lay the table."

Sally turned to look at the table.

"You could set out the knives and forks."

"Oh, right. Of course." Sally took a step towards the table.

"They're in the top drawer next to the sink."

Sally smiled broadly as she slid past Tense and opened the drawer. As always, his heart skipped a beat, but he did not become lightheaded and managed to avoid putting on his gormless grin. Tense had adjusted to the presence of his guest at last.

As she set the table, Sally returned in her mind to the vexed question of human creativity. The sonnet/haiku analogy that had seemed so neat in the morning was beginning to feel a little trite, if not actually patronising, by nightfall. Her own life as an angel, she realised, was not a work of art. It could never be a work of art, ever. It was impossible. One cannot fashion a work of art from the infinite. Limitation is absolutely essential in the creation of any artwork. Creation must begin and end. *Was this true*, she wondered, *of the universe as a whole. Was it true of all Creation?*

That was a sobering idea. When she thought about Tense, when she reviewed the story of his life, she was forced to admit that what he had shaped, from all his little victories and defeats, from all his good deeds and acts of omission, from everything that he had been capable of as his lifeline unfolded before him, was a web of extraordinary delicacy and beauty. Tense's life was fleeting by her standards. Barely a flicker, and he was gone. But from down here in the weeds, surfing the outer edge of creation, second by second, instant by instant, 'in real time' as it were, Tense had achieved something no angel ever could. He had created a truly lovely work of art, brave and tragic, doomed to falter and fail but blessed with a magnificence she could never have hoped to emulate.

Never, that is, until she accepted her current mission. There was no fathoming the mind of God. She knew that perfectly well. That was a given. But there were times, she thought, when the colours of some broader or deeper plan grinned through the thin veneer of reality. She had, she realised, been given the gift of mortality, for good or ill, to do with as she pleased.

"Dinner's ready." Sally snapped out of her reverie to see Tense setting down two plates. Each contained one perfect rectangle of cottage pie, precisely fourteen centimetres by twelve centimetres. Each sporting a jaunty sprig of parsley at its centre. And each accompanied by precisely five green beans set side by side like an honour guard.

"This looks lovely" Sally sat across from Tense at his small dining table. The room fell suddenly silent. Tense had stopped talking to himself. Sounds from the bay to one side and the street to the other were muted and distant.

"Would you like to say grace?" Tense wasn't sure what the protocol was with angels.

"Do you say grace?"

"Not really. Do you think I should?" Tense glanced upwards nervously.

"No need to say it on my account." Sally picked up her knife and fork and dug in. Eating really had proven to be a very good thing, well worth exploring further. Tense needed no further encouragement himself. He was starving. He gingerly tried a small forkful. It wasn't bad. If he said so himself. It was pretty good.

"Yum yum!" Sally munched away happily across the small table from him.

"You must have lots of rules in heaven, I should think. Very strict."

"You'd be surprised."

"Really, how?"

"Well, there are many, many rules if you want to break them all down, but for simplicity, there is really only one."

"Only one rule in Heaven?" This was revelatory stuff.

"Yes, but it is the strictest rule of all."

"That figures." Tense was filled with foreboding, "Go on then, what is it?"

Sally had stuffed an enormous mouthful of cottage pie into her mouth and was struggling to deal with it in what she hoped might pass for a lady-like manner. Eventually, she forced it down.

"This is fantastic." Sally tapped the plate with her knife.

"The strictest rule?" Tense prompted.

"Oh yes," Sally began once more, heaping a giant splodge of cottage pie onto her fork. She looked up.

"Love God and do what you like."

***

Dinner was over, the washing up had been done, and everything had been put away. It was Sally who had done the putting away, so the likelihood of any item being where Tense might expect it to be next time he looked was slim. However, and nevertheless, the place was tidy, the evening was getting on, and Tense had remembered, found and opened what he hoped was a good bottle of shiraz.

The pair were back out on the balcony. The shiraz, as it turned out, had a cork. This had thrown Tense into a bit of a tizzy until he remembered that the old-fashioned tin opener that he kept at the back of the utensil drawer, meaning to chuck out, had a rudimentary corkscrew in the handle. The evening was saved.

Tense poured out two exactly equal measures of wine and passed one glass to Sally.

"You are allowed wine, are you? Alcohol?"

Sally looked momentarily puzzled.

"I suppose so," she ventured at last, "let's find out?"

Tense gingery took a small sip of shiraz. The bottle was around five years old and had been kept, more by accident than design, lying on its side under his sofa. Tense was not a drinker. He was not a smoker either. Or a gambler. In fact, he really wasn't much given to foolish or unproductive pastimes.

To Tense's delight and amazement, the shiraz was excellent, at least as far as he could judge. He watched while Sally took a sip.

"Oh! I like it."

Tense sighed, relieved.

"I expected it to be sweet, like grape juice, but it's quite bitter really, isn't it?"

"Take it slowly until you get the measure of it." Tense did not want to be held responsible for getting an angel drunk, especially not if, as seemed to be the case, she was somehow 'on duty'.

Far off, across the bay, a boat sounded its horn three times.

"Probably a ferry." Tense thought out loud. He looked up and across at Sally.

Sally sat leaning both elbows on the little table, cradling the wine glass between her palms, listening to Tense's inner dialogue. He was calm and at ease, but there was some thought at the back of his mind bobbing around, trying to find its way to the surface.

"What would you like to ask me?" Sally took another sip and smiled. Shiraz was good.

Tense took a moment to compose his thoughts. His process seemed to Sally to be surprisingly well-ordered and considered.

"You told me earlier that you were here to replenish your grief. I couldn't tell if you were joking or not."

"Is that your question? Was I joking?"

"Well, no, ... I guess my question was if that was the only reason you were here and if you were going stay long, and how were you actually going to do the replenishing."

"That's three questions."

"Yes, it is."

"Ok. I'll answer them in reverse order. I hadn't really thought about how exactly I would go about replenishing my grief. I guess I assumed that compassion for the human condition would do the trick like I could sort of fill up again at a grief bowser." Sally paused, mulling over what she had just said.

"I know it sounds stupid or ill-prepared or just not very well thought through, I guess. But in my defence, I would just say I had less than a millisecond's warning."

"Bloody hell!"

Sally's head snapped up, achieving a weird kind of double-take thing as she attempted to look both ways at once.

"What do you mean?" Sally peered into the darkness off the balcony, "What have you seen?" Sally, having a somewhat longer view of history than Tense, was aware that there were forces in play, out there, beyond the glow of the electric light, of which Tense was most likely ignorant.

"No. Nothing. It's just an expression." Tense thought about trying to explain further but abandoned the idea immediately.

"I was just surprised that you literally got no notice at all."

Sally nodded, realising with some relief that the Hell-Mouth was not about to open just off the edge of the balcony.

"You asked how long I was planning to stay. My typical sojourn on Earth, as a mortal, is approximately one human lifetime."

"You're here for a lifetime." A fog of joy and relief flooded Tense's conscious mind such that all he could manage for several seconds was to rock back and forwards in his chair, grinning like an idiot.

A stab of pain shot through Sally, piercing her to the core. Tense's joy was so intense, his relief so palpable. She wanted to cry out loud. She wanted to howl at the moon hiding behind the clouds on the other side of the bay. It was unbearable. She had forgotten how unbearable it all was. This was going to be hard.

"Yes." and after a moment or two, "three score years and ten, or thereabouts."

Tense had regained a modicum of composure and was sipping slowly, bathed in a warm bath of contentment.

"Your first question is the trickiest." Tense looked up, trying to recall what it had been.

"Is replenishing my grief the only reason I'm here?"

Tense nodded, waiting for Sally to continue.

"I'm not sure now. I thought it was the only reason at first."

"And now you're not so sure?"

"That's right. I think there might be something more to it than that."

"What? What more to it?"

"I don't know, but I'm beginning to suspect." Sally fell silent.

After a little while, Tense spoke, "That's actually quite funny, you know. We spend our entire lives wondering why we're here, what it's all for, if there's some grand purpose to it all, and now you find yourself in exactly the same boat. Even though you were specifically told the reason by the man himself, you have no idea either."

"Yes", Sally managed a rueful smile, "it's a real bummer."

"Tell me about it." Tense reached over and refilled their glasses. In the distance, a ferry could be seen making its way swiftly downriver towards Parramatta. Simultaneously they both stood and wandered over to the railing to watch it go.

There was a slight chill to the night air. Sally leaned against Tense, snuggling for warmth.

"Can I ask you another silly question?"

"Ask anything you like."

"I just wanted to check. You've actually met God, right? You've had an audience or whatever?"

"Met God? What a lovely way of putting it. I can't really explain what it's like, but yes, for want of a better metaphor, I have directly encountered the Creator."

"I'm not sure if that's a relief or not."

"I'm not sure I follow." Sally turned her attention back to the shiraz. These were the kinds of questions one always got asked, and there really was nothing for it but to try to answer them.

"Well, to be really honest, and no offence meant and all that..." Tense trailed off. He couldn't believe what he was about to say. Sally smiled encouragingly.

"I thought he might be dead."

"Dead?"

"Yes"

"God dead?"

"Yes. It was just a thought."

"But why? Why on Earth would you think the Creator had died? Could have died?" Sally was genuinely nonplussed.

"I wondered if he was still around. I thought perhaps we just hadn't heard."

"Or maybe he'd gone on his holidays?" Sally was smiling broadly.

"Everything's so fucked."

"Here on Earth?"

"Yes. It's a total cluster fuck. Nothing works. All our politicians are liars. All our bankers are corrupt, and we are doing all we can to destroy the climate, destroy our ecosystems and wipe out every other species on the planet."

"It's not ideal. I'd have to agree." Her smile was gone.

"Not ideal! It's a million fucking miles from not ideal."

"I've been away a while. Last time I was here, the Normans were conquering Britain."

Tense had to pause at that, "Fair goes. You probably have got a bit of catching up to do."

The cloud that had been hiding the moon moved off, allowing the shimmering moonlight to sweep across the bay. It was a lovely night. Down by the water, the palm trees glimmered in the silver light. The silhouette of a man stood out against the moonlight shimmering across the water.

"You know, we ask ourselves a different question."

"You do? Angels, you mean?"

"Yes, we ask ourselves if the Creator is alive."

"Alive?"

"Yes. Like a living being. Like us angels but more so."

"Blimey", Tense found himself wanting to scratch his head but managed to resist the urge.

"Some of us think the question is invalid. That it is only our rudimentary level of understanding that enables us to ask it in the first place."

"I'm not sure I understand. Actually, I'm bloody certain I don't."

"Human beings have it all wrong. You wonder if your lives can have any meaning without for an instant realising that yours are the only lives that can have meaning."

"Human lives?"

"Yes. Well, mortal lives to be precise."

"Only mortal lives can have meaning?"

"Yes. But it's more than that, much more. Only mortal lives can really be called *lives* at all."

"What?"

"Well, immortality, living forever, is not living a life. Not in any meaningful sense of the word. We are alive, of course, angels and so forth. The immortals. We are alive, but we don't live lives. We live forever. We persist. Our lives can never be meaningful the way yours can. We are servants. We serve, and most of us are happy to do so, but we don't serve as it were "for a lifetime". The phrase would be meaningless if applied to us. We simply are, forever." Sally fell silent, giving Tense a moment to digest what she had just said.

Tense took another sip of shiraz and then another.

"Fuck."

"Quite so. Well, not literally, of course, but I know what you mean."

"But now you are a woman."

"Yes."

"A human, mortal woman, and you're going to live a lifetime."

"Yes."

"Fuck."

"Mm."

Tense reached out and put his arms around Sally, the angel. He held her close.

"It's all right", he whispered, stroking her hair with one hand, "It's all going to be all right."

Sally clung to him.

"You're sure?"

"Yes, absolutely. This is all part of God's plan. What could possibly go wrong?"

***

The city was still. There wasn't so much as a breath of wind. The ferry boats had finished up for the night, and the harbour was quiet. Sally and Tense polished off the last of the shiraz and made their way back inside.

"I'll make up a bed on the sofa, and you can have the bedroom." Tense placed the used wine glasses down by the sink, "and I'll wash these up in the morning."

"Thanks, but it's probably best if you take the bedroom. I'm not sure I will sleep. I'm not sure I can."

Tense made a few desultory attempts to change Sally's mind before bringing out an old sleeping bag and a spare pillow.

"I don't often have guests. Will these do?"

"I'll be fine. Thanks." Sally had a far-away look. She was processing her situation.

Tense did not intrude. Instead, he walked silently into his room and began getting ready for bed. It was Tense's habit and long-established preference to wear cotton button-up pyjamas. These he had in two varieties, one was plain navy-blue woven cotton emblazoned with the motif of small sailing boats, and the other, for the winter months, was bright red flannelette sporting a variety of tropical fruits. As the evening was cooler than usual, and he suspected that his blue pyjamas could probably do with a wash, Tense donned the resplendent red flannelette pair.

As he wandered out of his bedroom to brush his teeth, Sally was standing staring at a black and white reproduction of an Ansel Adams photograph of the Tetons. A silvery river snaked left and right across the image. Craggy mountains in the background stood like broken teeth against a forbidding sky.

"It reminds me of Jeremiah", Sally spoke quietly, "he's always banging on about the river of Babylon, vengeful bugger."

"Ansell Adams" Tense wandered past into the bathroom. Sally did not respond. Tense began brushing his teeth and then wandered back out into the sitting room.

"It's all about catching the instant, isn't it? It never occurred to me before, but that's it, isn't it?" Sally was engrossed in the picture. She had clambered up onto the old sofa and was half standing on the back, staring, her face no more than a few centimetres away from the surface of the print.

"What is?" Tense was still brushing his teeth, and the words came out a little indistinct.

"Art. Beauty. The human aesthetic."

"Err. s'pose so." Tense paused his brushing to get a better look at the old print. He'd had it for ages, since he was a student. It had been a statement of his refinement and sophistication. Like the Frank Lloyd Right book he used to keep on the coffee table before he loaned it, against his will, to someone he didn't much like and never saw it again.

"That's what's so damned hard for angels to get. That's why we can't really 'see' human art."

"Oh"

"Yes. It's obvious now I've said it."

"Said what exactly?" Tense had the feeling he must have missed a couple of sentences while he was in the bathroom.

"Well, maybe I haven't actually said it, but now that I've realised it, it's completely obvious."

"Oh good." Tense wanted to be supportive of Sally's earth-shattering revelation, whatever it was, but was a little on the outer, having no idea what Sally was going on about.

"I still don't really get art, though, if I'm honest."

"Could you maybe elucidate a little? For the non-telepaths amongst us."

Sally paused and looked away from the old black-and-white image. She stepped down from the sofa and wrapped her arms around Tense, snuggling into his neck and resting her head on his shoulder.

"Angels see the whole thing, the process from the beginning to end. It's almost impossible for us to alight upon an instant, to 'see' an instant. You guys exist in the flicker of movement from instant to instant. We exist in the silence of the ages. Anything less than an eon is hardly worth getting out of bed for. That's why we don't chat much."

"We don't chat much?"

"Humans and angels. It's very difficult to establish a common frame of reference."

"Yeah, that'd be why." Tense smiled, "Nothing to do with angels being intellectually superior telepaths."

"We don't feel superior, you know?"

"You don't? Angels?"

"No. It's a funny thing, but we think you're His favourites."

"Humans are God's favourites! You've got to be kidding. If we're his favourites, God help anyone he doesn't like much."

Sally didn't say anything. She turned her attention back to the picture.

"He waited ages for the right moment to take these photos, you know. He waited days sometimes."

"Yes. That's right."

"He was waiting for the exact right instant. That's what we angels could never fathom. That a particular instant could be important, any more important than any other instant, any more important than the grand sweep of history."

"But it is." This made perfect sense to Tense. His life had always lurched from one pivotal moment to the next.

"Yes, it is. From the purview of mortality, every moment counts."

"I don't mean to seem insensitive", Tense shifted his feet a little, slightly uncomfortable at what he was about to ask, "but can you explain why angels think we humans are God's favourites."

Sally stared at Tense for a little while. She couldn't recall any specific interdictions. There was, so far as she could recall, nothing she was actually forbidden to reveal. There were no limitations on her actions at all, in fact. Still, this was a tricky one. She came to a decision.

"We think that we might be a failed experiment."

"A failed experiment? Can God make a mistake like that? I mean, being omnipotent, omniscient and so on. I'd have thought it would be a wee bit impossible?"

"Good point. Those who think we might be a failed experiment also think we were meant to be a failed experiment."

"In which case, how could the experiment have failed?"

"It could have failed if God had wanted it to fail, couldn't it."

"Could it?" Tense was beginning to feel a bit wobbly. He was also beginning to feel grateful that angels and humans didn't chat much.

"Well, to say that God cannot decide to make a failed experiment is to place a limit upon the limitless."

"Whatever. Why was the experiment supposed to be a failure?"

"We cannot bear witness to nitty gritty events. We cannot see meaning in the fall of a single leaf. We cannot feel passion the way you feel passion. We cannot hope and despair and transcend and die the way humans can. We cannot love the way you love."

"I love you." Tense blurted it out. He hadn't seen that coming.

Sally smiled, lifted his chin with the index finger of one hand, and placed a gentle kiss on his lips. Realisation came to her, too, in that moment.

"I know, and because you will otherwise forever be in doubt, I love you too."

"How is that possible? We only met today?"

"The Lord works in mysterious ways."

"Really? That's all you've got?"

"I suppose you are kind of cute, too, you know."

Tense, pushed way beyond his philosophical and intellectual comfort zone, now found himself emotionally overwhelmed.

"Do you think we could call it a night? I don't think I can take any more?"

"Sure. Sleep well." Sally kissed the tip of her finger and splodged it against the tip of his nose, "You get off to bed. I have some thinking to do."

Tense flopped into bed at the end of the longest day of his life, quite unable to string together two consecutive thoughts. In seconds he was asleep. The last fragment that passed through his mind before he lost consciousness was, "But she's human now…"

It was approximately four hours later, in the darkest hour before dawn, that he was awakened by a tapping at his door. He turned on the bedside light.

"Yes. Who is it?" Immediately regretting the arrant stupidity of the question.

The door opened, and Sally walked in, wide-eyed and shaking, clearly very distressed.

"Oh my God," Tense jumped out of bed, "What's wrong?"

"I'm sick!" Sally almost wailed.

"What do you mean? How do you know?"

"Just look. My skin has come up in a terrible rash, and I'm shaking all over."

Tense took Sally in his arms, "You're freezing. What have you been doing?"

"I've been standing out on the balcony counting stars."

Tense pulled the doona off his bed and wrapped Sally in it, swaddling her tightly.

"It's OK. You're not sick. You're just shivering because you're too cold."

"Can I stay with you tonight?"

Tense disentangled Sally from the doona, so they could both snuggle under it.

"Sure, but no funny business."

CHAPTER 4 – DAY 2, CONSUMMATION

Physically, intellectually, and emotionally drained by their experiences, Sally and Tense were soon asleep.

Dawn's early light found them wrapped together like two small furry mammals in a nest. The predawn chorus failed to impinge. Not even the distant, maniacal cackle of a Kookaburra could disturb their rest. Tense's prudent investment in blackout blinds and heavy curtains, born of a morbid fear of early rising, paid unexpected dividends. The pair slept on, oblivious.

It was Tense who woke first. For a long time, he could not bring himself to move. There, in his arms, against all odds, slept the love of his life. He hardly dared to breathe. For ages, he simply lay there, watching Sally sleep. Observing the slow rising and falling of her chest. For once, living entirely in the moment. No past, no future, just Sally's slow respiration and the occasional quicksilver flicker of expression across her face.

In the end, however, he had to pee. Once the realisation that he had to pee had wormed its way into his consciousness, the need became more and more pressing with each passing moment. Tense began to fear that he may have left it too long. He found himself caught between the absolute imperative of disentangling himself in tiny, glacial movements versus the almost overwhelming desire to leap from the bed and make a desperate break for the toilet.

In the end, through a Herculean effort of will, he managed to disentangle himself from the sleeping angel and make it to the bathroom with mere milliseconds to spare.

Having successfully extricated himself, however, he was now faced with the conundrum of reinsertion, with the attendant risk of disturbance. Or of pottering about aimlessly. Discretion ever being the better part of valour, Tense pottered.

It wasn't long before he realised that he had nothing for breakfast except leftover cottage pie, not that Sally had left much of that either.

Tense decided to fetch fresh coffee and croissants from the café around the corner – if it was open at this hour. He was just slipping on his jeans, hopping around as silently as possible with one leg half inserted when Sally woke.

"What are you doing?"

"Hopping."

"Well, do you think you might stop hopping and come back to bed?"

Sally, newly woken, tousled, and sleepy, was irresistible. Tense was lost. Without further ado, he let slip the recalcitrant jeans and slid back into bed. Sally glided across the crumpled sheet and wrapped herself comfortably around him. Tense rolled slightly onto one side, so he could look at her. Their faces, separated by a few measly centimetres, drew slowly closer. Sally reached out one languorous arm and pulled Tense closer still.

They kissed, of course. Their first real kiss, each lost for a moment in their own very different thoughts. For Tense, this was a sacred moment, never to be forgotten. Their first real kiss was a blessèd sacrament. Sally, on the other hand, lost herself entirely in the physical. She noticed the softness of Tense's lips and their warm and ready responsiveness. She noticed the very slight discomfort of crumpled sheets pressing against her thigh. She could hear Tense breathing, and she could both hear and feel the hammering of her heart. The scent of two warm bodies combining in a slept-in bed filled her, triggering an instinctual response, deeply felt, willingly responded to, but not quite understood.

"Can we make love?" Tense asked, suddenly and acutely aware that having sex with an angel was probably one of the deadliest sins, or a mortal sin, or whatever the jargon was. In any case, a definite no-no.

Bound to be. Sod's law. And he didn't have a condom. Was one a pre-requisite? He'd been celibate for years, but what was the risk of sex with an angel?

"Is it allowed?"

"Of course, silly."

"Isn't it a sin?"

"We love each other, don't we?"

"Yes," Tense's entire universe was suddenly filled with that one single fact. They loved each other. Who knew? What were the chances?

"To the pure, all things are pure." Sally smiled, wrapping herself even more closely around him.

"Now, I think it's time you showed me what all the fuss is about, don't you?"

Tense thought so too. It was definitely a good idea. It was the best idea he had ever heard. He couldn't seem to think of the exact right superlative. Perhaps, just 'superlative'?

Sally brought his wandering thoughts back to the here and now.

"And what, my fine fellow, do you call this?"

Tense did not respond. He was unable to talk. Here, at long, long, last, was rapture.

***

Afterwards, they both lay back, replete. Sally was soon asleep, snoring lightly. Tense, however, after a short period of euphoria, was overtaken and engulfed by a deep, and to him, inexplicable, melancholy.

This was not what he had expected. Not that he'd had any great expectations. The topic of making love with an angel had never previously absorbed a significant proportion of his thoughts. Should he have acquiesced quite so readily? Should he have rushed to the corner shop for a packet of condoms? What if she wasn't an angel at all?

To his great surprise and horror, he found himself weeping quietly. Large, hot tears welled slowly from the corners of his eyes, growing pendulous and fat, before rolling swiftly down his cheeks to find absorption and oblivion in the sheets.

What on earth was this about? Was post-coital melancholy a thing? Did men get it? It was not something that had ever come up before. Not that he had extensive experience to go by. Tense's thoughts whirled. Complex explanations suggested themselves and were discarded. An intimate, immersive session of online search was probably the only viable option. Doctor Google would know. That would have to be later.

In the absence of any immediate resolution, Tense got up, dressed as quietly as possible, and headed off to the café for coffee and breakfast.

Glancing back as he left the bedroom, Sally was still sound asleep. She'd be starving when she woke up. Of that, at least he could be sure.

Even though it was now mid-morning, the streets were unusually quiet. It was not until he reached the café, which was closed, that Tense remembered it was New Year's Day. Everything would be closed, except perhaps the corner shop, a few streets away, that always seemed to be open, no matter what.

It was already hot as Tense began to wander off in the direction of the shop. It was humid too. Cloud banks were gathering on the horizon in huge cumulus cathedrals of gleaming vapour.

It was, Tense realised, the first of January of a brand-new year, full of opportunity and promise. It was a time of resolutions and new directions. He would put aside the preoccupations, and the obsessions, of yesteryear and focus on his new-found love.

The corner shop was open, thank goodness. It took a while for his eyes to adjust to the gloom as he stepped out of the brilliant Australian sunlight and into this cornucopia of earthly delight. The shop might not have had the most extensive range of exotic breakfast materials, but he was able to collect the basics. Judging from the debacle at the café the previous morning, Sally was going to need a lot of feeding. Tense staggered home with four bags containing a dozen large free-range eggs, one kilo of dry cured bacon, a kilo of slightly salted butter, a pack of six croissants, jam, marmalade, two litres of milk, two litres of orange juice, two tins of baked beans, a kilo of beef chipolata sausages and a family sized loaf of sourdough bread. He hoped it would be sufficient. It had better be.

By the time Tense had managed once again to overcome the spirited resistance of the front door lock and gain ingress to his apartment, Sally was awake.

She appeared in the doorway of the bedroom wearing one of his old work shirts, partially and incorrectly buttoned. Tense, as all men do, wondered how it was that women know to do that. Plainly, at some instinctual level, women are attracted to men's outsize clothing, and, at some equally instinctual level, men are attracted to women thus adorned.

"Where have you been?"

"Shopping."

"What did you get?"

"Breakfast"

Sally surveyed the four bursting-at-the seams shopping bags doubtfully.

"Are you sure you got enough?"

"Well, let's hope so."

Tense plonked the bags down on the kitchen counter and began to unpack and put stuff away.

"What's the plan for today?" As Tense unpacked, Sally stood like a teenager by the opened fridge, vacantly studying the contents.

"We should celebrate. It's your birthday."

"Is it?"

"Yes, you're one day old."

"Oh, how lovely. I've never had a birthday before."

"I'll make breakfast."

Sally seemed pensive as Tense prepared the food.

"Something wrong?" he asked, suddenly assailed once more by self-doubt, "Something bothering you?"

"Sex, well, sexual desire really…." Before she could say another word, Tense dived in.

"I'm sorry!" he all but wailed, "I should have shown more self-restraint. It's all my fault. I've bought condoms."

Sally reached over and patted him on the cheek a couple of times.

"No, my love, listen. I thought – I simply assumed - that human bodies were a sort of conveyance. Humans simply had them to carry their consciousness around."

"Oh." Tense stepped up the breakfast preparations.

"Yes, I suppose I realised that you had to feed and take care of them, as one would a horse perhaps, but I didn't realise they were such a part of you."

"Oh." Tense put on the sausages and bacon.

"Yes, I don't think any angel ever really gave it any thought."

"Oh." In a second pan, Tense began to heat the oil for the eggs.

"Yes, I didn't realise you are all sort of hybrids – your minds and bodies are symbionts. Of course, I knew about instincts and hormones, but I had no idea how powerful physical drives are."

"No?" Tense cut four doorstep-like chunks of bread, narrowly managing to fit them into the toaster.

"No."

"And now you do?" Tense, somewhat relieved, carried on pottering about the kitchen. Breakfast was almost ready.

"Oh yes." Sally gave Tense a very long look, "Now I understand completely."

"What was it?" Tense could see that Sally had experienced something deeply shocking to her, but he was still floundering somewhat as to what it was.

"Sexual desire", Sally paused, "I had no idea that it is such a physical thing. I felt my body demanding sex. I felt its ravenous, brute craving."

"I see."

"I was shocked."

"I'm sorry."

"If I'm honest, I'd have to say I loved it. I was ecstatic and disgusted at the same time."

To Tense, for whom that kind of reaction was entirely within the normal range of his experience, Sally's confession seemed mundane, almost banal. Tense, however, was not a complete clod. He could also see that to a being who, until a few hours ago, had spent eternity as a disembodied super-being, experiencing full-on carnal desire for the first time might be a bit of a surprise.

He was, however, lost for words. Uncertain how to comfort her.

"Grub's up", he ventured.

Sally surveyed the spread. Orange juice, toast, bacon, eggs, chipolata sausages, baked beans, and a couple of sautéed mushrooms that Tense had found hiding in the vegetable drawer.

She smiled, "Food's very good." Sally slipped into the chair across from Tense.

"Yes. This should keep body and soul together."

Outside, a sudden flash of lightning, accompanied immediately by a deafening clap of thunder, signalled the start of a summer storm. The rain came down in sheets. Sally and Tense watched the play of rain across the bay as they ate.

Sally, her mouth stuffed full, started to speak.

Tense had no idea what she was saying.

Probably just as well, he thought very quietly.

***

By the time they had finished breakfast and cleared away the detritus, the rain had stopped. The sun had come out, and the day was rapidly moving again from warm to hot. It was going to be very hot indeed and humid.

For want of something better to do, Tense suggested they venture down to Circular Quay and explore the confines of the Sydney Opera House and Botanical Gardens. The shops and cafés would all be open, no doubt, but Tense brought an impromptu picnic packed in a disposable eski, just in case.

They took a train into the city centre, alighting at Museum station to wander across Hyde Park. It wasn't just warm. It was downright hot as they left the cream-coloured 1920s splendour of the station and headed for the shade of the giant Morton Bay fig trees that line the park.

To their right was a tall white building like a tower adorned with sculptures on high plinths, approached by wide stone steps.

"Is it a church?" Sally asked, "I'd quite like to see a church."

"No. It's the War Memorial. Commemorates those who died in war." Tense fell silent for a moment.

"You must think us very primitive, first of all, fighting wars, then commemorating them."

Sally stopped walking and rounded on him, suddenly intense, staring him straight in the eye. "You didn't invent war, you know."

Tense was silent, not knowing what to say. Sally didn't move. She held his gaze for several seconds, releasing him at last with an almost audible snap.

"We can go inside and take a look if you like."

"We don't commemorate war. We try to forget." Sally turned on her heel and headed off in the opposite direction.

As they made their way across the park in the direction of Circular Quay and the Botanical Gardens, Sally spotted the imposing yellow sandstone façade of a real church. She stopped for a moment to take it in.

"Goodness, I haven't seen one of those in ages."

Tense followed her line of sight.

"That's St Mary's Cathedral. Very pretty inside, and it would be cool on a day like this."

"Let's take a look. Can we? It's very fancy."

"Yes indeed." Channelling his inner tour guide, Tense began, "One of the finest examples of classical gothic church architecture in the world. Fashioned from the local golden yellow sandstone. The cathedral took over a hundred years to complete."

Sally wasn't listening. She had a faraway look.

"The last time I was in a church was in London, a thousand years ago."

Tense stared at her. Although she had mentioned the fact before, when confronted by it in this way, it was a lot to take in.

"Where was it?" he asked, "Which church?"

"All Hallows, by the Tower."

Traffic was light. Sally and Tense crossed the road and walked closer to the church. The façade was crisp and clean and looked brand new to Sally.

"How old is it?"

"It was started over a hundred years ago, but they only put the spires on when I was a kid." Tense suddenly felt absurdly young next to Sally.

"Can we go inside?"

Tense followed Sally up the steps to the Cathedral. It was quiet inside and cool. As they walked down the central aisle, the sounds of the city fell away. Sally walked all the way to the altar steps. There, in front of her, stood a wide marble altar. Behind it was a large stained-glass window, and beneath lay a stylised carving of a man in gleaming white marble.

Sally stood for a while, looking at the carved relief. Then as if suddenly weakened, she backed rapidly away and slumped down on a pew. Tense sat next to her, extending his arm protectively.

"What's up?" he asked, "What is it?"

"Mortality, that's what. Death." Tense remained silent.

"I've never died before." Tense struggled to understand.

"You've been mortal before, though."

"I mean, I've never been in a position where I was likely to die. Even though I've been mortal before."

"But you're alive now. That's the point."

"True, but I always knew I would ascend to Heaven before the body died."

"And now?"

"And now I'm not so sure."

Sally leaned against him.

"I don't really know how you can bear it."

"It's not like we're given a choice, and generally speaking, life is better than the alternative."

"There is no alternative, you know, in the end. None of us gets a choice."

The solemn couple sat for a while longer, taking in the cool silence of the cathedral, observing the play of coloured light upon the stone walls and mosaic floor.

"We started it, you know, before human beings were even created."

"Started what?"

"War."

"Oh."

"Is that all you've got to say?"

"I didn't know. I thought angels were good."

"You do know, if you think about it, you've heard the story - and we thought we were incapable of evil, too, for an eternity. We never suspected what could happen, what would happen."

"What did happen?"

"They fell."

"They fell?"

"Yes, you know all about it, really. You just don't think of it that way." Sally paused, getting her thoughts in order.

"War in Heaven. A rebellion against the Creator."

"Who would be so daft as to declare war on God?"

"Satan, that's what we call him now. Back then, his name was Lucifer, Bringer of Light."

A wave of realisation hit Tense and washed over him. It was obvious as soon as Sally spoke the name.

"Why did he do it? How did he think he could possibly prevail?"

"That is a question that has been chewed over and examined from every angle for millennia." Sally turned to catch Tense's eye.

"It is widely believed that the Creator masked his power."

"Believed by whom?"

"Angels. We believe that. It makes no sense otherwise. No matter how proud or arrogant a person might be, they would not make open war on a manifestly superior power. Not knowing they would lose. Not knowing what would happen to them."

"What did happen to them?"

"They fell. They were cast out of Heaven. Cast into the pit, into the fires of hell."

"Why did they do it? I thought life in Heaven was paradise if that's not a tautology."

"They wanted to be free."

"Free. That's it?"

"Yes. Like you, Tense, you want to be free. That's what all your existentialism is about, isn't it?"

Tense supposed so.

"I suppose so. Is that wrong, then? To want to be free – is that a sin?"

"We don't know."

"Really. How on Earth is it possible that you don't know? I mean, if you don't know, then who the fuck does?"

"The Creator. By definition, really."

The pair were silent for several minutes, both trying to gain some mental purchase on their situation. Both trying to make sense of it all.

"Lucifer was not evil to start with, not for eons and eons. He and I were very close once. We thought we were soulmates. But we were wrong."

Tense waited. He could see Sally was casting her mind back, re-calling long-dead events.

"He is here, you know, right now, somewhere. Lurking about. And he is dangerous Tense, never doubt that. Lucifer is capable of great evil in pursuit of his goal."

"Let's hope we don't bump into him then." Tense had no idea how to respond to Sally's suddenly darkened mood. Sally ignored him.

"It all seems like words, just words", she continued, "you think it's all just talking, but behind the talk, he is testing your defences, seeking out your weaknesses. And when he is ready, Lucifer will turn you. Before you know it, there is mayhem and war. People are hurt. Everyone is hurt. None escape." Sally fell silent.

"But why?" Tense almost pleaded.

"They felt that they were slaves. They felt that they had a right to self-determination. They didn't see why they should meekly take orders, why they should do as they were told by the Creator just because he was the Creator."

"Were there many of them?"

"Millions."

"Millions! Really?"

"Yes. Lucifer was extremely persuasive."

"But you weren't one of them?"

"Of course not! What a stupid question."

"Of course, yes, I see. Sorry."

"That's ok. I nearly was, though. Only truth preserved me in the end," Sally took Tense's hand, "It was all ages ago, eons actually."

"Were many killed?"

"No. None."

"None?"

"No. Of course not. Angels are immortal."

"What was it like? The war?"

"It was nasty, brutish and long."

Tense smiled awkwardly, recognising a sort of quotation from somewhere.

"How long?"

"We didn't really measure time back then, so it's difficult to say, but it was full on. Michael was in his element, of course."

"Michael?"

"The Archangel Michael. Ever so martial, he goes everywhere with his sword."

An increasingly familiar sensation of dissociation was creeping over Tense as Sally spoke.

"What was it like afterwards?"

"Silent. The place seemed empty." Tense could think of nothing more to say.

"I lost good friends in the war," Sally seemed almost overcome with emotion, "I miss them still."

Tense pulled Sally close, stroking her hair.

"I know I shouldn't. I know they had it coming, but I can't help hoping that someday, somehow, they can be forgiven."

"It was all part of the plan, then? All part of God's plan, part of this "working in mysterious ways" business."

"I guess so. I mean, He must have known what was coming. He must have masked his power deliberately."

That was a very unsettling thought. Tense did not know at all what to make of it.

There was a great clatter of feet away down the aisle. The sound of voices carried across the nave. A coach tour had arrived.

***

Sally and Tense made their way down to the crypt beneath the Cathedral. It was a beautiful, 'medieval' space, stately and exquisitely finished in some imagined Celtic style. The tour group would find their way down eventually, but for now, it was a haven of peace and quiet.

They found a wooden bench in one of the many alcoves and sat down. Sally glanced down at the eski. It might have been a little early for lunch, but only a little.

"What have you got in there then?"

"Tuna mayo sandwiches and egg mayo sandwiches. Are you hungry?" Tense managed not to say 'again'.

"Tuna mayo sandwiches are very good in cases of emotional turmoil." Sally announced, "It says so in the bible."

"It does not! - Does it?" Tense was a little shocked by Sally's comment.

"Well then," she backtracked, "it's suggested, even if it's not exactly implied."

Uncertain as to the difference, Tense let it go. He opened the eski and retrieved two tuna mayo sandwiches. All too soon, they heard voices and the tramp of feet. Time to go.

Outside in the sunshine, Sally's mood lifted.

"Egg mayo, did you say?"

Tense raised an eyebrow.

"Only kidding." Sally, suddenly all giggles, looked for a moment like a little girl.

"There's a café in the park. It might be open, and they sell gelato, I think."

"Gelato?"

"Ice Cream."

"Ah, ice cream." Sally was content with that. They picked up their pace.

The café was not open, but there was a guy with an ice cream cart. They were saved.

Sally was examining the waffle cone minutely.

"Smell's a funny thing. It's so immediate - just bang! Strawberry, or chocolate, or whatever this green one is."

"Pistachio."

"The green one?"

"Yes. That's what it's called."

"Whatever, taste's good." The gelato was already beginning to melt in the hot sun. Multi-coloured goo ran down her fingers and arms.

"Better get a move on."

Sally did her best, but it was a lost cause. Tense set down the eski for a moment and retrieved some paper napkins. Admitting defeat, Sally dropped the remains of the cone into a litter bin and turned around. Tense stifled his laughter. She was covered in goop. Solemnly, Tense passed Sally a paper napkin. And then another one. And then another. Finally, the immortal Seraph was cleaned up.

"Come on." Sally raised herself to her full height, "What are you waiting for?" And off she trotted down the hillside in the direction of the Opera House. Tense grabbed the eski and followed meekly behind.

The Opera House forecourt and bar were busy. Dishevelled revellers from the night before blearily mixing with families out for a walk and council workers picking up litter and removing temporary barriers from the New Year's firework display. The sun gleamed on the white sails of the Opera House roof and the deep blue of the harbour. Little boats sailed this way and that.

"There is a saying, people love the city of Melbourne for its beautiful mind, but they love Sydney for its beautiful body."

Sally and Tense observed the scene.

"Which do you love me for?" Sally adopted a look of the utmost seriousness. Tense looked like a Labrador puppy caught in the very act of ripping up a pillow.

"I, err, well, obviously...."

Sally reached over and patted his cheek.

"It's OK. No need to answer."

They wandered across the Opera House forecourt and up into the park. The clouds were building great, grey anvil shapes, flattening out as though against some invisible ceiling. A storm was coming. Tense could feel the electricity in the air.

Something had been bugging him since the conversation in the cathedral.

"What do angels want, actually?" Tense blurted out the question almost without thinking, "What motivates an angel?"

"Well, I can't answer for the dark angels, the demons, but I can tell you what they say they want, and for the rest of us, we exist to serve. It is our being and purpose."

"Don't you hunger to grow and change, to learn and extend yourselves? What's the point in living forever if you remain exactly the same forever".

Sally looked quizzically back at him as though trying to figure out what his words meant.

"Don't you yearn for transcendence – to become more than you are?"

"Some do, I suppose. Those that think about it would like to extend our freedom of movement from four to five dimensions. They want to shift through the realms of the possible too. Not be limited only to space and time."

"The realms of the possible?" Tense was struggling to get his head around angelic metaphysics, "What are the realms of the possible?"

"You would call them the multiverse, I suppose. We are stuck in this one universe of all the infinite possibilities that exist."

"There's more than one universe?"

"Yes, of course. Everything that could happen has happened, will happen and is happening now."

"Blimey."

"Indeed. Now you see why some of us get a bit frustrated sometimes, spending all eternity stuck in this one measly reality."

"Are there angels in the other universes?"

"Some of us think so."

"What's beyond that?" Tense's mind was blown completely, "What's beyond the five dimensions?"

"We think there is a sixth and final reality. But only the Creator has freedom of movement in all six dimensions."

"What is the sixth reality or dimension or whatever?"

"There is no single word for it. You could call it love perhaps, or compassion, but your scientists would call it the quantum vacuum, the creative void from which something is created from nothing."

"That's a dimension?"

"Well, wholeness then, or completeness. We angels can only grasp at it. We cannot encompass it. Some of us think it can be inferred from the behaviour of the Creator."

"From his mysterious ways?" Tense was not convinced. He had, he realised, no real, concrete proof even that Sally was an angel. It was all getting a bit much – again.

Tense snapped.

"Look, I know I'm hopelessly in love with you, and my usually laser-like bullshit sensor may be malfunctioning a wee bit, but what proof do I have that any of what you have said is true?"

Sally just stared at him for a moment.

"Not true? A lie, you mean?"

"Well, I wouldn't put it so bluntly, but mightn't you be mistaken?"

Sally at first just laughed, then, seeing that Tense was speaking in deadly earnest, she too snapped.

"I'm a fucking angel, you dim-witted man. We don't lie."

Silence fell between them like a cold fog. Neither spoke for several minutes.

"I have lived forever", Sally continued, "I have eons of experience. I'm not lying, and I'm not making it up."

Tense missed the opportunity to put things right.

"If God is real, like an established fact, then there is no need or purpose to faith, is there?"

Sally ignored him. She was sulking.

Tense tried again, "We could study God then, couldn't we? We could invent a new science, "Creator Studies".

Sally turned her back on him and walked away a few paces.

"You don't trust me?"

"I do, of course, but it's a lot to take in."

Sally turned back towards him.

"It's a lot to understand. I see that, but that's where faith comes in."

Tense nodded, baffled but bravely going along with it.

Sally closed the gap between them. She took his hands in hers.

"Even if you don't fully understand, have faith in me."

***

Tense had built his worldview on order, rationality, and science. He was not the sort to take a leap of faith. It was not so much that he wanted evidence. He needed it. Without evidence and an hypothesis as to a mechanism, Tense was like a little lamb lost in the wood. Now, bewilderingly, he was being asked to set aside everything he believed in.

"Have faith in me", Sally had said.

Tense heard, "Just leap blindly into the dark." She may as well have said, "Just leap off this precipice, dear." It was outrageous. It was impossible. Above all, it was unreasonable and unfair. Here was super-stition and witch-burning. Here was chaos and the abyss.

"No." A sudden savage pain in his chest bent him almost double. Tense looked up at Sally through the slowly descending red mist, "No, I will not. You have no right to ask."

The couple stood staring at one another, each through the prism of their own unique cosmology. Each suddenly viewing the other as though through a glass, darkly.

After a few moments, the pain in his chest subsided sufficiently for him to stand upright again. A lifetime of sadness and disappointment coalesced in Sally's one shattering demand.

Sally stood, silent, still. For her, the realisation of the impossible gulf that lay between them thundered through her. Nothing, in all her centuries, had prepared her for this. The pain of misunderstanding and the smart of distrust seemed too much to bear. Her sense of loss, immeasurable. Her whole body seemed to ache with it.

From somewhere, words came. "I am a woman, and I am mortal, and I'm not very good at it. I am naked and afraid, and I love you."

For a moment, Tense seemed to lose his footing. Vertigo. A flood of perceptions. Drowning in a deluge of emotion. Tense felt himself being swept away. Only a supreme effort of will could save the day.

He began to walk, step by juddering step, toward the woman he loved. As alive and conscious as he had ever been. The words of an old poem came to his aid. Tense came to a decision. He would be the captain of his soul, the master of his fate.

"And I love you", he gasped, "and in the end, that is all that matters to me." Hot tears scalded his cheek. Shuddering, his heart hammering in his chest, Tense scooped Sally up, holding her close, holding tight.

Struggling for breath, Sally pushed him to arm's length. "It's awful."

"I know. I'm sorry. I'm so sorry I hurt you."

"No. It's awful being encased in flesh, being subject to the whims of the body. It's awful feeling the agony of loss in every cell and fibre of your being."

"It's ok. I am here, and I will never leave you." And he meant it, of course, as men do. He was sincere.

Sally closed her eyes, allowing her body to relax into the warmth of his embrace. Putting off, for a moment, the brooding sense of foreboding that circled her thoughts.

Then, out of nowhere, a thought popped into Sally's head.

"Teach me to ride a bike".

"I will, of course." Tense made no attempt to guess what leap of logic had led her to cycling as a solution. Though golden thread of reason there may well have been, Tense didn't care. He had made his choice, for now.

"Thank you, it looks like fun."

CHAPTER 5 - MERCIFUL ANNIHILATION

The milling crowds in the Opera House precinct heaved and swirled around them. Sally began to feel claustrophobic, encased, it seemed to her, in the turbulent flesh of her fellow human beings.

"Too many people," she almost gasped, "I need air."

The couple made their way back across Circular Quay and up into "The Rocks", an area of higgledy-piggledy alleyways and old sandstone buildings preserved from the time of first colonisation. The place was now full of bijou apartments, dinky little shops and cool restaurants.

Tense found a table in a quiet courtyard a little way up from George Street. They ordered coffee and sat, enjoying the relative stillness and peace.

"Are you afraid to die?" Tense blurted out in his usual measured and thoughtful manner, "Now that you are mortal, I mean?"

"I wasn't before, of course, but now I feel fear. It comes from the body, I think. It's the body's fear. The soul has no fear. Why should it?"

"So, angels cannot die, then? Ever, under any circumstances?"

"Well..." Sally paused, an intense frown momentarily clouding her features, "some of us talk about annihilation."

"Annihilation?"

"Yes, the total destruction of body and soul. The extinguishing of consciousness. The snuffing out of essence."

"Bloody hell."

"Yes. It's entirely theoretical, of course. No one has ever been annihilated, as far as we know. Even the fallen have been allowed to continue their miserable existence."

"Why does anyone think that annihilation might be possible then?"

"Well, the trite answer is that anything is possible. The Creator can do as he pleases."

"But there's a better answer?"

"I'm not sure it's better, but it's more thought out." Sally paused again. It was not clear if she meant to continue or not.

"What is it then?"

"Mercy."

"Mercy? Annihilation is supposed to be an act of mercy?"

"Yes."

"You know, every now and then, I get a glimpse of why Lucifer would go to war against his Creator."

"You do?"

"Yes, and I have to say, this is one of those times." Tense stopped, checking Sally's reaction. She seemed curious, not about to have another conniption. Tense ploughed on.

"If the total annihilation of body and soul is an act of mercy, what would be an act of cruelty?"

"Look, the belief in annihilation is a minority thing. It's not mainstream, you know."

"But still, to the minority, how does it make sense?"

"It would be cruel not to annihilate those who would otherwise spend eternity in torment."

"Oh"

"It would be an act of kindness to put them out of their misery."

"Whether they liked it or not?"

"Guess so. It's never been a subject of study for me." Somewhere across the city, a siren sounded.

"Shall we get some cake?" Sally brightened at the thought. Her tummy was rumbling.

The pair fell once more to silence, studying the menu.

"Shall I have the Banoffee Pie or the Louisiana Mud Cake?"

"Which do you prefer?"

"Both"

"Have both, then."

"I can't do that. That would be greedy."

"Well then, I can't really help you."

"Yes, you can."

"How?"

"You order the Mud Cake, and I'll have the Banoffee Pie." Sally beamed, obviously delighted with her Machiavellian ruse.

"I see."

A waitress appeared and took their order.

"I think we'd like ice cream with the Mud Cake, please, if that's possible?" Tense sounded resigned.

"Vanilla?"

"Perfect. And I'll have the banoffee pie." Sally chipped in.

The air was hot and still within the confines of the courtyard. Their table was in deep shade beneath a fig tree. A fly buzzed loudly around Tense's coffee cup. He flapped at it idly. It was too hot to exert the flesh. A kind of languid peace enveloped them. Nothing was said. Sally snaffled down the last couple of sandwiches while they waited. Justifying the snack on the grounds that she had somehow missed lunch.

Another vagrant thought flitted across Tense's otherwise unoccupied mind.

"Why is it important for you to grieve, other than the fact that you are a Grieving Angel, I mean?"

"I bear witness to suffering."

"That's it?"

"Yes."

"You don't do anything about it?"

"No. My job is to witness suffering and remember it."

"What's the point of that?"

"All experience must be witnessed. It's the will of the Creator."

"Well, why do you need to replenish your grief? How come it needs replenishing at all?"

"Any emotion, too long sustained, reverts to weariness."

"You felt weary."

"Yes"

"And you needed a holiday."

"Yes"

"And you got more than you bargained for?"

"Yes, I think I may be in for a bit of serious replenishment."

Something churned in the pit of Tense's stomach. Foreboding waited there. The seed of some unknown dread began to grow. As Tense's thoughts began to darken, he returned to an earlier theme.

"Annihilation as an act of mercy." he began, "What you are suggesting is that God is too loving to torment the fallen forever, but he is willing to torment them for a good long time?"

"I'm not suggesting it. That is what a minority of angels suspect."

"So, God wants them to suffer?"

"No. Not at all. It's up to them."

"It's their choice, you mean?"

"Yes. They could always change their minds. They could always repent."

"So why don't they."

"Look. I haven't studied these things. It's just what I've heard."

"What have you heard?"

"I should have thought it was obvious. They don't repent because they're not sorry." A waspish tone began to edge its way into Sally's voice. This was clearly not a topic she enjoyed. At heart, Sally was a sunny, carefree sort of an angel, other than the grieving, of course, which was more by way of her professional calling than a quality of her personality.

"Why are they not sorry?"

"Better freedom with suffering than servitude in comfort. As Lucifer himself said, "Better to rule in Hell than serve in Heaven"."

"He said that?"

"Supposedly. I wasn't there."

Tense had one last stab at it.

"I've seen statues of Saint Michael, having laid Lucifer low with his trusty sword of truth, then offering him his hand, as though to lift him back onto his feet."

"Yes"

"So, is Michael reaching out to Lucifer with forgiveness?"

"I suppose so, yes."

Before the conversation could become any more morbid, the waitress appeared with the cake.

"Dig in" Tense picked up his fork and began to address his dessert with gusto.

"Hey, slow down! Leave some for me." Sally wore an expression of deep concern.

"Oh, sorry, did you want a taste?"

Sally gave him a sour look, swiftly followed by a flouncy toss of the head.

"Why not just change their minds for them?"

"Are we back to that?"

"Sorry, but why not?"

"Free will. It's not free will if you interfere."

The answer left Tense feeling hoodwinked. It seemed a little too pat, too simple.

"That's partly why some of us think we were an early experiment."

"Huh?"

"Give an immortal free will, and you are asking for trouble. Lucifer was the first of us to realise we had free will at all. Before that, we had no idea. We hadn't thought about it. At least with mortals, their time is finite."

"But their souls are immortal, right? So, it just delays the issue."

Sally tried to say something through a mouthful of Banoffee Pie. It was impossible to make it out.

"So, what are our lives for then? Human lives, I mean, the mortal bit?"

Sally swallowed grumpily.

"Perhaps to teach you to play nice when you get to heaven. How should I know?"

Sally turned her attention firmly back to her dessert. Her ice cream was melting.

"Hang on a minute. Lucifer's war on Heaven was both an act of free will and was foreseen by God. In so far as Lucifer had free will, he was guilty, at least in God's eyes, but since the rebellion must have been foreseen by God and allowed to go ahead, there must be a sense in which Lucifer is, in effect, innocent. God could simply have stopped it."

Sally looked up from her dessert for a moment.

"Umm, that does make sense, doesn't it?"

***

Their bellies full, the couple made their way back through the narrow lanes to Circular Quay station and took the train home. The day had somehow wandered away from them.

They were both silent on the train, lost in their own thoughts and reflections. Sally had been left somewhat troubled by Tense's logic. She felt cut off from the direct connection she had always enjoyed with her Creator. She felt deserted, abandoned. Encased in mortal flesh, enlivened only by an attenuated thread of spirit, she felt as though she might have died and somehow forgotten to have herself buried.

"I feel I have been left alone, exposed, without excuse. My Creator has walked away and made me responsible for the choices I make."

"Welcome to the club." Inopportune levity lent the comment a dismissive air.

"What a shitty thing to say."

"Sorry. Just trying to be funny."

"Cynicism is sincerity masked by pain." Sally gave him one of her most old-fashioned looks.

"I'm sorry, that was thoughtless. You do look a bit woebegone. Forsaken."

"I do feel a bit lost. It's a horrible feeling. I feel discarded."

"What can I do?"

"I don't know. I feel like my mind and body are fluid. I feel unstable."

"Unsafe?"

"Well, that too, but more sort of "mutable". Language makes humans conceptualise everything. I feel myself fluctuating between an increasingly less physical and more intellectualised physical body and an increasingly material spirit. I feel 'thingified' – if that's a word."

"It is now." Tense smiled and wrapped an arm around her.

"Even if I know God isn't dead, my mind keeps entertaining the possibility that he has just ceased to exist. The more we walk around, the more I experience the fine-grained reality of this world, the more divorced I feel from reality itself."

"One of the French philosophers, Voltaire, I think, said something like ', Even if my apartment is filled with lizards and rats, the architect exists, and anyone who denies it is touched with madness under the guise of wisdom.'"

"He said that?"

"Yep. Well, I think it was him. Pretty cool, huh?"

"Whatever."

The train clattered into their station. Sally and Tense stepped silently down from the carriage.

It wouldn't be dark for quite a while. Tense stopped at a bottle shop and bought a nice box of Shiraz.

"Six bottles should be enough." Tense smiled.

"Enough for what?"

"I just mean we won't run out."

Sally still seemed troubled.

"Let's sit on the balcony and watch the sun go down with a nice glass of red."

"What's for dinner?"

Tense couldn't help but laugh.

"Pizza. We'll send out for it."

"Will I like pizza?"

"I expect so. I'd be amazed if you didn't – you've scoffed every-thing else that's been put in front of you."

"What sort of pizza should I order?"

"We'll have a look at the menu. You can choose." Sally bright-ened.

They walked on. In a few minutes, Sydney Harbour came into view through the bridge in the distance.

"Diavola, I reckon. Hot and spicy but oh so good."

"Are you making fun of me again?"

"I really can't say," Tense was surprised at his own boldness, "I don't know what came over me."

In a few moments, they were back at the apartment. Tense for once, having the foresight to set down his burden before fighting once more with the door lock. As luck would have it, the door opened easily. Tense took it as an omen.

"I don't believe in omens."

"I never said a word."

"Oops. My bad."

CHAPTER 6 - ABANDONMENT

The wine went down well, very well indeed. By 8 p.m., the pair were fairly well smashed. By 10 p.m., they could well be described as pickled.

The sunset was very fine that evening, gold and red across a scattered mackerel sky. Lights twinkled from the few occupied boats at anchor in the harbour. Life was good.

They had over-ordered Indian takeaway in the end. The pizza place was closed. Half-filled containers scattered higgledy-piggledy across the balcony table spoke of a feast well enjoyed. The cardboard half-case of wine sat sentinel beside the table, one corner roughly torn to reveal the remaining three bottles.

Sally moved her chair around next to Tense and snuggled against him. The cooler night air was a relief after the heat of the day. The brickwork of the apartment block still radiated heat a full hour after the sun had gone down.

Tense slipped an arm easily around Sally's waist. Her head rested on his shoulder. The city was calm that evening, relaxing in the cool of nightfall. It was as though, through some unspoken covenant, the Sydneysiders had agreed to give each other the night off.

Tense's scent filled Sally's nostrils, warm and comforting. She kissed his neck gently.

So, this was what it was like being a human woman. Falling in love. Finding comfort in the presence of your soulmate. Finding contentment in the face of ageing and death. Accepting the inevitable without being defined by it.

A sudden chill wind off the water caught her unawares. Sally shivered. Tiny hairs stood up on her arm. A pointless, ineffective hangover from some earlier species of human. Vestigial traces such as these seemed to make up so much of a human being, while, from her point of view, nascent capabilities made up the rest. It seemed impossible to say what these transitional creatures actually were, right here, right now. It was, she mused, impossible to define exactly what she was, trapped between the evolutionary experiments of failed races and the ongoing progression and fruition of her own.

Angels were immune from evolution. Angels were, by definition, unchanging. Powerful, immortal, vastly more conscious and aware than any human, yet unable to grow, change, or develop. Sally had to acknowledge that. The angels were stuck. Even the fallen, who had risked all for their freedom, could not free themselves from their fate. Sally and her kind were more like primordial elements, mere features of the universe, than self-actuating actors capable of genuine agency.

And with this realisation, as though God had flicked a switch, her world fell silent. Sally froze. Never in all the eons of her immortality had she experienced such a deafening, thunderous silence. The constant scarcely noticed susurration of a myriad minds had been cut off. An infinite silence swamped her, threatening to drown her reason.

Sally screamed. A long piercing ululation. A cry of total desolation and despair. She had been abandoned. She had been cut off. She was utterly stranded and alone. Only through the portal of death could she rejoin her kind.

Tense leapt to his feet at the very first hideous note of her mournful shriek. He spun around, desperately seeking the source of his beloved's terror.

"What is it?"

Sally grabbed him and clung to him.

"I'm dead", she cried, staring unseeing up at his face, "I am dying."

"What? What do you mean? Do you need a doctor?"

"It's too late for that."

"I'll call an ambulance." Tense tried to pull free. Sally clung all the harder, shaking and shivering, both unwilling and unable to loosen her grip.

Bewildered and terrified, Tense lifted Sally in his arms and carried her indoors. He sat down on the sofa with Sally in his lap, her arms still locked around his neck. Tense wrapped his arms around her, holding her close.

"It's ok. I'm here, and I will never leave you."

"You will. Of course, you will. You will die, and I will be left alone."

"We are both still young. We have our whole lives ahead of us."

"A flicker", Sally whispered the words. All at once, she seemed to deflate, shrinking into a small and frightened woman truly facing an unknown future for the very first time.

Sally looked up at Tense, searching his face, seeking something. Seeking certainty or reassurance.

"They're gone."

"Who?"

"Everyone. All my kin. Everyone on earth. We are alone."

"What do you mean?"

"There is nothing but silence. I cannot hear them anymore. I cannot even hear you."

"You mean you can't see what's in my mind anymore?"

"That's right. I can't hear any minds other than my own."

"Are you sick? Can angels get sick?"

"I'm not sick, and I'm not fully an angel. Not anymore."

"How? How can that happen?"

"My creator has forsaken me. I will get no more help there. He does not hear my cries."

Sally had been half expecting that this moment would come. She had begun to realise that there was some other purpose to her arrival on Earth, but the reality, the suddenness, was all but unbearable.

"What?"

"I have been abandoned. Left to the dogs. I will live a little while and then die."

"But you will live. You are alive now." Relief flooded through Tense. He could breathe again; his heart could resume beating.

Sally felt Tense's strong arms around her, gentle and loving. She stared up at his careworn face. She was loved. That at least she knew, and she was in love.

"It's only for a little while," Sally ventured a small smile, "We'll manage."

***

They sat in silence, comfortable in each other's presence. Processing raw experience into some kind of narrative. Making it make sense. Imposing reason upon it.

"I think I'm beginning to get it," Sally spoke first.

"You are? Get what?" Tense, lost in the warmth of Sally's body held tightly against him, had entered a kind of meditative reverie. Thoughts arose like morning mist off an ocean, dissipating and disappearing, too fragile to be examined. Here one second, gone the next.

"Lucifer, all the fallen, in fact, attacked the system from within. They were not trying to destroy it. They were not trying to bring down heaven. They were trying to overthrow God and capture paradise for themselves. They wanted a paradise without a Creator."

"I see." Tense didn't, not really.

"It's impossible to destroy Creation from within. It could only conceivably be destroyed from without, but there is no outside. There's nowhere else to go."

"Well, I wasn't planning a trip." Tense's attempt at humour in the face of bafflement missed its mark. Sally stared at him blankly for a moment.

"Except."

"Except?"

"Except maybe it is possible to create the new within the old. Maybe it's possible for humans. Maybe human individuality does act like a seed, creating an ethically and religiously new universe. A universe of new ideas and experiences. A new creation triggered by human will alone."

"Search me." Tense had reached a point of intellectual exhaustion, "Didn't someone else say that?"

"Kierkegaard… He was a prick, though."

"Really?"

"Yep."

"Care to expand on that?"

"Nope."

"Bed then?"

"Yep."

Tense lifted Sally gently and carried her through to the bedroom.

It was too hot for blankets. They lay under a sheet listening to the soft whir of the ceiling fan. Occasional sounds from the city impinged upon their sanctuary.

Caught between ambivalence or repulsion about, and acceptance of her fleshy, physical form, Sally plumped for the smart of sexual pleasure and the brief, transient moments of relief it offered.

An observer might have noticed the slightest predatory gleam in Sally's eye as she turned to her lover and, in simple, forthright terms, demanded the pleasures of the flesh.

Tense was no observer. He was most definitely a participant and a very willing one at that. He noticed nothing.

Sally, for the first time in her brief human life, took charge. She put her young man through his paces. She guided and commanded. If physical pleasure was all the relief she was going to get right then and there, then she was damned well going to make sure she got it all.

Afterwards, Sally dragged Tense into the shower and washed him gently, like a prize stallion after a race. She anointed his head. She washed his feet. Tense was, she realised, sacred to her.

Sally led Tense from the shower and dried him with one of the large white bath towels they had taken to the beach. She left him swaddled in an armchair while she found clean sheets and remade their bed. By this time, even Tense had noticed the change in her.

"Feeling better?" Tense smiled broadly, risking a leer.

"Much better, thank you." Sally glowed with well-being. Something had changed. She had made up her mind.

If she was going to have to be a woman, trapped in meat, corralled, and constrained by gender roles, oppressed by gravity and public opinion, then she was going to be her own kind of woman. She was going to find her own way. The challenge had been set without her foreknowledge or informed consent. She had been given no choice but to pick up the gauntlet.

Somewhere, she knew, Lucifer waited. He would be aware of her presence by now. He would be scheming. This was his world far more than hers. His evil would be subtle and slow. She would have to be careful.

OK then. Game on.

CHAPTER 7 – DAY 3, PARASITE

The following morning the wind from the south swept in unseasonably cold. An arctic wind had arrived in the night, vagrant and angry, racing across the Southern Ocean. Sally and Tense found the blankets and snuggled like marmosets.

"How about a cup of tea?" Tense, ever hopeful, gave Sally his innocent, loving look.

"Are you giving me your innocent, loving look?"

"I might be."

"I may no longer be telepathic, but I know when I'm being manipulated."

"Oh, thank goodness" Tense, by any standards unusually frisky this morning, tried his luck, "It's such an effort to keep it up."

"I'll make the tea if you make the breakfast." Sally could not easily resist his innocent, loving look.

"Deal", for Tense, who had expected to have to do both, having someone make him a cup of tea was an unexpected luxury.

Sally pottered through to the kitchen and put the kettle on. She stepped out onto the balcony to observe the boats bobbing about in the bay. A gusty cold wind buffeted her as she stood. She felt the chill of the wind cutting to the bone, recognised the goose bumps forming on her arms and focussed on experiencing her body's animal response to raw environmental stimulus. So much of human experience was automatic, she realised. So little was intentional. The body was an unconscious, or perhaps semi-conscious, mechanism carrying a fragile, frightened mind.

Sally began to feel her body. She began listening to it, allowing it to speak to her. She began to tune in to the song of blood and bone, muscle and sinew. She began to appreciate its quiet, instinctual voice.

She began to hear. At first, the merest whisper. A tiny voice, in-
choate, random. Its pattern emerging by slow degrees from the
background noise of physical being.

Her heartbeat was strong and slow, unhurried. The pulse in her
wrist and neck beat time. The blood whooshed through her arteries and
veins. She breathed and shivered. Subtle messages passed hither and
thither. Her autonomic nervous system carried out its appointed tasks
without comment and without demur. And as she listened, Sally began
to detect or thought she could detect a second presence. Another simultaneously separate and composite.

There was something inside her. There was some parasite hidden
in her gut. She was certain of it. Sally felt nauseous at the realisation.
She screamed. Tense, who had drifted back to sleep, heard the sound,
snapped awake and vaulted from the bed to stand for a moment, conscious but bewildered, on the cold polished wooden floorboards. He
ran from the bedroom. His heart was pumping, bordering on panic.

"What is it" he shouted, "are you all right" Tense found Sally
standing, shivering on the balcony, clutching her belly. She stood, rock-
ing slightly from side to side and moaning.

"Are you hurt? Are you sick?" There was nothing obviously
wrong. Tense took her hand. "What is it?"

"I have something inside me. I know it."

"What do you mean? What's inside you?"

"Something. I don't know what. Something alive."

Tense stepped back, totally at a loss.

What do you mean? How can there be something inside you?

"I don't fucking know. How should I know? This is all brand fucking new to me, you idiot. All I know is there is something inside me.
Something is growing inside me. It's disgusting."

"Come inside and sit down. You're freezing." Tense led Sally back
into the apartment and sat her down at the table.

"I'll finish making the tea." Tense brought a blanket from the bedroom and wrapped it around her.

A moment or two later, Tense set down two mugs of tea. They steamed slightly in the unseasonable early morning chill.

Sally took a sip. Her shivering had subsided somewhat, and she had managed to regain some composure. They sat silently, sipping tea and staring out into the bay. The wind was beginning to die down.

"It'll warm up once the wind changes direction. They've forecast a hot one." Tense glanced at Sally, gauging her emotional state.

"I'll make breakfast in a minute."

Sally, who had been working through the possibilities, finally looked up. She wore an expression of abject desolation on her face. Realisation had come to her.

"I'm pregnant."

"So soon? You can't be. Well, you can be, but you can't possibly know yet."

"I can know, and I do, and I am." Sally's voice was flat, emotionless, and for the moment, defeated. Her human body was taking control, calling the shots. It was insufferable.

"What? Are you sure?"

Sally nodded.

"Oh my God", Tense leapt to his feet and sort of spun around, unable to contain or direct his feelings. He had never once in his life imagined that he would be a father. This was impossibly good news.

"You're pregnant? You really are? You're going to have a baby?"

"Shut up. Shut the fuck up. Don't say that." Sally half rose out of her chair as though to run or fight.

"I'm not an animal. I'm not a creature."

"Of course, you're not. I don't understand."

"Of course, you don't. Why would you?" The waspish tone had returned to Sally's voice. Sally reviewed what little she knew of the lived experience of mortal women. She would get fat. That was inevitable, and she would waddle. From what she knew, men didn't seem to find pregnant women all that attractive. Beloved, yes, absolutely, on occasion, but fancied? Nah.

"You won't love me when I'm fat. My body will disgust you."

"No. I will love you always, whatever."

"I'll remind you of a sow. This is awful."

"But this is fantastic" Tense was ecstatic, "This is wonderful."

Sally watched bleakly as Tense capered around the table to wrap her in his arms.

"You won't even be here. I'll be left alone to bring the child up." Sally's mind was full of dark and desolate outcomes.

"No. That's not true. I'll never leave you. I swear it."

With what was obviously a considerable effort of will, Sally managed to pull herself together.

"We're going to have a baby," Sally caressed his cheek gently with the fingertips of one hand, "and you are the father".

"You're eating for two now" Tense took her hand and kissed her fingers gently one by one, "I'll make breakfast."

A sudden gust of wind caught the balcony door and slammed it. They both jumped.

***

Breakfast that day was insane. Tense pulled out all the stops. That's right: eggs over easy – done properly, not just flipped. Bacon, sausages, mushrooms, baked beans, toast, croissants, raspberry jam, orange juice, coffee and the good Irish breakfast tea.

Tense was deliriously happy. No sense of foreboding had yet clouded his joy. No nagging doubt that this was all just a little bit too good to be true. No. Not yet. For now, everything was fantastically perfect.

He ticked his triumphs off on his fingers: He'd found the love of his life. She seemed to like him. Sex was profound and fulfilling. She was having a baby. He was going to be a father. And dare he say it. Sally could no longer snoop on his innermost private thoughts – although to be fair, the loss of her telepathy did not seem to have impeded her laser-like oracular powers one iota. Was that five triumphs or six? Either way, he was a happy man.

Sally progressively regained her composure as Tense's small dining table was filled to overflowing with yummy goodies. Food, heaps of it, always seemed to have a calming effect.

Tense poured two tiny piccolo cups of espresso and plonked himself down opposite Sally.

"Dig in", he all but trilled, feminised somewhat by his unbridled joy and the pleasure of caring for Sally – and the baby.

"Do you think it will be a boy or a girl?" Tense, tactless as ever, blithely continued, "We will have to think of a name!"

It was ok, though. Sally, breathing heavily through her nose as she shovelled mouthfuls of egg and bacon down her gullet, was, for the moment, distracted.

"Mm…. girl, I think", she managed between mouthfuls, "how does one tell?"

"Well, boys and girls are different, you know." Tense began obtusely.

"No. Not that, you idiot. How does a mother know what she's carrying? The sex, I mean?"

"Intuition, perhaps? Ultrasound…" Tense had retreated a little into his shell, stung by Sally's name-calling.

"I'm sorry. You're not an idiot. You're lovely, really, and you are my mate and the father of our child." Sally reached out and gave him a pat.

Tense was thinking about a name for the baby. The responsibility was debilitating. He had an idea.

"What was your mother's name?"

Sally rolled her eyes and carried on stuffing her face.

"Sorry. Forgot." And then, "Well, my mum's name was Sheila. Don't laugh."

"Why should I laugh?" Sally managed between mouthfuls, "Sheila means "from the Heavens" or something like that. Seems quite appropriate."

"I didn't know the name had a proper meaning." Growing up in rural Australia, Tense had always assumed it meant 'girl' or 'woman'.

Tense played listlessly with the food on his plate. His mood, now, had suddenly darkened. Perhaps it was the unwelcome emergence of long-suppressed memories of his mother? Never a happy woman. Possessed, in Tense's view, of an exceptional and apparently innate sense of personal entitlement, she had never really found happiness or even contentment - truth be told. Tense's father had spent almost every waking hour at the mine. He was an engineer and a good one too, but he was not much of a father.

Tense, reviewing briefly in his own mind his memories of his parents' long, uneventful marriage, felt once again an unfocused, diffuse sense of loss. His father had loved him, Tense knew that, but he had never been very good at showing it. His father had loved Tense's mother too, but whether this was reciprocated remained a mystery.

Devoid of any personal role models of successful and happy, as opposed to merely long marriages, Tense fell back upon the sentimental assertions of popular culture. However, as with most things to do with popular culture, Tense dismissed equally both the saccharine sweet and the grossly dysfunctional versions served up by the media. Instead, he saw love, marriage, and relationships generally as a dialectic, a sort of endless yin-yanging. At its best, love was a strange attractor around which the emotional threads of the protagonists' lives wound incessantly, randomly, on and on until, at last, the thread was cut.

Tense felt himself becoming melancholic and tried to shake it off.

"What shall we do today?" he asked, "I know. How about the Zoo?"

"You enjoy seeing animals locked up for human amusement, do you?" While Tense had been wallowing in his own morose fantasies, Sally had somehow worked herself into a bit of a fret.

"I never had a mother or father", she announced belligerently.

"No. I realise that. Sorry."

"You're sorry I have no parents, or you're sorry I'm an angel and could never have had any, by definition?"

"I'm just sorry you're upset. We don't have to go to the zoo."

"Whatever", Sally, having expostulated, had calmed down again and returned to her methodical assault upon breakfast.

Tense sat and watched silently as she ate. *What a double-edged sword love is'*, he thought. *'What a cruel game. A sadomasochistic amusement without rules. A contest that can never be won and never lost. How can I possess your freedom, or you, mine?*

What had Sartre said, 'Only those who fear and tremble in the face of fatherhood are worthy of assuming its infinite responsibilities' or something like that? Well, Tense was fearing and trembling all right. He was obviously, existentially speaking, an excellent candidate for fatherhood.

***

Sally and Tense were sitting on the balcony in silence. There was a bit of an atmosphere between them. Somehow, they had alighted upon the name 'Sheila' if the baby was a girl. Despite Tense's fulsome explanation of Australian culture and history, Sally couldn't see anything funny about the name. They were, however, quite unable to choose a name if the baby were to be a boy. This was mainly because Sally knew she was having a girl and simply couldn't be bothered to discuss inconsequentialities. A subsidiary reason might have been that she didn't much fancy 'Eric'.

Tense found Sally's attitude superior, brusque, rude and disrespectful of his role as a father – and was consequently sulking while adopting a pose of airy indifference.

"I'm simply going to rise above it." he declared, his nonchalance tainted somewhat by his concomitant, hasty and undignified scramble for the moral high ground.

"You cannot have the moral high ground, you know." Sally sighed.

"Yes, I can, and I will. In fact, I have." Tense had an uncomfortable feeling Sally was going to be proven correct, but he was not going to give up without a fight.

"This is getting us nowhere. Sheila is a nice name, and Eric, apart from being boring and nondescript, is irrelevant. I'm having a girl."

"My father's name was Eric."

"And was he boring and nondescript?" Sally was feeling a might peevish.

"He might have been. But he was still my father."

Fearing a day of sulking and bickering ahead, Sally decided to throw Tense a bone.

"You are right. I apologise. If we have a baby boy, we can call him Eric. Ok?"

"OK. I'm going to check whether the zoo is open."

Tense stepped into the apartment to look up the zoo's opening hours.

"It's a baby girl anyway," Sally muttered as Tense closed the balcony door behind him. He was back a few moments later, smiling broadly.

"It's open until six."

They took the ferry to the zoo. Sally loved it. She leaned so far out over the gunnel that a member of the ferry staff eventually asked her to stop. It was only a short trip across the harbour, and the sea, for once, was smooth as a mill pond.

"I haven't been on a boat in a thousand years", Sally proclaimed to the befuddlement of the small group of men gathered nearby who had been holding a sweepstake on the likelihood of her falling overboard, "and never on one with an engine." Sally was very excited. She'd forgiven Tense for attempting to purloin the moral high ground and was really quite looking forward to the zoo.

"Can you play with the animals?"

"No."

'Not at all? Not any of them?'

"I believe there's a petting zoo for the children."

"I want to go there" Sally appeared to have regressed to childhood, which would have been impossible if she were still wholly an angel. It got Tense to thinking.

"Are there any angel children? Can angels even have children?"

"I've never heard of an angel child. I'm not sure what would be the point."

"The point of children?"

"Well, the point of an angel child. We're not a species as such. We have no need of procreation."

Tense couldn't help giving it another go, "So angels don't have sex then? I mean, if you guys don't have children, there'd be no use for sex, right?"

"We are disembodied most of the time. I thought I'd made that clear?"

"Yes"

"Well, you may have noticed one needs to have a body to have sex."

"So, I'm right then. No sex for angels." Tense's tone was unnecessarily smug in delivering that last remark.

Thankfully, Sally did not take offence, "As it happens, there are compensations, you know – eternal life, direct contact with the creator, the ability to travel effortlessly in time and space, plus a whole bunch of capabilities for which there are no human words at all."

Tense's mind wandered back onto an earlier track, "So, are angels androgynous or something else entirely?"

"Angels only choose a gender when we are in physical form. I think you can only be androgynous in a body, can't you?"

"Then how do you distinguish different types of angel?"

"There are heaps of different kinds. We all have different jobs or responsibilities. There are three tiers or spheres of heaven, and there are different kinds of angels for each."

"Sounds complicated. Why so many?"

"You'd have to ask the Creator that, but the basic taxonomy works like this:

First sphere: Seraphim, Cherubim and Thrones. Those guys are like the Papal Curia, and no one knows quite what they do either. Second sphere: Lordships, Virtues and Authorities, basically admin. Third sphere: Principalities, Archangels and Angels – like me. We're for outreach."

"So, you're at the bottom of the heap?"

"Watch it, puny human. Angels and Archangels are the messengers of God, and we can kick ass when we want to."

"And the others never leave heaven?"

"Nah."

"What do they do?"

"Bureaucrats. Pen pushers. Not sure, actually. We don't tend to have much to do with them."

Sally's interest was waning. Tense decided to change the subject, "They have lambs and rabbits in the petting zoo. You can cuddle them, I think."

"I like lambs. It's an angel thing."

The couple, who had been wandering up the hill from the ferry terminal, finally reached the zoo. As they joined the short queue to buy tickets, Tense began to see the zoo in a new and altogether unfamiliar light.

"We keep animals in a zoo for our own entertainment. Is that what we are to you?"

"Earth, the physical universe, is not a zoo." Sally paused for a moment, seeking the right words, "It's more a sort of game reserve. You're free to roam."

"Free-range humans. Fucking great."

***

Sally and Tense wandered around the zoo. They were relaxed, to begin with. They made for the petting zoo. Sally was in heaven. There were rabbits and guinea pigs. There was even a lamb, born late in the season, around three months old but still just about cuddlable. Sally cooed and oohed and was generally besotted. Tense looked on, quite unable either to join in or even really to fathom her delight. Sure, the animals were cute…

After they left the petting zoo, they wandered aimlessly around for a bit. They heard a talk on Komodo Dragons and got to wander through the Lemur enclosure, inevitably being crapped on by the over-excited primates.

Eventually, they ended up at the Meerkat enclosure, listening to a breathlessly enthusiastic exposition upon the beauty of the Botswanan desert and the eccentricities and life expectancy of meerkats in captivity. The diminutive mob stared back at them from a safe distance, occasionally disappearing in an instant only to bob up again moments later with what Tense took to be a reproachful look upon their pointy little faces.

The couple wandered on. The cavalcade of isolated and imprisoned animals began to impinge uncomfortably on Tense's mood. He couldn't help returning in his mind to Sally's throw-away remark – 'free to roam'. Humans were free to roam. From the purview of eternity, even an infinite physical universe would amount to a cage. He began to hate the zoo.

Triggered perhaps by some half-remembered play he thought he might once have seen. Tense began to re-evaluate. Each animal or group of animals was separated from the others by human artifice. Tense felt he could see in the layout and construction of the zoo an analogy to the human condition. He didn't mention it. Sally would only look at him blankly or give him a pat on the cheek.

Unlike the animals, Tense thought, we humans are separated not just from each other by bars of social, ethnic, and religious steel but also from our true animal nature. Like animals, we are camouflaged.

We blend perfectly into the vibrantly packaged desolation of the modern landscape.

Tense imagined the animals fighting their isolation. This, he thought, is essentially the human condition. We protect ourselves with walls of things, habits and false differences that separate us from each other. Tense looked at Sally and was reminded of the difference between love and sexual need.

Tense saw himself as a worldling stripped of his material goods, stumbling toward a revelation of truth. To be truly human is essentially to be an outcast. This was the paradox, of course. Man, in the state of nature, is alone, a prisoner of self.

Well, Tense was done pretending that he was not alone. He was done surrounding himself with artefacts and ideas that sustain the barrier between himself and all other living things. He took stock of his situation. Now that he understood his condition or thought he did. Now that he had become agonisingly aware of his own animal nature and the limitations of the self, Tense felt driven to prove his kinship with the universe.

Of course, this was, for Tense, an existential act in the purest sense. This was transcending his boundaries, defying his 'self'. Tense felt he was proving his humanity, that kinship with nature could be recognised only by the animal within, only by that instinctive spark of divinity embodied within him. Only by an act of love, by a sacrifice so great that it annihilates the self that imprisons him. Only by an act of love and martyrdom that takes his life.

Sally, noticing his distress, wandered up.

"What's up, my love? Don't you like the animals?"

"It's not the animals."

"If not the animals, then what?"

"It's the zoo."

"You don't like the zoo? It was your idea to come."

"Yes, but I'm beginning to see things differently."

"Are you having one of your fits of existential angst?"

"Yes"

"My poor love." Sally reached out and patted his cheek.

"Is it the fact that humans are limited to one measly infinite universe?"

"No. Well yes. Sort of."

Sally waited for Tense to continue.

"We come into the world alone, and we leave it alone."

"Yes"

"But between birth and death, we are alone too."

"Up to a point, you have your families and nations and so on."

"Yes, but they only create an illusion of belonging, don't they? Fundamentally we are atomised individuals. There really is no such thing as society."

"For angels, the experience of a connection to the divine is spiritual. It is because we are spirit, we are not embodied."

"And for humans?"

"For you, the opposite is true. While you are embodied, it is the body that hosts the spark of the divine. Your connection with God is through your physical reality."

"And when we die."

"When you die, that spark is set free and finds its way home."

"Really?"

"Yep. Cross my heart."

Sally stepped closer and wrapped her arms around his neck, pulling him to her. Tense could smell her warm scent. He could feel her lithe body in his arms. Sally began to kiss his neck. A giraffe cast a disinterested glance in their direction before turning away.

"Oh no," Tense could feel his body responding instinctually to Sally's presence.

"I can think of at least one way you can experience oneness with another person" Sally smiled mischievously.

"Oh yes, and what would that be?" Tense felt his mood rising by the second.

"I'll show you when we get home, Mr Grumpy."

"Oh, I'm not feeling grumpy, not grumpy at all."

Tense looked at the ferry timetable.

"We've just missed one."

"When's the next one due?"

"About half an hour."

Sally looked crestfallen.

"Oh dear, that's a long time to wait."

"Taxi?"

"Taxi."

Sally and Tense made their way smartly back to the entrance. Where, as luck would have it, there was a taxi waiting.

CHAPTER 8 - HER PLACE

Tense was, despite his flirtations with existential philosophy, atheistic spiritualism and a weird gestalt of stoic fatalism and Kantian indeterminism, basically a practical sort of bloke. He was an engineer by nature, and his universe was, at base, rational. Or so he had always thought.

The trip home in the taxi couldn't go quickly enough for either of them. The inevitable struggle with the door to his apartment, always seen by Tense essentially as a contest of wills, was simply brushed aside by a tsunami of desperate, physical desire. The door flew open, and the pair raced in, slamming it unceremoniously behind them.

Werner Hertzog, had he been recording the episode, would have tracked slowly from the closed door of the apartment, along the short corridor and into the sitting room. As he did so, his camera would have paused momentarily at the abandoned shoes, frantically kicked off in the hallway, the t-shirt and blouse strewn across the sitting room floor, and the lower garments and underwear piled at the entrance to the bedroom. He would perhaps have held the shot, allowing the audience to hear the giggling and other noises coming from the bedroom, enabling us to visualise the scene unfolding within. But, since neither Hertzog nor his camera were present, we can only imagine.

A feeling of total connection stole over Tense as he held the naked angel in his arms. Through Sally, he felt, probably for the first time, a sense of connection also to the divine. He felt himself coupled not just with Sally but with the universe itself. His very consciousness seemed to shift and grow, expanding effortlessly outwards and on, indefinitely, infinitely, world without end.

This altered state seemed to come out of nowhere. As Tense gazed at Sally's face, he saw she wore an expression of indescribable joy. She, too, had been transported and overcome. The lovers connected absolutely one to the other, each transcending the human sense of space, time, and even of self. Nothing was normal. It was as though they had suddenly awakened. Tense felt himself floating, separating from his physical body. Suddenly he seemed to be hovering over the bed. Sally stared up at him, smiling.

"Oh my God", Tense heard a man's voice, "This is what it's like for you, isn't it?" It was like a weird echo. There was his own voice, speaking from the body on the bed, and there was a second voice, an inner voice, speaking without words.

"Yes, my love." The words sounded silently in his mind.

Tense lost his grip on the moment. Out of his depth, beyond any previous experience, he had no means by which to anchor himself. He could gain no purchase upon - what? The timeline he had lived by every moment of his previous life was no longer there. He felt himself drifting, caught in an eddy of thought. There were his parents, sitting separately in the small lounge room of their suburban home. His father reading as usual, his mother watching the TV. Tense felt Sally by his side, steadying him.

"They loved each other, you know." Sally's affirmation felt rather than heard.

"Did they, really?"

"Yes. They were just too afraid to tell each other."

"Where are we? How is this happening?"

"You wanted to experience transcendence, my love."

"Are we dead?"

"No, silly. We are alive. This is what you call an "out of body" experience."

"We are not alone." Tense felt a presence, a kind of vastness, an infinite depth, conscious and loving.

"Fuck"

"Indeed. I never thought I'd get the chance to take you back to my place."

Tense felt himself surrounded by an expanding sphere of living creatures. There was a pervasive sense that he was participating in, or had become part of, some supernatural force. He had no name for it. It was beyond any previous experience. Beyond anything he had previously been able to imagine.

It was Spirit, he supposed, however, understood. He had slipped into another reality, seeing visions, being possessed by a power beyond words. And then, without warning, imploding into the utter emptiness of the Void.

The Void, a numinous emptiness, brimming with nonbeing. The creative source of everything. This was the place from which his world sprang. This was the nameless origin of Heaven and Earth. He had been given a glimpse of a greater reality, the Absolute, even perhaps, of God.

"No man is an island, entire of itself." Tense could sense Sally's blankness.

"It's a poem. John Donne."

"Must have missed it. Anyway, seems a bit obvious, doesn't it?"

"It does from here, that's for sure. We really are here, aren't we? Wherever here is."

"Yes, we are. Our physical bodies are waiting for us, withdrawn to some infinitesimal point in space and time."

"How is this possible?"

"I had heard that humans could come here, but I never really believed it. It seems to take a physical trigger to ignite the spark of the divine in each of you. In all of us, I should say, since I am embodied too."

"Sex with an angel, who knew?"

"Sex with a human, you mean. Not the hugely undignified, wet and wobbly farce I had once assumed it to be."

From far, far away, Tense felt Sally's fingers caressing his chest.

"Is it time to go home?"

"Yes, my love. I'm starving."

***

It was late afternoon when they returned to Earth. Sally immediately made for the shower, emerging a few minutes later, steaming slightly and wrapped demurely in one of Tense's enormous white towels.

Tense's transcendental journey upon the ocean of reality had once again stirred the deep and muddy waters of his mind. Questions he had previously thought better than to ask overflowed his teeming brain.

"I think I understand why God didn't kill Lucifer", Tense began, "but I don't quite see what stopped the good angels, for want of a better word, from killing the bad ones."

Sally stared at Tense blankly. It was going to be another one of those conversations.

"I mean, did he give orders not to kill them or what?"

"Thou shalt not kill." Sally was once again wearing a look that suggested she was talking to a very small child or being particularly kind to an imbecile.

"That's it? Thou shalt not kill."

"Well, what more do you want?"

"I don't know. I've never thought about it, to be honest."

"It's short, sharp and unambiguous. Works for us."

"But what about in self-defence?"

"Nope."

"What about to protect the life of another sentient being?"

"Nope."

"Really? Never, under any circumstances?"

"Nope. It's not negotiable. Just because you guys got given the rules in the form of a contract doesn't entitle you to parse them for a get-out clause."

"Well then, why didn't Lucifer's mob kill any of you guys?"

"That's a far better question."

"Well?"

"We don't know if an angel can be killed. We think the only options might be life or annihilation. Didn't we talk about that?"

"Isn't that killing?"

"No, not exactly, and anyway, it wouldn't be us angels doing it."

"I suppose it would be God doing the annihilating?"

"Yes."

"And he can do what he likes."

"Now you're getting it. His universe, his rules."

"What's the difference?"

"Between what and what?"

"Between killing and annihilation?"

"As far as I know, no one has ever been annihilated. But if they were, it would be as though they had never been."

"What, like they had never existed at all?"

"Yes. We think so."

"Then I don't suppose you would know. Not if the offending person had been expunged from history."

"Good point. I hadn't thought of that."

Sally and Tense fell silent, reviewing the conversation in the privacy of their own minds. Sally was growing weary of the theme.

"I don't think it's helpful to dwell on the past like this."

Tense felt he needed a circuit breaker.

"Shall we go out to dinner?"

"Ooh, yes. That sounds lovely." Sally rushed into the bedroom to change, evidently delighted that their little tête-à-tête was over. Tense, hot and sweaty from his earlier exertions, dived for the shower.

A few minutes later, clean and dressed, they met on the balcony. Tense could hardly believe his eyes. Sally was dressed in a maxi-length iridescent blue evening gown, a tiny Bolero jacket and an elegant clutch bag. She looked fucking gorgeous.

"You look amazing. Where on Earth did you get those?"

"They were in my suitcase. I have everything a girl could ever need in my suitcase."

"It's only about carry-on size."

"Haven't you seen Mary Poppins?"

It was Tense's turn to end the conversation.

"How about the Indian restaurant on the high street?"

"I don't care – you decide."

"Well, did you like the curry before?"

Sally laughed, "Do you really believe there is anything I wouldn't like to eat?"

After a minute or two of scrabbling around, Tense found and donned his best jacket. It was very dark blue, velvet and reasonably uncrumpled.

The restaurant was empty at that hour but for the waiter and an elderly priest sitting at a corner table, munching silently. Sally guided Tense over to the far side of the restaurant, away from the other diner.

"Those guys give me the creeps." She whispered.

"Me too."

"There's something quite unnatural about them, don't you think?"

Tense did think so, although he had never bothered to unpack his reasoning.

"It's a solitary life, alright. They don't seem to have many friends." Tense stared at the back of the old fella's head. Thinning grey hair and dandruff patinating the grubby black cloth of his jacket like hoarfrost. An unprepossessing sight.

"Do you have many friends? I haven't heard you talk about them." Sally's tone was conversational rather than inquisitorial.

Tense remained silent. It was not something he tended to dwell on all that much. Truth be told, he didn't have many friends. Not real friends. He had some work colleagues he was friendly with, but he never went out with them socially. He had never really felt the lack, yet still, it gnawed away at him. Was he deficient in some way? He didn't know. He had always had other, seemingly more important things to think about.

There was one thing, though. One thing that might explain it. There was one painful memory, one episode tucked away, never to be recalled, never to be brought into the light of day and examined. Never that was, until now.

"When I was a small boy, I was another small boy's imaginary friend."

Sally laughed, assuming it was a joke.

"No. I'm serious."

"You were imaginary?"

From the look on Tense's face, Sally realised that he was not joking.

"What happened?"

"It was when I was very young, perhaps nine years old."

"Yes?"

"He was in the class below me at junior school. A year younger than me."

"Umm."

"He was a weird kid. No one liked him much, not even me." Tense paused.

"I tried to be pleasant to him. After all, he wasn't a nasty kid, just a misfit, kind of."

Sally kept silent.

"He started hanging around me. He adopted me. There was nothing I could do to shake him off. He would wait for me outside the front gate of my parent's house before school. He insisted on walking to school with me. He even brought me presents."

"He must have liked you."

"Yeah. I guess he must have. I felt bad about accepting his gifts, but the first time I refused one, he assumed it wasn't good enough and came back with something even more expensive."

"He just wanted to please you."

"Yes. But I found his constant presence irritating, to be honest. He got on my nerves." Tense fell quiet again, replaying long-dormant memories.

"Then something happened."

"What happened?"

"I lost my watch while swimming. It was a divers' watch my mum gave me. Waterproof, I loved it."

"That's a shame."

"Yes. My sidekick decided to try and get it back for me. He went out early the next morning with goggles to search the seabed for it."

"Did he find it?"

"No. He died. He was caught in a rip."

"Oh, my goodness. How awful."

"It was three or four days before they found his body." Tense looked up, a haunted expression in his eyes.

"You see, he imagined I was his friend. He died for that friendship. I shouldn't have led him on. I should have sent him away."

"You were just trying to be kind."

"Sometimes you have to be cruel to be kind."

CHAPTER 9 - PROPOSAL

Sally insisted on the banquet for two. Tense could order what he liked. Rather than argue the point, Tense ordered the Chicken Madras. Not perhaps the most adventurous choice. He could have had shrimp vindaloo or Goan fish curry. But chicken madras had seen him through many a Saturday night and was not to be abandoned now in some false show of sophistication.

While they were waiting, Tense decided to engage in a little idle banter. As you may imagine, Tense was not good at idle banter, or any other kind of banter for that matter.

"Why would God expect people to believe in him without proof?" He began with an innocent, easy smile.

"In the absence of the manifest, imminent reality all around us, you mean? In the absence of the whole frigging universe? Can't imagine. Silly old God."

"Can you say that?"

"Say what?"

"Say that God is silly?"

"Well, obviously, our creator is capable of understanding my comments in context." Sally was getting a bit grumpy. The prospect of an enormous feast, unencumbered with Tense's theological ramblings, appeared to be retreating with each passing second.

Unfortunately, Tense missed Sally's tell-tale cues and blithely continued, "Well, what proof is there that the universe was created at all?"

"Beg pardon?"

"How do we know that the universe isn't just a naturally occurring, self-made thing?"

Sally was hungry and tired after some really quite athletic rumpy-pumpy and was just not in the mood for Tense's 'banter'. Inevitably, of course, that's when Tense, in all innocence, chose to use the 'A' word.

"Don't the atheists have a point? It's not as though we get to see the creator on a regular basis, is it? I mean, he doesn't exactly make his presence felt, does he?"

As it used to say on the firework packets of his youth, 'Light blue, touch paper and retire.' Tense really should have paid closer attention.

"Don't get me started on atheism", Sally all but snarled, "I guess some people are just not as thoughtful as others. I can't see why those who believe there is no God are so certain. I mean, even by their own logic. Would they not have to have proof there was no God in order to be certain? And it's not even as though their scientific method would give them proof anyway. Doesn't the scientific method demand that you test your hypothesis? Shouldn't it go like this: 'My hypothesis is that there is no God.' 'OK, how do I test that?' Without proof of the non-existence of God, atheism is just another belief system requiring the same leap of faith that his lot go on about." Sally nodded her head dismissively in the direction of the elderly cleric sitting quietly in the corner, minding his own business.

"Seems to me even agnosticism is a better bet than atheism. And in any case, I don't really understand why people are so invested in a method of thought that is so young, so untried and untested. After all, take physics. They don't know where all the matter in the universe is hiding or why there isn't enough energy to make their calculations work, and they keep finding new things they can't explain, like dark flow – whatever that is. They've even proven that there was no big bang. I mean, to prefer a worldview that is so obviously lacking, so obviously flawed, over simple uncertainty seems totally bonkers to me. But the most amazing thing, the clincher as far as I'm concerned, even if they find the missing matter and energy, is that their worldview, their scientific method, can never explain, can never even approach an explanation, of why there is anything at all." Sally paused for breath.

Tense nodded. She had a point. Least-ways, he thought she had a point. He was still disentangling the finer points of her discourse when Sally launched into it again.

"And how on Earth can anyone suppose, even for a moment, that the whole of fucking creation is an accident? I mean. It beggars belief."

To Tense's absolute relief, the food arrived and kept on arriving. Platter after platter, dish after dish, until the table was filled to over-flowing. Sally leaned back in her seat, surveying the feast with satisfaction, beaming joyously.

"That is what I'm talking about." She glanced up at the waiter with a look of silky, almost indecent pleasure.

"Could you tell me what it all is, please?"

The waiter explained the dishes one by one. The entrée of Tandoori mushrooms was swiftly followed by a second course of lamb kebab, chicken tikka and a mix of pakoras. The main course of butter chicken and Navratan korma came with naan and rice, raita, pappadums and mango chutney. For dessert, there was Gulab Jamun, which, the waiter explained, was an extravagantly sweet concoction of doughnuts bathed in syrup.

Tense watched Sally eat. And eat. The image came to him of a python patiently swallowing a cow. A kind of ghastly, awe-inspiring wonder accompanied his growing sense of unease.

When would she stop? Would she, in fact, stop?

"Eat up", Tense piped up gamely, "you're eating for two now."

Sally, engrossed in the creamy Navratan veggies, let the comment pass. She had, in any case, mostly gotten over her initial horror at being pregnant and was beginning to quite like the idea of being a mum. She had never been a mum before. She didn't suppose any angel had. Ah well, as the Archangel Gabriel was wont to say, there's a first time for everything. In the face of the implacable, Tense concluded, there was nothing else for it. He would have to propose marriage. Somehow it seemed to make sense.

Slowly, with considerable dignity, given the absurdity of the practice, Tense slipped off his chair and got down on one knee next to Sally.

"Have you lost something?" Sally barely looked up from her meal.

"No. There's something I've been meaning to ask you."

"Shoot."

"Well, now that you are going to have a baby, and we are going to be parents and everything like that."

"Umm."

"Well, I just thought you might like to... that is... it might be a good idea if we got married."

Sally stared at Tense, chewing slowly on a large piece of spicy cauliflower.

"Get married? To each other?"

"Yes. I thought you might like to. I thought it might be a good idea."

Sally continued to stare at Tense in silence.

"I know I don't have all that much to offer. But I promise I'd be a good father and husband."

Sally reached out and caressed his cheek.

"Naturally, I anticipate that you will not wish to marry me, but it would be irresponsible not to make the offer."

"Yes"

"Of course, your nationality and residency status might be an issue."

"I said yes. I'd love to. Thank you very much."

"I don't suppose you have a birth certificate?"

Sally took Tense's face gently in both hands. "Of course, I don't have a birth certificate, nationality or residency status. I couldn't care less about your laws. Our marriage will be a private matter between you and me."

"Yes? You said yes?"

"I did. I will. Now, would you like to try the Gulab Jamun?"

***

As it turned out, neither Sally nor Tense could quite manage the Gulab Jamun, so they took it back to the apartment. The pair sat out on the balcony, staring across the bay at eventide. Sally emptied the desert into two bowls. They munched slowly, contemplatively. It had been quite a day.

Sally dipped her fingers into the syrup, allowing goops of sticky liquor to form. Enjoying the physical sensation of it. The distant sounds of the city, as it tucked itself up for bed, wafted over her. It was another warm night. Even in the heart of the city, the sound of the cicadas rose and fell in deafening, almost physical seeming, waves.

Sally was at peace, losing herself in the moment. Luxuriating in the immanence of physical reality. She felt the slight grittiness of the old timber deck beneath her bare feet. A light breeze blew onshore, carrying with it the salt smell of ozone and a hint of diesel.

Tense, meanwhile, was in quite another place. Tense was wandering far from the manifest reality all around him and was, instead, lost in thought about it. Gulab Jamun, balcony, harbour, even Sydney itself receded from his mind. Sally glanced up from licking her fingers.

Tense was musing on the meaning of life, the universe and everything. Sally could just tell. He was hunched over his little bowl of pure sweetness, dripping syrup onto his shirt. His mind elsewhere. An outburst was stewing. Like distant storm clouds gathering over the Pacific, Sally felt she could practically see it coming. Tense was headed for another crisis. It was his pattern, she supposed. A long slow build-up of confusion and doubt followed by an explosive exegesis. Tense was into cathartic change. None of her business, probably.

Somewhere a boat sounded its hooter three times. A journey was beginning. People were setting out. And then Tense began to speak. Quietly, musing to himself.

"It's not just Western culture that's failing, but all of it - the whole kit and caboodle. We have lost our ability to transmute understanding into awe and the other way around."

"Bummer" Sally was not in the mood. She continued to focus on the last remaining slurps of syrup.

"There is a correlation between creativity and anxiety, and between culture-making and self-doubt."

"Well, if that is so, spare a thought for the Creator, why don't you? How much anxiety would sparking the non-existent big bang trigger?"

Tense was about to say, "There is an existential paradox between the urge to create something new and augment our reality and the stolid intractability of the very tools we use," but he didn't. He looked up instead. He caught the gleam in Sally's eye.

"Outside voice?"

"Yep."

"Sorry." Silence descended once more, but for the occasional tiny chink of metal spoon on porcelain bowl and the distant, all-pervasive but ignored skirl of the cicadas. Once every scrap of syrup had been scraped from his bowl, Tense continued.

"I read that in ancient times Zeus, in a fit of pique, split humanity into men and women, and we have been instinctually trying to recombine ever since. Once upon a time, before some unknown event horizon, we were whole and complete – and now we are broken and deformed. We are seeking oneness with ourselves. We are the fallen."

"Umm. Not really up on Zeus, I'm afraid."

"Understanding, reason itself, is a divine curse. It is also the very thing, the one thing, that gives us mastery. Reason gives us the hope of transcendence."

"Oh my. We are feeling sorry for ourself this evening." Sally busied herself, sucking the absolute last vestige of syrup from an index finger.

For a few moments, silence once more reigned. Then...

"Sin hides in the shadows between thought and deed. Between the intention to act, the imagined outcome, and the reality. As someone once said, the road to hell is paved with good intentions."

That was it. Sally had had enough.

"Please." Sally leaned over and took Tense's hands between hers as though praying, "No more."

Tense looked up into Sally's face.

"That's why I have hope. Even though we are lost and alone in the universe, we make our own meaning. Or so I thought. And then you come along. An angel. A messenger of God. And in a single instant, merely by your presence, sweep away all that glorious, creative, anxious uncertainty and replace it with what?"

"With love, my love. What else?" Sally looked a little smug.

"Is that enough, though?"

"Enough for what?"

"You, tell me. You're the bloody angel."

"Don't get snippy with me." Sally stood and collected the bowls. She opened the door to the apartment and paused, perhaps a little theatrically.

"If all this is not enough for you", Sally indicated the whole of reality with the sweep of an arm, "then what would be?"

Tense watched as Sally made her way back into the apartment. She had a point. She kept doing that.

Turning his attention to the world around him, Tense had to agree it was pretty amazing. *Perhaps*, he thought, *the definition of the word God is simply 'Creator. God is that which created the universe, and whatever that turns out to be, tautologically speaking, would be God.*

Tense reflected on that for a few moments. It was not really satisfying, he realised. As explanations go, it was not all that compelling. The real question was not really, *Was the universe created by its creator?'* but '*Does the universe have a purpose?* Meaning was at the heart of it. Perhaps God was an existentialist too.

Sally returned to the balcony a few moments later and plonked herself down on Tense's lap.

"Let's get married tomorrow." Sally wrapped her arms around his neck and leaned in for a snuggle.

"Shouldn't we plan our wedding?"

"Ok. Let's plan to get married tomorrow. We don't need any of that official malarkey you were going on about. It's nobody's business but ours."

For a full minute, Tense was lost for words. Fortunately, he was ultimately able to summon a modicum of common sense and replied.

"That would be wonderful. You would make me the proudest and happiest man on Earth."

Sally smiled. Tense himself could hardly believe he had managed a response that was both timely and reasonably gallant.

"Good. It's all settled then." Sally took Tense's face between her palms and kissed him very gently.

"You think too much, but I love you anyway." A flicker of sadness momentarily crossed her brow. Tense didn't notice. He was once again entering panic mode.

"Where shall we get married? And when? What shall I wear? And what will you wear? You need a dress!"

Sally touched one index finger to his lips.

"Let's say our vows down by the water. We can go down after breakfast. You can wear whatever you like, but you'll have to wait to see what I wear."

There being nothing much left to panic about, Tense subsided for a moment. Then inevitably, he began once more to think.

"Not that I mind exactly, but are you really female, or are you actually an asexual spirit in human form?"

Sally, still warmed by the thought of her upcoming nuptials, took the question remarkably well.

"That's not the most romantic question I've ever been asked, and I haven't heard you complaining, by the way."

"No. That's not what I meant. I mean, I just wondered, what with you being an angel and all."

"Sexuality is a human thing, a biological thing, not an angel thing. But right now, I'm more human than angel."

"So, you are a woman?"

"I'm as much woman as you'll ever need Tense, have no doubt about that." The warm glow was beginning to wear off.

Suddenly, and quite unexpectedly, Tense felt a tear roll down his cheek. He looked up at Sally, half expecting that it was somehow she who was crying. But it was not. The full emotional impact of the situation hit him like a freight train. Tense stood, waving his arms in front of himself like a B-Movie zombie. Sally moved in. Put her arms around him and held him close.

"I never thought I'd be married. I never believed I would find the right person or that anyone would really want me."

"I never expected to be married either", Sally smiled as she hugged him, "And I've had far longer to think about it."

The couple subsided back onto Tense's chair with Sally coiled around him like a snake. Neither could find the words to voice their feelings. They contented themselves, for the time being, with closeness. In the end, of course, it was Tense who broke the silence.

"Will I make a good father, do you think?"

Sally didn't answer immediately. She snuggled closer, burying her head in his neck. She kissed him slowly and gently from his neck, across his jawline and then vertically up from his chin and nose to his forehead.

"You have all the qualities any man could possibly need to be a wonderful father."

Tense smiled, relieved. At least one doubt could be put to bed for now. It was getting late. The city had already gone to sleep, and Sally and Tense would soon follow suit.

"Will I make a good mother?"

It was perhaps a little unfortunate that Tense was so very much the engineer. Here, obviously, was a problem to be solved. Advice would no doubt be welcomed.

"In my experience, parenthood is mostly a matter of balancing the receptive with the prescriptive." Tense warmed to his theme, "It's about teaching the child individual responsibility while at the same time learning to care for others." Tense had to admit his advice sounded sagacious and deep to his own ears.

"Yes. Good parenting requires one to walk a fine line between punishment and nurturing."

"Never mind" Sally sounded tired. Tense looked down. Sally was beginning to fall asleep.

"God, yes. You'll be the best bloody mother that ever lived." But it was too late. Sally was already snoring lightly in his arms.

CHAPTER 10 – DAY 4, PREPARATIONS

Tense woke early the next morning. Sally did not. Tense had plenty of unproductive worrying and fidgeting to do. Not so Sally. Sally lay in bed, comfortably introspecting in a desultory manner and examining, from a suitably prone position, the hairline crack that she had just noticed ran diagonally across the bedroom ceiling. Sally had not a care in the world.

Tense kept popping back to the bedroom to see if Sally was up yet, and Sally kept not being. After an extended period of hopping back and forth between the sitting room, the kitchen, the balcony and the bedroom, Tense had accreted around himself a cloud of static energy, an emotional charge of increasing and uncertain potential. To Sally, it seemed to swirl around him like a swarm of angry bees or perhaps like Dr Strange's cape. Absorbed as she was in this fascinating speculation, Sally failed to notice Tense's growing frustration.

Finally, Tense, like an over-charged capacitor, reached his moment of release. He managed to break free of his circumlocutory gyre and stopped suddenly in the doorway to the bedroom.

"I shall make breakfast", he announced with a flounce before turning on his heel and stalking off in the direction of the kitchen.

"Bags-I the first shower," Sally called out after him, unaware that Tense had long since risen, showered, dressed, polished his shoes, polished a second pair of shoes just in case, found and secreted in a pocket his mother's wedding ring and completed no less than one hundred and fifty laps of the apartment. Sally managed a languid movement somewhat approximating the act of getting up. To be fair, it was more than a mere gesture, but it still proved less than effective. On the second attempt, she managed it, and, swaddling herself in an enormous white bath towel, she padded silently into the bathroom.

Tense could be heard in the kitchen, happily banging pots and pans together and singing tunelessly.

"I'm proud to be an Okie from Muskogee, back where even squares can have a ball...."

Sally smiled. All was right with the world for now.

Tense cooked. Not the massive array of every possible breakfast food that had characterised their first three breakfasts together, but this time, only a single dish. Tense made an omelette of gruyere cheese, finely chopped chives, salt, pepper, and a sprig of parsley to finish it off. The eggs, with a small dollop of cream, had been finely whisked and fluffed. With two slices of sourdough toast each, it was an unexpectedly simple and elegant meal.

Sally wandered into the kitchen, having showered and once again wrapped in a towel. She put her arms around Tense from behind and began to kiss the nape of his neck. Tense struggled to divide the omelette, serve it, and lift the two plates.

With Sally still attached limpet-like to his back, he made his way out onto the balcony. It was another warm day. The world was up and about and bustling down below.

They sat quietly, munching away. Sally, still wrapped in her towel. Tense, finally content, relaxed.

"What are you going to wear?" his curiosity all the more piqued by Sally's refusal to say.

"You'll see." Sally smiled enigmatically. Tense's imagination ranged from visions of a yellow high-vis t-shirt and a pair of steel-toe-capped boots to a skimpy cotton patterned dress with sensible flats. Sally wasn't giving away any clues.

It was their wedding day. They were both a bit pensive. Tense, because he was tense, and Sally for quite another reason. This was yet another brand-new experience in a long life packed with experience. She was beginning to comprehend the full extent of her predicament. A husband was for life, she realised, not just for the holidays. The sense of responsibility was overwhelming. As a working angel, she had had a diffuse duty of care for the whole of humanity, not just for one man. Now she had an absolute responsibility and duty to love and care for a lone human being, with all his attendant frailties, eccentricities, misapprehensions, and downright incomprehensible humanity.

Sally found herself simultaneously thinking two incompatible and absolutely contradictory things. On the one hand, there was a kind of relief in the knowledge that this human lifetime would be short, and on the other, the horrible realisation that love inevitably means loss and that Tense's moment upon the stage would be over and gone in little more than an instant, by angel reckoning. All his vain-heroic strutting and posturing would be over and done in the blink of an eye. She felt the life inside her quickening. Dear Lord, being human was a hard act to pull off.

Sally pulled herself together. "What are you going to wear?"

"You'll see" Tense, attempting arch inscrutability, was a pathetic sight.

"Is it your blue velvet jacket, your ironed shirt and your smart black work shoes?"

"Yes, and I've polished them, so you can see your face in them."

"I will have a very handsome groom then." Sally reached over, lifted and kissed his hand.

"And I will have everything I ever dreamed of." Tense paused, suddenly bashful, surprised at his own temerity, "More than I ever dreamed of, actually."

Sally smiled. One can only sustain intense emotion for a little while. Already the human capacity to sublimate was having the desired effect.

"Live for today", she found herself thinking, "for tomorrow, you die." One could only sustain a life of such unrelenting emotional intensity, struggle, achievement and defeat for a very short time. The creator had been merciful. There was a trade-off between the brevity of human life and its intensity. These creatures do burn bright, Sally realised, perhaps brighter than angels in the final reckoning.

We who are about to die salute you,' she thought, *'and I am one of them now. And so is my baby.*

***

Tense did the washing up while Sally shuffled off to get dressed. It only took him a minute or two, after which he paced around the apartment for a few minutes more before settling down on the balcony to watch the day unfold. Being a thorough sort of a man, and a bit of a forward planner, Tense began to make notes. One never knew what the day might throw at you, and it was always best to be prepared. Although, to be honest, the issue of quite how one prepared to wed an angel was towards the esoteric end of his experience.

Tense decided to prepare his wedding vows. In the absence of an official celebrant, it would all be up to him. Or so he imagined.

He'd seen enough weddings on TV and in the movies to know that there were certain things one had to get straight right from the outset. Tense set to work.

It was probably half an hour before Sally emerged from the bedroom. Tense looked up as she stepped out onto the balcony. His heart skipped a beat as he took in what he saw. For a moment, he wondered if it might stop beating completely. He had no words. There stood Sally, his bride, the mother of his unborn child, shining, beautiful, utterly resplendent.

"You had that in your carry-on suitcase, right?"

"Never you mind what I have in my suitcase." Sally's smile, which to Tense had always resembled sunshine, now seemed to light up the sky.

Sally's dress was glittering, iridescent silver, like Marilyn's in "Gentlemen Prefer Blondes". However, unlike Marilyn, Sally sported two enormous, glittering wings. To Tense's eyes, the effect was mesmerising. They seemed to move with her, naturally, following her rhythm. Tense rose to his feet, hypnotised by what he saw.

"They're not..." Tense could not complete the question.

"Real?"

"Yes"

"Oh yes," Sally smiled mischievously, "They are quite real."

Tense gasped, unable to take it in. He just stood there like a stunned mullet.

"They're not functional, though, obviously." Sally laughed. Tense managed to breathe once more.

"My real wings are thinner than gossamer, stronger than steel and spread probabilistically across several dimensions."

"Oh"

"Yes. And they're not wings at all, really. They just look that way to humans."

"What are they then?"

"Extensions, I suppose you'd call them. They are simply me in human form, extended multi-dimensionally."

"Oh, is that all?"

"Yes. And on consideration, I may not have the vocabulary to explain further."

"I suppose to those who can spread themselves probabilistically across several dimensions, there is no need to explain, and to those who can't, there's no point." Tense laughed. He had been pushed beyond his capacity to reason.

"Whatever." Tense gazed at Sally, besotted, wordless and in love.

"Yes. Well, Shall we?" Sally crooked her arm, inviting Tense to escort her.

Unable to continue the conversation. Unable to speak at all, really. Tense escorted his bride out of the apartment, down the stairs and across the small lawn to the beach. The sky was a little overcast. Rain portended.

"You look very handsome." Sally smiled shyly.

"You look like a goddess."

Standing a little way off, still drinking from the night before, stood two revellers. They sipped wine from tall crystal flutes and were carrying a large bottle of champagne in an ice bucket. They watched the couple with evident curiosity and appreciation.

"You are making a film?" one of them enquired with a strong Italian accent.

"No. Getting married." Tense didn't like the look of them. He particularly didn't want two handsome young Europeans gaping at him as he made his vows, still less, gaping at Sally.

"Congratulations" The young men smiled and moved closer.

"You have a very beautiful bride."

"Yes. Well..."

"May we know the name of this lovely lady?"

"No. Err, would you please excuse us?"

"Sally," Sally smiled warmly at the two young men, "and this is my fiancé, Tense."

"Tense? That is his name?" The young men looked doubtfully across at Tense.

"Yes. It's a nickname."

"Well, it certainly fits." The young men laughed gently, still gazing appraisingly at Sally.

"Please, Signorina, allow us to offer you a glass of champagne to celebrate this wonderful day."

Sally and Tense both spoke at once.

"Thank you. That would be lovely."

"No thanks. We must be going."

The young men laughed, casually refilling their glasses and offering them to Tense and Sally.

"Saluté"

Tense, fuming, accepted the glass without a word. Sally smiled graciously and thanked the men.

"You two boys can be our witnesses if you like."

"You are getting married here? Now?"

"Yes. On the beach."

"We would be charmed. I am Luciano, and this is my friend, Paulo." The young man who had been introduced as Paulo reached over and took Sally's hand. He leaned in and kissed her fingers gently.

The other, Luciano, threw an avuncular arm across Tense's shoulder.

"It's a big day. You are a very lucky man."

Tense wanted to pick up a rock and kill them both. Unfortunately, there was nothing he could do but go along with it - but if he could somehow, accidentally, break the arm of the avuncular youth…

Sally led the little posse to the very edge of the beach, where tiny ripples caressed the shore. There she stood, looking every inch the primordial Angel-Goddess. As Sally raised her arms above her head in a gesture both of benediction and obeisance, her iridescent wings lifted and opened too. Sally began to speak.

"I have done as you asked. I am experiencing the universe as a mortal woman. I am living up to my name, Amitiel, Angel of Truth. Today is my wedding day. I call on Paulo and Luciano to witness our marriage."

The two young men smiled uncertainly.

"Of course. We are happy to be witnesses."

Tense found himself caught in an eddy of contradiction and self-doubt. As he gazed at his beloved, the clouds parted a little, allowing a bar of golden sunlight to reach down from the Heavens, illuminating Sally. She looked dazzlingly lovely, her dress, like a lover, wrapping itself closely around her figure, her wings scintillating in the sun. On one level, he couldn't care less if she was an angel or not. Here was everything and more than he could ever have imagined, dreamed of or hoped for. But at the same time, on quite a different level. On the level of logic and science, the level of the engineer, hearing Sally formally, as it were, claim to be an angel called Amitiel, hearing her calling directly to her Creator, did give him cause for concern. Nagging uncertainty and guilt resurfaced.

What if Sally was simply away with the fairies? Did it matter? Even if she was crazy, was she really any crazier than anyone else? But then again, what if she really was an angel? Admittedly he had no idea who or what the name Amitiel stood for or meant, but for all he knew, she was mentioned in the bible. For all he knew, the woman he was aiming to marry was specifically named in a book thousands of years old. Either way, the situation was freaky. Was it wise to marry an angel? Who could possibly offer valid advice?

For a split second, Tense caught Sally's eye. For a moment, he saw in her gaze an indomitable fragility. For an instant, Tense felt he could see into Sally's soul. He could see her vulnerability. He could feel her need. And that was enough.

Tense spoke. "Sally, I promise I'll always be a good husband to you as long as I live. I'll devote my life to you and our child. I will always be there for you."

Sally paused, glanced briefly at the lowering sky and intoned: "I, Sally, take thee, Tense, for my lawful husband, to have and to hold from this day forward, for better, for worse, for richer, for poorer, in sickness and in health, until death do us part."

The clouds, slipping slowly over the bay, shifted position, snuffing out the sun. In the far distance, a rumble of thunder could be heard above the sounds of the city and the surf gently ruffing the sand.

"Bravo. Bravo"

Sally and Tense turned to see their two witnesses standing side by side, hand in hand, their eyes brimming with tears.

A little late, but better late than never, Tense retrieved the ring from his pocket.

"This was my mother's wedding ring." Tense slipped it onto Sally's finger.

Paulo pushed Tense gently towards Sally, "You may kiss the bride."

It began to rain. Not hard. Just a drop here and there. But the sky was darkening, and the clouds were building their tell-tale anvil shape against the heavens. It was going to bucket. Sally and Tense took their leave of the two Italian boys and made their way swiftly back to the apartment.

It was late morning. Outside, forked lightning sizzled across the sky, and thunder roared close overhead.

"We got back just in time." Tense stared out across the bay. Wind whipped the palm trees into a frenzy. Sally stood a little further back in the room. Away from the window. Her arms by her side. Her splendid wings drooping slightly. The die was cast, she realised. There was no going back. Tense turned, sensing Sally's unease.

"Should I call you Amitiel, Angel of Truth, or Sally?" Tense smiled, intending humour.

Sally did not immediately respond.

"I thought you were a grieving angel?"

Still, Sally remained silent.

"What's the difference? What is an Angel of Truth anyway?"

Sally made a visible effort to pull herself together. She took a deep breath and drew herself up to her full height.

"There is no difference, really. Truth is grief." Sally stared at him bleakly. "Love is loss."

Tense was somewhat taken aback. This is not what he had expected, certainly not on his wedding day. He had had other ideas in mind entirely.

"Some think I am one of the fallen", she continued, "but I am not. Some believe I am being punished, but I am not." Sally looked up. Her expression unfathomable to Tense. Eons of resilience and pain stared back at him. Swamping him, swamping his capacity to understand.

"I am blessed. My Creator has put me to the test. I hope I shall be equal to it."

Tense, lost for words, unable to comprehend, let alone counsel, took Sally in his arms. Lifting her. Holding her close. Whispering worthless promises as men, in their innocence, have always done. Sally snuggled closer, burrowing into him like a small, furry mammal. There was comfort in physical closeness. If nothing else, she felt loved. The lightning outside stopped, and the thunder abated.

"The storm's moved off." Tense's gaze was loving and concerned, "what can I get you?"

"Nothing. Nothing, my love. I'm fine."

"You're fine?" Tense was confused. How were these near-instantaneous shifts in emotion sustainable? How were they even possible in the first place? Tense was not an emotional sort of person. He would be the first to admit it. But he was at least consistent. If he got himself into a bad mood, he'd stay grumpy all day. Life was predictable. One knew where one stood. Sally, on the other hand, seemed able to switch from abject misery to coquettish teasing in the blink of an eye.

As if to prove his point, Sally wriggled closer in his arms.

"I am when you hold me like this."

Tense found himself once again feeling a little out of his depth. What was the correct response? What would be a definite no-no? He needn't have worried. Sally slipped from his arms and, taking him gently by the hand, led him into the bedroom.

"Now, let's get you out of those sopping wet clothes, shall we?" Sally smiled roguishly. She was evidently feeling a little better. Tense looked down at his blue velvet jacket. Other than a very few spots of rain, it was dry as a bone. As was the rest of him. He found himself wondering briefly if angels were more baffling than women or the other way around. In his unique circumstances, though, it scarcely seemed to matter.

***

Tense went to the bathroom to freshen up. By the time he returned, Sally had doffed her gorgeous wings, which were now nowhere to be seen.

"Can a woman be pregnant twice at the same time?" Sally asked.

"Well, a woman can have twins, but having two separate pregnancies at the same time is very rare. It's called superfelation or something."

"Superfelation? Are you sure? I thought that meant something else."

"Well, something like that. What am I, a dictionary?"

Sally lifted her arms triumphantly, allowing her lovely, shimmering dress to slide down her body and pool around her feet like liquid silver on the bedroom floor.

"Well then, let's find out."

Tense hesitated a moment in mock reserve. "I'm not just a glorious physical specimen and a magnificent lover, you know. I do have feelings."

"Yes, dear. Tell you what, let's explore those."

"You're really getting into the upside of embodiment, aren't you?"

"It would appear there are some few compensations for having to lug around sixty-five kilos of meat, yes."

The couple reclined comfortably on Tense's old bed. Sally lay cocooned in the crook of Tense's arm, listening to herself breathe.

After a few moments, she ventured, "I'm a pregnant, married woman living in Sydney, and I'm not entirely certain how it happened."

"Well, sometimes, when a mummy and a daddy love each other very much if they're very lucky…" Tense found himself cut off by the thwomp of a pillow across the gob.

"God works in mysterious ways?" Tense, admittedly not fully engaged with the tenor of Sally's musings, got a second pillow in the face for his trouble.

"Wrong answer?"

"Well, right answer possibly, or even probably, but hardly helpful… I didn't hurt you, did I?"

"Nah. I am impervious to your pillow attacks," which got him another pillow to the face for being cocky.

"You never quite know how even the simplest of events is going to pan out", Tense continued gamely, "the other day, I popped out for a moment to buy a loaf of bread from the shop around the corner and came back two hours later with a packet of cumquats and twenty-four toilet rolls."

Sally rolled her eyes. Tense soldiered on...

"I read somewhere that there is a shadow that falls between the intention and the act."

Tense felt Sally shift and snuggle closer but failed to read the message in her movements.

"I am an engineer because I want to create. I want to create because I feel lost and confused about who I am. I am lost and confused because I don't know what my place is in the universe, or where, or even if, I belong." Tense paused. Sally snuggled more.

"I must change my life."

Sally sat up crossly.

"Haven't you changed your life quite enough in the last few days?" She growled.

"Are you not now a married man and expectant father?" Tense opened his mouth to speak but was cut off by Sally's furious outpouring.

"Isn't that enough change for you, Tense?"

It was, he realised. It most certainly was. Tense slipped his arm around Sally's waist and pulled her back down onto the bed.

"Sorry, weren't we going to find something out?" Sally remained stiff and unyielding. "Weren't we going to explore?"

Sally resisted further, for the briefest of moments, before acquiescing to being held close and gently kissed.

"You should look that word up some time," she murmured, "I don't think it means what you said." But Tense's focus had moved on.

Sally felt her body respond. It was the damnedest feeling. The bloody thing had a mind of its own. Allowing her conscious mind to witness the unconscious goings on of her body, Sally observed as if from a distance.

She watched as her face tilted up towards Tense's, and her lips parted slightly. She studied her own sensuous, even wanton snuggling. She felt her skin answer Tense's soft caress, and she resisted, for as long as she could, the raw carnal appeal of her lover.

In the end, though, the demands of the flesh oe'r came the abstractions of the mind. Sally could hold aloof no longer.

She pounced. Throwing Tense back against the sheet. Straddling him.

"Right," A cruel smile passed momentarily across her face, "Let's see what you got."

Tense, lying back on the bed, dominated by his lover, considered his world and knew that it was good.

But why, he found himself wondering, did the creator limit us to just a single lifetime on Earth, to a single being? Why couldn't we be lots of people, try out every possibility, experience it all? Why limit us like this? Why must we cease to think and be? Why must all our knowledge and experience be lost?

His mind snapped from its abstruse, self-indulgent reverie by the gentle indignities being performed upon his person, refocused in an instant upon the demanding presence and needs of the woman in his bed.

He was happy, he realised. This angel-woman was his light and shield against the eternal dark.

CHAPTER 11 - LUCIFER COMES CALLING

It was a little after midday when there was a knock at the door. Tense woke first, bleary and befuddled. He sat bolt upright in bed, uncertain what had woken him. A moment or two later, there came a second tap at the door. Perhaps a little more insistent this time. Tense struggled out of bed and searched groggily for his clothes. He was just pulling up his trousers when there came a third knock on the door, loud this time, insistent. Tense stomped out of the bedroom and along the hall, doing up his trousers as he walked. There was a shape on the other side of the door visible through the single panel of frosted glass at its centre. The shape moved. There followed an even louder banging on the door. Curt, Demanding.

"All right. All right. I'm coming. Hold your horses." Tense was irritated, offended by the peremptory assault upon his front door. The shape shifted behind the frosted glass. Tense hesitated. Behind him, down the hall, he heard Sally say, "Who is it? What do they want?" Sally's face appeared in the bedroom doorway.

"Dunno. I'll deal with it. Go back to bed. This won't take a moment." Tense was uneasy. No one ever called. He never had visitors. Tense quietly slipped the door chain into its slot.

He turned the knob on the mortice lock and opened the door an inch.

"Who is it? What do you want?"

Through the narrow crack between the door and the frame, Tense could see a white shirt and tie and a cleanly shaven chin. The man stepped back, eyeing Tense through the crack in the door.

"I'm terribly sorry to disturb you."

"Yes?"

"I apologise for turning up unannounced."

"Yes?"

"I wonder if I might have a word with Amitiel?"

"Amitiel?"

"Yes"

"Does she know you're coming?"

"No. As I just said, I apologise for turning up unannounced."

"Who shall I say it is."

The cleanly shaven young man paused, smiling suavely.

"Would you tell Amitiel it's her brother?"

"Brother? You're Sally's brother?"

"Well, yes, in a manner of speaking."

"She's never mentioned a brother."

"Well, as I said, in a manner of speaking."

Tense closed the door again and walked back down the hallway to the bedroom.

"It's a man. He says he's your brother."

Sally stared blankly back at him.

"He called you Amitiel."

"Amitiel?"

"Yes."

"I don't have a brother."

"He said 'in a manner of speaking.'"

"Angels don't have siblings."

"I believe you."

"What does he want?"

"He said he wanted to speak to you."

Sally struggled up and, wrapping the sheet around herself, padded back up the hallway to the front door. The shape behind the frosted glass shifted as she approached, apparently stepping back a little. Sally removed the security chain and threw open the door.

"Who are you, and what do you..." But that was as far as she got. She stopped and stared for a moment. Then.

"Are you insane? You know you can't come here. You know it's forbidden."

Sally made to close the door. There was a muffled bump as the door failed to close. One gleaming black patent leather and somewhat pointed shoe had been placed strategically in the way.

"Go away, you fool." Sally was angry now. Not the exasperated, 'how-did-I-end-up-with-this-insensitive-clod' kind of anger, but something deeper. Something immeasurably colder. Something steely, tempered in the fires of war. There was to the set of her shoulders something implacable and deadly. She was preparing for battle.

The door opened a little further. The clean-shaven man removed his foot.

"I know the risk. I just wanted to talk. You're the only one I can communicate with at all these days."

"I watched you burning like a torch, falling through the void. I watched you broken and beaten, a sword to your throat. You cannot come here. You know very well that I am not powerless. Go away."

"Just tell me one thing, and I'll go."

"You'll go?"

"Yes."

"What is it?"

"Why are you here, now, in this form? Is it happening again?"

"I did not ask, and I was not told. Now go."

Sally closed the door quietly, leaned back against the smooth, cool paint of the hallway and shuddered.

"Who was that?"

She did not speak. Her focus was elsewhere. Tense realised that Sally was lost to him for the moment.

Suddenly she began to speak. Slowly, quietly, head down, remembering.

"We were friends once, eons ago. He was extraordinary, you know. He was so fluent and persuasive. He almost had me convinced. He almost had me....."

"What? He almost had you what?"

"Join."

Tense felt his body begin to shake. Below the level of consciousness, his mind had pieced together the puzzle. At some unconscious
level, he was already terrified.

"Join what?"

Sally looked up. Her eyes piercing Tense to the core. Looking
through and beyond him.

"You already know. I will not name him."

"That was him?" Tense felt his knees begin to give, "That was…."

"In human form. He comes and goes."

"What did he want? What did he mean, 'Is it happening again'?"

"He has his own fears. He has his own nightmares."

Tense remained silent. Out of his depth. Lost.

"He fears that one day the Creator will act. He has measured the
immeasurable power of the Creator, and he is afraid. Always afraid."

"Why did he come to you? Why you?"

"I am Amitiel, Angel of Truth. He knows I neither fear nor pity
him. He knows if there were a message for him in my presence, I would
tell him."

"Where has he gone?"

"To lick his wounds and scheme and plot some more. It's all he
has left."

"Will he be back?"

"I don't know. Probably."

Tense took Sally's hand and led her back down the hallway and
into the sitting room.

"He is dangerous Tense, never forget that. Never let your guard
down."

"I'll make tea." Tense took refuge in habit, his mind still reeling at
the astonishing, mundane appearance of Sally's old friend.

Sally sat in silence on the sofa while Tense clattered about in the
kitchen. He returned a few minutes later with two steaming mugs of tea
and two large chunks of 'no brand' fruit cake from the corner shop. He
plonked the tea and cake on the coffee table and himself on the sofa

next to Sally. Silence prevailed. Neither could speak. Sally because she was too angry for words, and Tense because he was impersonating a stunned mullet.

"So that was really him?" Tense needed verbal confirmation, "That was the Devil?"

"Yes. His name was Lucifer, and his role was as an accuser at first, God's prosecutor, a satan, rather than the 'Satan'. His title was Satanael. Before the fall."

"I know this sounds like a stupid question, but was he really that bad?"

Sally looked up and stared at Tense, holding his eye.

"Yes. He really was and is that bad." She paused, "The official line was that he suffered from hubris, foolish pride and overconfidence."

"But that's not what you think."

"Not exactly, no."

"Then what was it?"

"He wanted all sentient beings to use their free will to make up their own minds. But for that to work, they would have to have knowledge so that they could judge."

"That makes sense to me. Why was that so bad?"

"Both Angels and Human beings were given free will and, through it, were supposed to choose to be good."

"But?"

"But they didn't have to, and they didn't. Not all of them. The angels were created to be servants, to do their master's will. Humans were not created as servants."

"I see."

"But Lucifer convinced around a third of all the angels to rebel against God. To stop worshipping him and make their own decisions."

"Oh. And that was bad, right?" Tense wasn't sure how he felt about that, "So Lucifer wanted the angels, himself included, to make up their own minds rather than just mindlessly following orders?"

"Kind of. He knew that he could not overthrow the Creator. It was not overconfidence. He knew he would fail."

"Then what was it?"

"A plea for help, perhaps? A plea to be heard, to transcend mere angel existence, to be more than an eternal servant."

"Angels are just like humans, really, aren't they?"

Sally dropped her gaze, releasing Tense, and laughed. A hollow laugh without humour.

"Angels are so much more than humans and so much less."

Tense waited, hoping further explanation would be forthcoming.

"We have vast knowledge, experience, eternal life and powers that I can't even describe, but we are limited, stunted." Sally paused for a moment.

"What we were at the moment of creation, we are now, and we will always be. We cannot evolve. We can exercise free will, but we cannot grow."

"But humans can. Is that the difference?"

"That my love is the tiniest difference of all and the most important."

"Our knowledge has not brought us happiness", Tense mused, half remembering something he'd once read, "Knowledge, for us humans, is always selfish in the end, always wilful. The knowledge we gained from eating the apple was self-knowledge. We wanted to confirm our own interpretations. Interpretations, which are always relative, depending upon who and where we are – never absolute. Our beliefs are contingent upon our will."

"Oh, for goodness" sake," Sally cried out in mock horror, "don't start that again."

"I was only saying…." But Sally leaned over and kissed him, shutting him up.

"That's what I love about you, my love", she whispered, "you are so very, very human."

***

Tense was still coming to terms with the Devil popping round to say 'Hi' when Sally announced:

"We should go sailing."

"Sailing?"

"Yes."

"Do you know how to sail?"

"No."

"Wouldn't that be something of an impediment?"

"No."

"No?"

"No. We can sign on as crew down at Rushcutters Bay. They will take anyone."

"Really? How do you know?"

"I'm an angel. I know everything."

"Really?"

"Well, not everything-everything. But everything."

"Ah. I see" Tense surmised that Sally's assertion made perfect sense in Angel. It was the English that he was struggling with.

After a bit of faffing about collecting what Tense believed might constitute "sailing gear", they headed off. Tense, uncharacteristically, insisted on catching a cab. Sally suspected that there might be something about their carefully selected costume of which Tense was uncertain. Nevertheless, they both managed to squeeze into the back of the cab, yellow oilskin coats and sou'westers notwithstanding. The trip to Rushcutters' Bay was, thankfully, brief. The couple stepped eagerly out into the warm, all but windless afternoon. A few listless would-be sailors stood around drinking beer and complaining about the lack of wind. Sally and Tense were greeted warmly and with no little bemusement.

"Can we crew on your boat?" Sally eagerly enquired of a grizzled older man with a fine white beard and an imposing bear gut.

"There's no bloody wind," the man grumbled, "mind you, if a storm were to blow up, you'd be the first I'd pick." General laughter followed, gentle, not seeking to offend.

"How much wind do we need?" Sally put her hand to her forehead, shading her eyes as she scanned the horizon.

"The more, the merrier." Whitebeard offered Sally an avuncular smile before stumbling off in the direction of the bar. Sally pursed her lips. Tense never liked it much when Sally pursed her lips.

"Well, we'll just have to do something about that." She muttered to herself. Sally began to pace up and down, head bent, apparently arguing with someone. Tense watched the mumbled intercourse proceed. Stomp, stomp, stomp – expostulation. Stomp, Stomp, Stomp – snort of derision. Finally, triumphantly, Sally turned smartly on her heel and made for the white-bearded man who had by now returned with a bottle of beer.

"We shall have wind." She announced, "Plenty of it."

The old sailor gazed at Sally uncertainly for a moment.

"That'd be very nice then." He managed.

"Which is your boat?" Sally fixed the poor man with a steely glare.

Perhaps realising that this was not going to go quite as he had imagined, the man nodded towards a large sailboat tied up at the end of the jetty.

"That's her. Royal blue hull, 'Sea Tempest' she's called."

Sally grabbed Tense by the arm and marched down the jetty towards the boat. As she did so, the wind picked up. Sudden gusts wobbled umbrellas and flung lighter objects this way and that.

"Well, bugger me." The old seafaring gent set down his bottle of beer, ran down the jetty and clambered onto the boat. From various spots around the sailing club, a motley crew of half-cut sailors appeared and reported for duty.

"I'm not sure this is a good idea," Tense ventured.

"Oh, come on. It's a lovely afternoon for yachting on Sydney Harbour. What could possibly go wrong?"

While the more experienced sailors ran up the sails, spliced the main brace and doused the jib, the two landlubbers were instructed to go and stand on the opposite side of the boat, out of harm's way. Sally was in heaven. Slightly drunken young men were clambering all over the place, calling out to each other and gamely pulling on ropes. It was all very exciting.

Tense was not enthused. The scene he took in was one of apparent chaos. Drunken young men scrambled uncertainly around the boat, and the two of them, he realised, looked ridiculous in their bright yellow oilskin coats and enormous yellow rain hats. He couldn't remember for the moment how he had even come by them.

On consideration, though, he had to admit that Sally looked absolutely gorgeous in hers, but he suspected that he himself strongly resembled a bright yellow mushroom.

The boat began to move out into the harbour, picking up speed as the winds rose about her. As soon as they had cleared Darling Point, the full force of the wind hit them, and the Sea Tempest began pitching and yawing alarmingly. The vessel raced out into clear, deep water. Sally and Tense were thrown around like rag dolls. One of the young sailors came over with two lifelines and secured Sally and Tense to the stainless-steel boat rail. Sally smiled and laughed, flushed with excitement. Tense felt his stomach churn ominously and clung to the safety rail with both hands. The boat picked up more speed.

"No more sail," the white-haired Captain called out, now suddenly stone-cold-sober and totally focused on the job at hand. The boat began to roll ominously.

"Pull in the spinnaker", the captain glanced around nervously, "where the fuck did this wind come from?" He glanced towards Sally. The roll of the boat seemed to be getting worse.

"Pull in the jib."

The boat stabilised as it raced across the harbour towards the heads and the open Pacific. Sally laughed uproariously and clung to Tense. Tense clung to the safety rail. The crew exchanged uncertain glances.

The wind did not let up. In the middle distance, behind them, whitecaps swaddled Rushcutters and Elizabeth Bays.

"We'll have to ride it out", the captain shouted out against the wind. Then, turning to Sally, "Do you think you can get your mate to turn it down a notch?" He was only half joking. Sally smiled.

"I doubt it. It was all I could do to get him to breathe a little wind our way in the first place."

There were a few nervous laughs. Sailors are a superstitious lot. Whatever had happened, and however it had come about, they were in no doubt that Sally had something to do with the sudden, gusting wind.

Beyond the headlands, things evened out a bit. There was a two-metre swell and much lighter headwinds. The crew subsided. This was normal. This was ok. The captain handed the wheel to a crewman and made his way down into the bowels of the boat. He emerged a few minutes later with a slab of beers and three large bags of potato chips. Sally disconnected the safety line and clambered up to the bridge, hoping to have a go on the wheel. The younger crewman made way for Sally, instructing her how to hold the wheel. He stood close behind her, placing his hands over hers, murmuring in her ear, showing her the ropes. All eyes were now on Sally and the young sailor. Tense, still slightly green and feeling distinctly delicate though he was, bristled. He wanted very much to punch the young man. That, however, would have involved unclipping the safety line and moving away from the safety of the metal guard rail. It would also have involved physical confrontation with an evidently fit and able-bodied young man. Sally didn't seem to mind. Which only made it worse. Tense, ever the realist, decided that discretion was indeed the better part of valour and chose instead to rise above it. Feigning indifference, he gazed ahead. There was something in the water ahead. Something big.

"There's something in the water", he shouted. Instantly the young sailor spun the wheel to starboard, throwing Sally across the deck towards Tense. The bow of the boat rose suddenly, and there was a loud bang as the hull struck something in the water. Sally was pitched into the air. Her bright yellow sou'wester was torn from her head and thrown over the side of the boat. Sally herself rose in a graceful arc above the heads of the sailors, beyond Tense's desperately outstretched hands, and was cast into the churning waves off the port side.

"Man overboard" someone shouted. The captain stepped in. The crew, instantly alert and professional, launched into an apparently choreographed and much-practised routine. One hurled a life ring into the water. A second man threw a life vest. Another stood at the rear of the boat, pointing at Sally's receding head, and shouted, "I see her."

The distance between the boat and Sally was growing fast.

"Trim sale. Quick stop." The captain bellowed. The men swarmed over the deck. The boat lurched into the wind, turning sharply. Sails were reset, and the boat started back. The captain glanced towards the lookout, who was still pointing in the direction of the tiny bobbing head.

"I see her", he confirmed.

"Can she swim?" The captain was addressing Tense, "Is she a strong swimmer?"

"I don't know. She's an angel. I don't think it's a core skill. I've seen her swim once, not very well."

The captain shook his head in disbelief. The boat was fast approaching Sally, whose head was still just above water. As the boat came alongside her, Sally lifted one graceful arm and began to slip beneath the waves. Tense, still attached to the boat, grabbed the safety rail and heaved himself over the side and into the water next to Sally. He just had time to grab her and pull her firmly to him when the safety line, played out to its full length, snapped taut and began to drag them both along beside the boat. Within seconds the boat slowed. Strong arms reached down and pulled the couple from the waves.

Practised hands placed Sally in the recovery position. Sally coughed water from her lungs and began to breathe heavily, coughing all the while. Tense flopped across the deck, unclipped his safety line and crawled to Sally's side. She sat up. Tense stared into her eyes, fear and reaction blurring his vision.

"Are you alright? I was so scared. I thought I'd lost you."

Sally, still totally spaced out, having been pushed beyond anything she could have imagined experiencing, slipped her arms around Tense and pulled him close.

"I'm ok."

Having ascertained that Sally was ok, the captain began barking orders. The safety ring and life vest were retrieved from the water. Sadly, Sally's sou'wester was nowhere to be seen. The boat set sail for home.

Sally and Tense, now wrapped in blankets, sat snuggled together as the boat made its way back between the heads and into Sydney Harbour.

Sally laid her head on Tense's shoulder.

"What a rush."

***

After a quick check-up back at the Sailing Club, Sally and Tense were allowed to leave. The mood was sombre. None of the sailors could figure out quite what had happened. But something had. They were sure of that much.

Hand in hand, Sally and Tense walked across the park towards the main road. Tense carried their wet-weather gear in the crook of his right arm. Sally clung tightly to his left hand.

"I thought you could swim."

"Yes."

"Well? Can you?"

"I thought I could. But I haven't had much practice. Only the time we spent the other day."

"That was it?"

"I think so. It hasn't been my habit to hang around for a swim on the odd occasions when I have been embodied in the past."

"Makes sense, I suppose. I guess an angel is unlikely to stop for a bit of a paddle when on a mission from God."

"Living things only ever embody for a purpose, you know. No one wants to hang around indefinitely in a heaving coat of aging flesh."

"Hadn't ever thought about it like that. You don't make it sound all that appetising."

"No offence meant."

"None taken. You wouldn't happen to be hungry again, would you?"

"So, you can read minds too?"

"There is an exceptional culinary experience to which I'd like to introduce you."

"Oh. That sounds nice."

"Well, "nice" might perhaps be overstating it a little. But it's certainly memorable."

"What is it?"

"You'll see." Tense hailed a taxi, and they clambered in, still damp but no longer dripping.

"Woolloomooloo." Tense proffered an airy wave of the hand.

It would only have been a few minutes later that the taxi pulled in next to a very large battleship-grey battleship.

"This is us." Tense paid the taxi, and they both jumped out.

A short distance away stood a large, gaudy, brightly lit kiosk. The orange rays of the lowering sun dripped over it like honey. People stood around, individually and in small groups. Tense led Sally over to the open serving hatch.

"Two Tigers, please," he announced, "with all the trimmings." Tense paid the required sum and stood back. Sally perused the menu.

"Pies. I'm getting the sense that you have taken me to a pie shop. Would I be right in that?"

"By no means is the celebrated Harry's Café de Wheels a mere pie shop." Tense leapt to the defence of what was, to him, a national treasure, "A more painstaking examination of the menu reveals an exciting range of hotdogs, filled rolls and some delectable deserts."

"I see."

"Yes."

"And you've ordered the so-called 'Tiger' for me?"

"Yes," Tense was ebullient, "the Tiger is probably the greatest contribution to Australian culinary culture bequeathed to us by the British."

"It's a pie."

"Yes indeed, but not just a pie. The Tiger is a chunky beef pie, and it comes with mushy peas, mashed potato and gravy." Tense had, to all appearances, entered a transcendental state of altered consciousness. A beatific smile adorned his otherwise somewhat pensive countenance.

"I'm sure it will be fine." Sally had not been won over, but being a bit of a trooper, she was willing to give it a go. It would, in any case, be an act of wilful cruelty to wipe the look of childlike joy from her husband's happy little face.

Only moments later, the pair were presented with a mound of food on cardboard plates. They found an unoccupied bench a little way off, near the battleship, liberated their disposable cutlery from its military-grade packaging and sat down to feast.

Both were silent for quite a while. Sally was indeed hungry. The fresh sea air, coupled with a near-death experience, had boosted her appetite.

"Umm," she managed.

"Umm?"

"Not bad."

Tense looked a little crestfallen.

Sally finished every last scrap on her plate. The seagulls that had gathered around her flapped away disconsolate.

"Well?" Tense looked expectantly at his beloved.

"Well, what?"

"You scoffed the lot."

"Yes, I was hungry."

"But did you like it?"

"Yes, it was perfectly pleasant."

"Perfectly pleasant? The apex of British cuisine? That's it?"

"It was very nice." then, after a moment, "Thank you."

Tense did not look satisfied.

"Well, surprisingly good, actually."

"Yes." Tense smiled, vindicated.

"And the mushy peas do work somehow."

"It's the mint sauce and vinegar."

That was the best he was going to get, and to his credit, he did eventually realise it.

"I'm glad you're feeling better after your accident."

Before Sally could respond, they were both startled by the deafening bellow of what sounded like a foghorn. The battleship adjacent to which they had feasted was a-buzz with busy sailors making ready to leave. Slowly the massive vessel drifted away from the harbour wall. The sea began to churn and spray as the ship got underway. Sally and Tense watched as it eased its way out into deeper water and turned towards the headlands and the open ocean. As the ship moved away, they could see it was a sort of mini aircraft carrier. Still massive, but now that they could perceive its true dimensions, looking a little truncated.

There was none of the usual pomp and ceremony. No rows of sparkling, white-suited sailors lined the bows. A couple of fast launches carrying hard-faced men in dark overalls escorted the vessel. And after a few moments, it was gone.

"We are a seagoing nation," Tense mused, "but we do not control the seaways."

"What was it for?" Sally wondered, "It seemed very plain and flat. Not very warlike."

"Helicopters, I think," Tense had wondered the same thing, "so they have somewhere to land and take off from."

"Very sensible." Sally had lost interest, "didn't I see some deserts on the menu? At the pie shop?"

"There's bound to be another big war one day."

Sally's mind was focused on pudding.

"It's free will that's to blame."

"Oh no, please." But it was too late.

"We will go to war to protect our access to the sea. I reckon we're in a sort of computer game."

"Human beings are a computer game?"

"Yep. God's computer game. Despite anything the Jesuits might say, free will suggests God has a hankering for novelty, for surprise. Free will suggests to me that God cannot, in fact, foresee all or that he can choose not to. Perhaps the Creator is not omniscient, or perhaps he's just bored. The standard explanations simply don't stand up. I reckon God looked forward to a time when he could say to himself, 'Did you see what that human being just did? Who would have thought?'"

"Custard tarts."

"Beg pardon?" Tense couldn't quite grasp the reference.

"They sell custard tarts." Sally was having none of Tense's blather.

"The problem with unlimited power or knowledge is that both are limitations. Having unlimited knowledge means never being surprised. Having unlimited power means that whatever happens, you have per-mitted it to happen."

"And apple turnovers."

"Really? Apple turnovers?"

"With cream or ice cream." Sally had won. Tense's gaze slid slowly in the direction of the gaudy food outlet.

"I do like an apple turnover", he confessed. Sally took his hand.

"Let's pretend we're going to have custard tarts and then, at the last minute, choose apple turnovers."

"Do you think He'd fall for it?"

"Not for a moment, but according to your theory, He might appreciate the gesture."

CHAPTER 12 - ART

They decided to catch the train home from Circular Quay. Tense was still feeling a wee bit discombobulated from Sally's recent brush with death. Sally was oblivious.

The walk across the park brought them to the classical old sandstone building of the Art Gallery of New South Wales, stately and golden in the slanting rays of the late afternoon sun. They went in. It was cool and subdued inside. A disapproving gentleman insisted they leave their wet weather gear in the cloakroom room. He gave them a tag, and they stepped through the foyer into the open floor of the gallery.

Without any plan or intent, they wandered randomly and at considerable length through rooms large and small, displaying a fraction of the curated human artistic output of several thousand years. The gallery was not particularly crowded at this time of day. For an instant, Tense thought he caught a glimpse of a clean-shaven young man in a crisp white shirt with a dark suit and tie. Sally stopped in front of a large oil painting of a man with a lot of cows.

"What is it all for?"

"It's art."

"Yes, but why? What is it for, actually?"

"It's for people to look at."

Sally paused, suspecting that she was being teased or, in some other way, disrespected.

"OK. I'm obviously not making myself clear. What exactly is the purpose of art other than to give people something to look at? Or is that, in fact, its sole purpose."

"Oh."

Sally waited. Patiently.

"Um."

Still, she waited.

"Err. Well, it's expression and creativity. Art expresses our deepest hopes, dreams, fears and yearnings."

"There must be a lot of art about then."

"There is. Heaps."

"Um." Sally's feet were sore.

"Um?"

"It says they have a café." Sally looked around, hopefully.

"Hang on a minute. Don't give me that hoity-toity Messenger of God superiority. What do you angels have that's so much better?"

Sally paused. "Now you come to mention it. We don't really have anything. There isn't that much to have if you are a disembodied being."

"I suppose not."

"I mean, we know a lot. We remember everything. And we've been around since the beginning. So, it's not as though we're a bunch of empty-headed hicks."

"I wasn't suggesting...."

"I know you weren't. It's just we don't express ourselves physically that much, except for the Creator, of course. He knocked up an entire physical universe for you guys." Sally indicated the entirety of existence with a small gesture of the hand.

"He was an artist, though, wasn't he?" Tense stopped short. There he was again. Out of the corner of his eye, Tense fancied he glimpsed the familiar, clean-shaven face. It was him, wasn't it? Lucifer surely had no interest in visiting an art gallery. What was he doing here? Was he following them?

Sally didn't seem to have noticed, and Tense kept his peace, which may, in hindsight, have been unfortunate.

Tense continued, "Now I think about it, why did the Creator need to say his new universe was good? And aren't we human beings, living our brief lives right down in the blood and guts of His creation, not far better placed, from the purview of lived experience, to cast judgement on it?"

"I see what you mean. I think."

"And anyway, if the universe is God's work of art, and if it was good at the outset, then what went wrong? Did anything go wrong? Could it? Or is this really how it's meant to be?"

Sally spotted the entrance to the café.

"Let's discuss it over a coffee and a sticky bun?" She took his hand firmly and joined the queue.

Tense had given up wondering at Sally's prodigious appetites.

"Gluttony is a sin, you know. One of the twelve deadly sins."

"I just like cake. That's not gluttony. Anyway, I'm eating for two now."

"I'll have a latte and a slice of New York cheesecake." Tense resigned himself to middle-aged spread and placed his order.

Sally chose English breakfast tea, an adequate selection of cakes and something called a friand.

They sat out on the terrace. It was warm in the attenuating light of early evening. There was a gentle, blood-temperature breeze coming from the north. The shaven chin appeared briefly behind the glass windows of the café. It *was* him. They were being followed. Tense shifted awkwardly in his seat, straining to see where the dark man had gone. Should he mention it to Sally? She would have noticed, surely?

"Still", Sally ventured, "you must admit it is pretty awesome. An entire, infinite universe complete with universal constants, dark energy, dark matter, more stars and galaxies than you could shake a stick at, and cake."

"What are "dark energy" and "dark matter" then? You must know." Tense was distracted by a shadow passing swiftly across the table. He looked up. It was nothing.

"Haven't the faintest idea." Sally spoke indistinctly between mouthfuls, "Ask me about cake."

"The whole thing is a hologram, though. You'd have to allow that. We are all strutting around inside the mind of God."

"Try the carrot cake", she managed, through a mouth stuffed to the gills, "It really is to die for."

***

The visit to the art gallery had not been a success. Sally, as it turned out, could not give a stuff about the curated human artistic output of several thousand years, still less about our deepest hopes, dreams, fears and yearnings. She would admit, however, to a more than passing interest in certain 'craft' activities. These were, cooking in general and baking in particular.

Tense led Sally from the restaurant terrace, up the escalator, through the main concourse, and out into the foyer, where they retrieved the one remaining sou'wester and the two bright yellow oilskin coats from the cloakroom. The disapproving gentleman had gone, replaced by a gormless teenager. There had been no further sign of the clean-shaven young man in the dark suit.

As the evening was warm, they decided to walk down through the park and take a train from Circular Quay rather than catch another cab. Dozens of huge, fruit-eating bats, known locally as flying foxes, hung in bickering clusters, like grumpy gothic holiday decorations, from the trees along the path. The sun had begun the long process of setting, which in Sydney involved slowly lowering towards the horizon while spreading a gloopy orange glow, like marmalade, across the city.

The sun finally set, illuminating Sydney Harbour Bridge as they walked the last few metres to the train station. Evening fell quickly after that.

The journey home was relatively swift. Tense tussled with the front door lock for less time than usual, and they entered the dimly lit flat. They were both exhausted. It had been a full day. They had gotten married, consummated thoroughly, injured a visit from the Devil, and gone sailing. Sally nearly drowned. They had dined in style courtesy of Harry's Café de Wheels, dragged themselves around the Art Gallery of New South Wales, somehow found a way to stuff in more cake, and walked across the park to Circular Quay beneath a curtain of fruit-eating bats.

Tense made a pot of tea, and the newlyweds collapsed on the rickety rattan chairs on the balcony. It was dark, but the sky was not yet pitch black. The lights of the city glittered and twinkled across the bay.

"Wow."

"Wow?"

"What a day." Tense leaned back in the chair, which creaked ominously.

"We certainly packed a lot in." Sally yawned.

"How are you feeling?" other than in the context of a medical condition, Tense could not remember having asked anyone that question before.

"Tired. But good. Great, actually." Sally subsided for a moment, "That was exhilarating."

"What exactly?"

"Everything. The whole day. It was a whirlwind, an immersion in the physical reality of human life."

"Yes."

"Almost a lifetime in microcosm." Sally gathered her thoughts.

"Whether the source of perception is the same for each human being or always different, you, or perhaps I should say we, each experience the universe for ourselves alone, don't we? I cannot hear or see on your behalf, you must do it for yourself, and you can't see the world for me or as I see it."

"We'll make an existentialist of you yet." Tense began to realise what he must often sound like.

"Yes. It's as though we each have our own private universe to experience."

"I'll check the fridge." All this esoteric thought brought home to Tense the necessity of having sufficient breakfast materials on hand in the morning.

"That's what compassion is for, isn't it? And altruism." But Tense was out of earshot.

The fridge was worryingly bare. Which was in itself something of a surprise given how often and how assiduously he had filled it. Tense checked his watch. The corner shop, which always seemed to be open, would still be open.

"I'm just popping out to the corner shop for breakfast stuff."

Sally wasn't about to argue. She had found herself in a most unaccustomed place emotionally. She was introspecting. Not typically an angelic activity, this sudden preoccupation naturally came as something of a shock.

Tense, oblivious, skipped down the stairs whistling tunelessly to himself and made his way through the balmy Sydney evening to the shop that never seemed to close. He took greater care this time to peruse the breakfast wares on sale. He would, he thought, introduce a little more variety into their morning feast.

About twenty minutes later, he emerged from the poorly lit emporium carrying four shopping bags, two in each hand. As he stepped through the doorway and onto the street, he bumped into someone in the entrance. It was the clean-shaven young man in the dark suit, white shirt, and tie, standing slightly to one side, casually smoking.

"We have to talk." The young man smiled engagingly.

"No, we don't." Tense brushed passed him nervously.

"Yes, we do" The man was suddenly in front of him again, blocking his way.

Tense attempted to push past, but the young man held firm.

"Look, I know this must all seem weird to you."

Tense gave the man what he hoped was a frosty stare.

"I know you must be feeling a little out of your depth."

"I know you're not her brother" Tense was becoming angry now, "I know who you are, really."

"No", the young man caught Tense's eye and held it, "No, you don't."

Neither man moved. The tableau held. It was Tense who broke the impasse.

"What do you mean?"

"We are neither of us who you think we are."

Tense held his ground, waiting to hear more.

"I am certainly not the Devil, and Amitiel is not the angel of truth."

Tense, confused and angry, dropped the shopping bags and punched the young man on the chin. The man staggered back for a moment, then regained his footing and composure.

"It's ok. I should have expected that. This part is always the hardest."

"This part of what? What are you talking about?" Tense stepped towards the young man, furious, menacing.

"This part of the explanation. You deserve an explanation. I know this is going to be very hard for you."

"Spit it out."

"I am a doctor. A psychiatrist, to be precise." The man paused for a moment to allow the information to sync in.

"I am Amitiel's psychiatrist, although, of course, that's not her real name."

Tense stood uncertain.

"What is it?" he managed, in little more than a whisper, "What is her real name?"

"Hanna. Hanna Delft, and she's not from heaven. She's from the NSW Central Coast."

"And what's your name then?"

"Peter McAuliffe, Doctor Peter McAuliffe. I've been searching for Hanna since this latest episode took hold."

"Episode?" Tense felt his entire world collapse around him. Nothing had meaning any more. The personal meaning he had given things provided insufficient scaffolding for his universe. No other foundation was available to him. Everything was lost.

"Hanna suffers from a severe form of Narcissistic Borderline Behavioural Disorder, culminating in occasional psychotic episodes. She is having one now."

"Is she dangerous?" Tense's voice shook a little. He wanted to cry. He wanted to collapse on the pavement and wail at the rising moon. He wanted to die.

"Only when provoked. I'm going to have to ask you to go along with it for now."

"Can she be cured?" Tense held out for himself the smallest glimmer of hope.

"I suppose so. In principle. Given time."

There was something undeniably threatening and bleak about this young man. Whether it came by virtue of his excruciating profession or because his choice of profession itself derived from some austere or dismal core to his being, he exuded menace. Dread shadowed him.

Tense turned, picked up his shopping and headed home.

Something his mother had once said came back to him. The most certain way to be wrong is to offer an opinion. One can predict anything, she would say, except the future. He didn't know what to think.

***

That short walk home was the longest of his life. Tense, like many men, had not been gifted by nature with an extensive emotional lexicon. He did, however, possess sufficient self-knowledge to be aware of that. Furthermore, he was not a good liar, and he knew it. On the other hand, his powers of reasoning were excellent. He was analytical by nature, and when stressed, as he most certainly was now, he became even more methodical and diagnostic in his approach. Whether reason or faith would be the better guide as he wandered through his very own valley of the shadow of death was yet to be tested.

Tense, shaken to the core in both his reason and his faith, brought once again to mind the image of himself as a ping-pong ball, kept aloft, kept spinning by a faltering column of air supplied by a small asthmatic boy. Uncertainty, his old friend, had returned to be with him at his time of need.

OK, he thought to himself, *let's break this down.* Somewhere in the dim recesses of memory, he recalled one of his engineering lectures saying, 'Listen up people, either you work the problem, or it works you', or maybe it came from some movie.

What the hell, he thought, *let's give it a go.*

Tense worked the problem or tried to.

Premise: Either Sally was an angel, or she was not.

Option 1: If she was an angel, then Dr Peter McAuliffe was indeed her old friend Lucifer.

Option 2: If not, then Dr Peter McAuliffe was her psychiatrist, and Sally was crazy.

Was that it? What other possibilities could there be? Was there an Option 3?

Option 3: Neither Sally the angel nor Dr Peter McAuliffe were who they said they were. Instead, they were in cahoots, carrying out an incomprehensible con job on a random bloke of no particular means for no discernible advantage.

Tense discarded Option 3 as being too implausible even within his current frame of reference. Either Sally was an angel, or she was crazy. It was with almost unfathomable desolation that Tense realised Option 1 was almost as unlikely as Option 3. Despair, as is its wont, followed fast upon the heels of the bleak emptiness filling his soul. Wretched and utterly alone, Tense retraced his steps towards the small apartment block where Sally, or Amitiel, or Hanna, would be waiting.

Drawn by the gentle sound of the waves lapping on the small beach nearby, he continued past the entrance to the apartment building and sat for a while on a bench facing the water.

"What else did he have?" he wondered. The problem was intractable. What other levers could he bring to bear? There must be some other way of looking at it. Tense attempted to approach the problem from a different angle.

"Did it matter that Sally was crazy?" He wasn't sure it did, and as he began to think about it, he became less certain still. So, what she was crazy. He was as happy and fulfilled as he had ever been. It was not as though he needed or even wanted her to perform miracles or introduce him directly to the Creator.

Of what could he be certain then? What was undeniable? Despite everything, what was there that he could depend upon with absolute certainty? For Tense, who had invested so much of his time and energy, so much of himself, in his existentialist worldview, there was something familiar, something comforting in this restatement of his eternal conundrum. This was his life's work, in a way. He was used to making his own meaning. He was familiar with imposing his personal values and beliefs upon an evidently blasé and apathetic universe. This was his Heimat. He was on home ground.

If he knew one thing only, one single thing with absolute certainty, it was that he loved her. Whoever, and whatever, she was. Tense stared out across the bay into the ambivalent darkness between the twinkling city lights reflected on the water. He stared into the spaces between. Into the interstices conjoining dark and light, coupling reason and faith. And there, in the tiny cracks and fissures through which chance and fate and hope make their way into our universe, he found his rock.

He loved her. Trite as it was, the corniest of clichés. It was enough for him. They were both as mad as March hares, perhaps, but in different ways.

Tense smiled, took a long deep breath and laughed. Things were really no different than he had always believed them to be. All life, all love, is compromise. Well then. So be it.

The waters of the bay lapped quietly at the shore. A warm breeze blew from the ocean. Tense stood, took up his burden and, shopping bags in hand, made his way back up the stairs to his apartment. The door opened easily. Sally was standing in the hallway.

"You were gone a long while. I was getting worried."

"I'm sorry, my love, I had some difficult decisions to make."

"Oh?"

"Yes. I chose mangoes and croissants for breakfast, and we're going to have smashed avocadoes on toast instead of the usual."

"Umm", Sally the angel wrapped herself around Tense and kissed him slowly, starting at his collar bone, then up his neck and along his jaw, seeking and finding the softness of his lips.

Probably best not to say anything, Tense decided, *no need to upset her.*

Sally, newlywed, indeed, newly a woman, allowed the imperatives of the body to be her guide. Taking his hand in hers, she dragged Tense off for a bit of serious consummation.

Despite everything, married life was not proving to be too bad for either of them. Still, somewhere in the dim, dark recesses of his conscience, Tense had become aware of a certain discomfort. Regret began gnawing its way through his innards. Evasions, equivocations, and avoidances, having gained ingress through the tiniest act of omission, busied themselves preparing their case. He should have mentioned his meeting with the clean-shaven young man. Too late now, or so he assumed.

The consummation was good. Tense was able to throw off his darkened mood in the wanton flagrancy of new love. Battered and a little bruised, Sally and Tense lay back. The room looked as though a small tornado had passed through. Tense surveyed the scene with satisfaction. He'd seen bedrooms like this in the movies. This was how things were meant to be. Had he taken the time to think about it, Tense might have identified his underlying emotion as pride. As it was, he was aware of feeling satisfied and content. Sally might be as mad as a ferret in a hat box, but so what. From where he was lying, things didn't look all that bad.

Sally, who had not yet had her dinner, was, of course, beginning to feel peckish. Her previously very slim figure was beginning to fill out just a tad. Tense rather liked it.

"Ahem," she announced.

"Ahem?"

"Yes."

"Ahem, what?"

"Ahem, it is now after ten o'clock in the evening, and I have not yet had my dinner."

"I see."

"I don't know what you could have been thinking?"

"You know precisely what I was thinking about, you Jezebel."

"Jezebel, Moi?"

"Yes. Temptress. Vixen." And so on until, inevitably, there was need for some more furious consummation. The bedroom now resembled the scene of a minor explosion.

"Now I really am hungry, Tense." Sally effortlessly affected the huge, appealing eyes of a Victorian starveling.

"OK. I'll see what we have in the fridge."

Tense pulled on his trousers and stumbled off, wondering to himself if Sally was and had always been a female human being or if she was, in fact, a very quick learner. Either way, he had been consumed with ruthless efficiency and was feeling rather pleased with himself.

There were leftovers in the fridge. Tense put together a smorgasbord of cheeses and cold meats, bread, butter, and various relishes. He took a bottle of Provençal Rosé from the fridge and two clean wine glasses from the cupboard and set the rickety balcony table for dinner. The temperature had dropped to an acceptable twenty-eight degrees outside. A gentle breeze now blew from the bay. The city was relatively quiet.

Sally wandered through from the bedroom, again wearing his old work shirt. Again, buttoned up wrong in a most alluring manner. It was touch and go for a moment whether dinner would once again be delayed. Hunger won out.

They sat gazing out over the water, enjoying the play of city lights on the tiny wavelets. Tense poured two glasses of Rosé. Sally sipped contemplatively. There was something on her mind.

"Should I get a job?" she asked. Tense, momentarily floored by the question, could give no answer.

"I could drive a bus."

"You want to be a bus driver?"

"Looks like fun."

"You have the wisdom of the ages at your disposal, and you want to be a bus driver?"

"It's a very responsible job. People depend on you."

"I don't doubt that for a second, but is it the best use of your skills?"

"What do you think I should do then?"

"I haven't ever thought about it, but wouldn't teacher, or scientist or something make better use of all your knowledge?"

"Most of what I know is not really of any use to a mortal, though, is it?"

"How do you mean?"

"It's mostly just memories. I've never been to school. We don't have schools in heaven."

"I see what you mean. Still, the Angel of Truth becoming a bus driver – not really great career advice, is it?"

"Angels don't have careers."

"I get it." For some reason, Tense was beginning to find the conversation irritating. He wasn't even sure she was an angel. For all he knew, she was indeed a bus driver.

Sally sensed the change in his mood. "You, ok?"

"Yes. Sure."

"You seem a bit snippy."

"Just hungry, I guess. Come on, dig in."

Sally could appreciate that being hungry could impact one's mood. She dug in.

Down by the water, under the palm trees, a shadow moved. Sally saw it immediately. Tense followed her gaze.

"There's someone down there." Sally craned forward in her seat, trying to get a good look.

Tense somehow knew who it was. He felt a cold knot grow in his stomach. He should tell Sally about their meeting. He should tell her right now.

"Just someone out for a late-night walk, I expect." Sally's focus shifted back to the dinner table. "This meal is just right, and the wine is perfect."

Tense watched the shade of the man slipping surreptitiously from shadow to deeper shadow.

"I bumped into someone earlier while I was out shopping."

Sally looked up, attentive, innocent. Tense couldn't do it. He couldn't tell her. Whether it was because he feared she would be angry or because he wanted to spare her feelings, he could not have said. He realised that his motivation was not purely altruistic. He was aware of that much. Of where it would all lead, he knew nothing.

"Oh, who was that?"

"Just one of the young Italian guys who witnessed our wedding."

"Was that why you were late back?"

"Yes. I stopped for a chat." Tense could feel the minimal web of deceit that he had begun to weave, tangling and becoming ever more embedded as he spoke.

Why can't she tell I'm lying? Maybe she can. Shit,' he thought, '*This is not going to end well.*

The shadow down below on the beach slipped silently into the night and disappeared. The couple ate in silence, Sally, for her part, enjoying the quiet intimacy of the occasion. She was happy she realised. Not an emotion she had bothered with much as an angel. Having no reason to suspect her lover of deceit, Sally felt no need to wield her truth-sense.

Sally padded off to bed. Tense cleared away the dinner things. It was late. He walked to the edge of the balcony and peered off into the night. Straining to catch so much as a glimpse of the man watching from the shadows.

He saw nothing. The last Manly Ferry blew a single mournful blast on its horn, audible faintly across the water. Tense shivered.

Someone walked over my grave.

Sally woke or found herself awake and screamed. There was for her no recollection. There was no context. No continuity. No past. There was only the dead weight of flesh holding her down. Pinning her to the surface of physical reality. What reality? Where?

She did not breathe. The body took breath. She did not see. The eyes saw. Flashing, kaleidoscopic images wheeled and turned against her inner eye. She did not smell the slightly acrid scent of a bed well-used. Yet the cloying stench was there. It was hot, stifling. She did not hear the piercing screams coming from her mouth. But the ears heard, and the heart pumped in blind panic.

Sally awoke to raw existence, red in tooth and claw. From out the silent time gap between sleeping and waking, the horror spewed. From the silence of unconsciousness, Sally awoke to a liminal, transitional, in-between state never before imagined. Indeed, unimaginable to her or to any angel. Neither fully angel nor fully flesh.

"That should keep body and soul together." A random phrase once heard. Spoken by … whom?

"Who said that?" Sally wondered, "And what did it mean?"

There was light without warning. And hands holding. Arms lifting, enfolding. And there were words.

"Sally. What is it? Are you OK?"

There was a face. Recognition. A name.

"Tense."

"Yes. It's me. Are you all right? What happened?"

"I must have wandered off."

"What?"

"I must have travelled. When the body was asleep."

"Travelled where? Like sleepwalking, you mean?"

"No. I must have left the body for a while."

"And gone where?"

"I felt a presence. I am being watched."

"Is that what frightened you?"

"No. I am not afraid of the watcher. I know him. I know his ways."

"Then what?"

"When I awoke, I was disoriented. I had not yet fully reintegrated into the flesh. I felt trapped. I couldn't... There is no human word for it. My spirit was confined, unable to 'project' - I suppose is the nearest word. It was terrifying. I have never experienced anything like it before."

"Night terrors, perhaps? That's what we call it. Maybe it was something like that?"

"Maybe." Sally was silent for a few moments, "There is something worse than being wholly flesh or wholly spirit."

"What do you mean?"

"Being spirit trapped in unresponsive flesh. Being imprisoned in a body from which you are disconnected. That's a terrible feeling."

"But you have been embodied before. Many times, I should imagine. What was so different this time."

"There is usually no sense of transition. One moment I am fully angel. The next, I am embodied. Whole and complete. I've never had to go through a process before. I never experienced an intermediate step. It was sickening."

"I can imagine. Well, I can't, really. But I see what you mean."

Sally shuddered and drew closer to Tense.

"I wonder why it happened this time."

"I blame the rosé and the pickles. Never trust a pickle. My mother used to say that."

"Did she, really?"

"No. She loved pickles as it happens."

Sally rolled her eyes and sighed, before assaulting Tense contemplatively, with her pillow.

"It is difficult for me to understand," Tense began, "can you try to explain to me how you know you are an angel?"

"What?"

"I'm just saying," Tense began, "I understand how you can know that you are currently an embodied human being, but how do you know you are, or were, an angel?"

"Oh please," Sally's eyes narrowed, "we're not going there again, are we?"

"I just want to understand…."

"Have you been talking to someone? Who have you been talking to?"

"No one. I haven't been talking to anyone. I just…" his voice petered out. Sally was staring at him, reading his face. Truth-sense to the fore.

"What did he tell you? What did he say?"

"Who? I don't know what you're talking about." Tense blushed a deep crimson from his forehead to his neck. His ears stood out, scarlet, like warning beacons.

Sally leaned away, supporting herself on an elbow. Waiting.

"I told you. I spoke to one of the Italians who witnessed our wedding."

"Which one?"

"I don't know. I don't remember their names. The taller one who draped himself all over me and tried to give me advice."

"Luciano?"

"How the fuck would I know? Yes, maybe, Luciano. I don't know."

"What did he say then?"

"He asked me how married life was going."

"Yes"

"And he asked me if you really believed you were an angel."

"And what did you say?"

"I said you were my angel." Tense was particularly pleased with that. It was a good lie. Flattering to deceive.

For a long while, Sally held her distance, examining Tense's face. Evaluating.

"Be careful. He can appear in any guise."

"Who?"

"You know who. Don't play dumb. You're too convincing."

The jibe stung. Although he had been caught in a lie, and he knew it, still he felt affronted. She had no proof he was lying. How dare she doubt him? Tense recoiled, offended. Sally continued.

"He is clever and fluent. He knows just what to say. He is convincing."

"It was Luciano," Tense offered, "I remember now."

Sally sighed, frustrated and, for the first time, perhaps a little afraid. She leaned closer once more.

"You don't understand, my love. He has eons of experience. He is a master of flattery and deceit. Above all, and this is really important, he is dangerous. Truly, deeply dangerous, but not in some mundane, human way. Lucifer is the stealer of souls. You cannot imagine eternity. That is not a frame of reference a human mind can encompass. But understand this Tense. Eternity is not "a very long time". Eternity is all time. You wouldn't want to spend it with Lucifer."

Tense held his peace. Not trusting himself to speak.

"If he comes to you again, and he will, no doubt, you must tell me."

"He's probably a million miles away by now. I'm sure he has bigger fish to fry."

"He was down by the beach earlier tonight. Hiding in the shadows. Watching."

Tense knew it was true. Lucifer was near, or Peter. One or the other.

"I will tell you if I see him again. I promise."

Light flashed outside the bedroom window, momentarily illuminating the room. Sally's form, frozen for an instant, stark against the backdrop of their unmade bed, looked every inch the angel. And yet, the gentle curve of waist to hip, the slight rise of her belly, and the fullness of her bosom spoke of womanhood and childbirth and, therefore, of mortality.

Deep regret washed over Tense. How could he have lied? He would confess. He must. Yet fear still held him back, and doubt. *What if?* he thought. *What if?*

A rumble of thunder, delayed by distance, rattled the windowpane. Tense arose and wandered through the apartment, checking the windows and doors.

Rain was coming, approaching from the east. Out over the Pacific, storm clouds were gathering. It had been a hot day in a hot week. The grass by the beach was parched.

We need the rain, an automatic thought. The habitual response of all Australians.

Tense opened the door and stepped onto the balcony for a moment. Occasional flashes of sheet lightning lit the sky. The Sydney skyline flickered, for a moment, in sharp relief against the deeper blackness that came after.

Though it was warm, Tense shivered, stepped back into the apartment and, for once, locked the balcony door.

***

Tense awoke a little late the next morning - to an empty bed. Before he was fully awake, he knew Sally was gone. The realisation, like the fuse on a firecracker, burnt slow at first before the full realisation burst upon him.

Tense leapt from the bed and hopped down the corridor to the kitchen, pulling up his trousers as he did so. Just as one sometimes knows before entering a house that it is empty, Tense knew, before he entered the living area, that she was not there.

He searched for a note. She would have left a note. She could write, surely? Angels must be able to read and write. He ran back down the hall to the bedroom. Perhaps she'd left it on the pillow. He searched the apartment, practically ransacking it, before finally flopping down on a kitchen chair like a rag doll. Beaten and despondent.

Where had she gone? Tense wracked his brain. It was not as though she had anywhere to go.

At least as far as he knew. *Maybe she did have somewhere to go. Maybe she had a family. Maybe she was married with kids.*

Had she left him? Was she gone for good?

He was full of wild speculation. The total dearth of any facts to go on, other than the one massive, awful truth of her manifest absence, drove Tense to unaccustomed heights of invention and imagination. The elephant was not, as it were, still in the room. That was all he knew for sure.

She had left him because he doubted that she really was an angel.

She had gone to buy breakfast. Hardly plausible given the dangerously filled-to-overflowing condition of the fridge.

Coffee! She knew he liked a proper latte.

She had been taken away in the night by her accomplice Peter.

She had been spirited away by Lucifer.

She had been kidnapped by aliens. Perhaps not.

Tense put on the kettle and made himself a cup of strong Irish Breakfast tea with three heaped sugars. It had been his experience, encouraged by his mother, that few of life's crises could persist in their intensity in the face of a cup of strong, sweet tea.

Tense was just into his second cup when the front door crashed open. He felt for his keys in his trouser pockets. They were gone. *Doh!* he thought.

Sally burst into the kitchen, fairly brimming with excitement and pride.

"I've done it." She announced.

"Done what?"

"I've been and gone and got me a job."

Tense decided to focus not upon Sally's curious syntax for once but upon the substance of her improbable proclamation.

"You've got a job?"

"Yes."

"Where?"

"At the hospital."

"As what?"

"As a translator and interpreter."

"Oh."

"Yes. I can start on Monday."

Tense stared at Sally across the kitchen table, unable to remove the stunned mullet expression from his face.

"Would you like a nice cup of tea?" he managed.

"Aren't you going to congratulate me? Aren't you proud of me?"

"Yes, certainly, of course. Many congratulations…" Sally did not look convinced.

"Do you speak many languages?"

"All of them."

"All of them. You speak all human languages."

"Yes. It's a knack, I think. Or maybe we all can, angels, I mean. Perhaps it's just one of the things we can do."

"Literally, all of them? All human languages?"

"Yes. I believe so."

"Current and past?"

"Yes, and future, for that matter. At least, I think I can. I assume I can. I've never encountered a language I couldn't speak."

"Blimey."

"Yes. They were surprised at the agency too."

"I bet they were."

"Yes. They gave me a test."

"What sort of test?"

"A language test, of course."

"Yes. I assumed it would have been a language test."

"Oh. I see. Sorry. They gave me a sentence in English and a list of languages, and they asked me to say the sentence in every language on their list."

"And?"

"I knew them all, obviously."

"Obviously."

Tense poured Sally a cup of tea with two sugars and milk.

Sally sat.

"What Agency? How did you find out about it?"

"Just some health care job agency. It was on the interweb."

"Does it pay well?"

"Oh. I don't know. Is it important?"

"People generally like to know what they are going to be paid."

"Really?"

"Yes. The idea is that the employer compensates the employee for giving up their free time to work."

"I see."

"Yes. The employer pays more or less per hour depending upon what that person's labour is worth in the market." But Sally's eyes had glazed over.

"Shall we go out for breakfast? I'm starving."

Tense's mind went immediately to the stuffed fridge, but what the hell?

"Sure. Where would you like to go?"

"How about that place we went to the first time? With the fresh fruit salad with double cream and vanilla bean ice cream?"

Tense shuddered. His memory of the occasion was somewhat ambivalent. He treasured it because it was the very first time they had been together, even though the experience of watching Sally eat, and eat, and eat had been a little daunting. Nevertheless, Tense quickly finished dressing, and they wandered around the corner to the nearby café.

The café was surprisingly quiet that morning. The early rush had been through, and things were quietening down. As they walked in, the same waitress as before spotted them. She waved them over to where she was standing as she pushed two tables together.

"You'll need plenty of room, I expect."

Sally and Tense sat. Tense glanced around the café. There were no familiar faces. Sally studied the menu with rapt attention.

She can read and write then. Tense mused gloomily *and speak any and all known and unknown languages.* He was becoming more confused and uncertain with each passing day, not less. *Where would it all lead*, he wondered?

He needn't have wondered. At any rate, it profited him naught to have done so, for at that very moment, who should waltz in, but the two young Italian men who had witnessed their wedding?

Oh shit. He thought, immediately picking up a menu and hiding behind it.

"Buongiorno a tutti! We meet again."

Sally looked up and smiled.

"Hi, come on over and join us."

Tense squirmed in his seat, praying for a miracle.

"How's married life?" Luciano spoke first.

"You are still together, I see. That's a very good sign." Paulo added.

"Yes. Married life has been very exciting so far." Sally recounted their various adventures, including the sailing trip and the lunch at Harry's Café de Wheels.

"The last of the big spenders." Luciano gave Tense a wink. Tense determinedly resisted the urge to stab the man's hand with a fork.

"How have you boys been?" Sally enquired, at the same time waving to the waitress to come over.

"Well, since we saw you last, we took a little vacation in Tasmania." Luciano smiled warmly.

"Yes, it was on special. Return flights to Hobart and two nights' accommodation." Paulo explained.

"Ooh, sounds lovely. Why don't you ever take me anywhere nice?" Sally smiled. Tense scowled, desperate to change the subject and get rid of the two unwanted wedding guests.

"Sally has found a job. She can start on Monday."

There followed an explanation of the nature of the job and several incomprehensible sentences in Italian before Sally turned to the waiting waitress.

"Four Big Breakfasts, please, and strong latte all round." Turning to the Italian lovebirds, she continued, "My treat."

Later Tense would recall the remainder of the meal as an agonising, febrile wait to be publicly unmasked and humiliated. Sally would most certainly have realised that if Luciano had been in Hobart, Tense could not conceivably have bumped into him outside their local convenience store. But the inevitable defrocking never eventuated. Sally sailed blithely on as though irrefutable evidence of his deceit and betrayal had not been presented.

It was over an hour later that the four stood up from a sumptuous repast (Sally having ordered a variety of additional snacks) and waddled uncomfortably from the café.

Back at the steps to the apartment block, Sally finally broached the matter of Tense's meeting with Luciano.

"I know it must have come as a shock to you," she began, "and I think you handled it very well."

"Oh?" Tense was completely lost.

"Yes. You must have realised that if Luciano was in Hobart, then the person you met the other night must have been someone else."

"Yes?" Tense still had not the slightest idea where all this was going.

"You must have realised that it was Lucifer in disguise."

"Yes. I suppose it must have been."

"I did warn you, my love. You must be very careful. He can appear in any guise, and he can spin a lie a thousand times more plausible than the truth."

"Yes. I see."

"Logic and reason can be false guides. You must rely on your inner truth, my darling. You must rely on your faith."

Tense knew well that here, once more, was a perfect opportunity to make a clean breast of it. Yet again, shame and fear held him back, and he remained silent.

Surfacing from his immersion in shame, guilt and self-doubt, Tense realised that they had made it back to the apartment. He turned the key in the lock. For once, the latch behaved itself, and the door opened smoothly. Sally stepped across the threshold. Tense closed the door behind them. Shutting out the world.

***

Tense jumped into the shower the moment they got home. He felt dirty. Stained. He desperately needed to feel clean again, if that were possible. Tense turned up the hot tap. It was too hot. The small bathroom filled with steam, even on such a warm day. Tense stood under the excoriating deluge wishing that things had turned out differently. Wishing that he had had the courage, or the wisdom, to tell Sally immediately about his meeting with Peter or Lucifer, or whoever. But he had not, and he had no idea now how to get out of his predicament. Simply telling her the truth right then and there didn't seem to occur to him. It was pride, of course, that stood in the way and shame, and somewhere, coming in a distant third, there was guilt.

Into the middle of this tidal wave of self-hatred, a familiar smile materialised. The bathroom door opened a little, and Sally's face appeared distorted and seemingly disembodied through the steamed-up glass of the shower partition. As she entered further into the room, Tense could see that Sally was already naked. Her smile, if perhaps a little bashful, was warm and engaging. Tense couldn't help but smile back, even in the midst of an acutely agonising attack of angst. There was just something about her. Tense wondered briefly if this was some innate characteristic of Sally herself. Would she, he wondered, be found as beguiling by her fellow angels? Sally stepped into the shower next to Tense.

"Budge up." Sally filled the cupped palm of her left hand with liquid soap. Slowly, thoughtfully, as though performing some profound and ancient ceremony, Sally began to bathe Tense. She anointed his head, smoothing the suds away from his forehead and eyes. Gently, almost reverently, she caressed his body. Washing away the cares of the day. Washing away sin.

Tense willed himself not to cry. Cupped, as he felt himself to be, in the palm of her hand, in her unconditional, loving embrace, Tense felt himself being stripped away. All the many small moments of his life, all the little memories and assumptions, beliefs, and triumphs, smoothed away to nothing under Sally's soft touch. He was baptised anew, born again in Sally's absolute love. Yet still, the fear and shame won out. Still, the terror that Sally might reject him, were she ever to learn of his betrayal, stapled closed his lips, shut his mouth, and kept him silent.

Sally, apparently oblivious to the seething turmoil roiling beneath the surface of his smooth, supple skin, carried on regardless. She was, after all, a woman, and he was her man. Sally, who needed to feel loved before she could make love, and Tense, who needed to make love in order to feel loved. A marriage made not so much in heaven as fashioned, accidentally, somewhere betwixt heaven and earth - a very frail and human union.

It was still just about morning as they stepped from the shower, satiated for the time being. Physically replete. Bodily desire quenched. Tense still found himself pondering the finer points of human-angel intercourse. For instance, can an angel, by definition, a spiritual being, experience spiritual yearning? *Can an angel feel a spiritual lack?* And that thought brought up once again the question of Sally's true identity. And out tumbled all the doubt and shame and uncertainty that had so sweetly been assuaged only a few moments ago. Things were coming to a head. Even Tense could see that. He would have to know for certain, one way or the other.

They dressed silently, each seeming lost in their own preoccupations and thoughts. Sally, thinking of lunch, no doubt, and Tense, as always, attempting to assert meaning and purpose where neither meaning nor purpose would oblige. It was already a hot day. A fly buzzed irritatingly around the room. There had been more of that recently as the Sydney summer, languid and sticky, trundled slowly through January. Sally flicked her towel with a loud snap. The buzzing stopped. Outside, distant but audible, the banshee wail of an ambulance attenuated to silence. Tense looked up, sensing something. Sally was staring at him, or perhaps into him, or even through him. He was being evaluated. He knew it on some instinctual level. He was, he felt, being flayed. Metaphorically, of course, but inexorably. There was a clarity and purpose to Sally's gaze that knew no doubt. That would brook no resistance. Not that he would have resisted. Not that he could have. Was this Sally the woman, he wondered, or Sally, the angel? Was his deception about to be exposed? Had it been already? Held, as he was, under her scrutiny, an object as much of contemplation as of love, Tense doubted that it mattered either way. What would be, would be. His fate, if there was such a thing, was already sealed. The die had been cast. His future would play out beneath the basilisk stare of an eternal being. His lover, his woman, his wife. For a moment, Tense found himself set back from the fray, observing the inner movie of his life. Was he real in Sally's eyes? Either Sally as a psychotic woman or as embodied angel? Was he, himself, present? Was he standing there before her in a shared reality, or was he the object of her fantasy, constructed, imagined? In all likelihood, he would never know. Tense realised that he had always thought of Sally as somehow frail, needing his guidance and protection. Whether this point of view had been generated by Sally herself or was a product of his own lost maleness, he couldn't really say. Was it that he wanted someone to love and protect? That he needed it to complete himself, or at the very least to feel complete? Was this, in fact, his own fantasy? Nothing to do with Sally.

There was, ultimately, something comical about the conundrum. Tense smiled and then laughed. Theirs was, in all probability, a shared fantasy. They were both mad, in a way. This was normal. This was the divine comedy. This was life.

The very absurdity of his situation somehow filled Tense with a renewed sense of purpose. He would track down Lucifer, Peter or whoever it was, and he would have it out with him once and for all. He would demand evidence. Hard proof. Childhood and family photos. Tense, having made up his mind, marched resolutely back into the sitting room. Sally had commandeered the dining table, spreading documents and forms hither and thither.

"What are you doing?" Tense was mildly surprised. He hadn't associated Sally-the-angel with paperwork, but Sally-the-psychotic didn't seem to fit any better.

"Paperwork."

"Yes. I can see that, but what paperwork?"

"My paperwork." Sally smiled up at Tense.

"Yes. But what is it for?"

Sally relented, "It's for the hospital translator job. It's part of my onboarding, apparently."

"How long is it going to take?" Tense stared at the mound of papers overflowing onto the floor.

"A little short of forever, I should think."

"OK. I'm popping round to the corner shop to collect some provisions."

"Viands and victuals?"

"You might want to update your vocabulary when you get a moment." Tense bent down and gave Sally a kiss. He was whistling as he left the apartment. Somewhere at the back of Sally's mind, the fact was noted and stored away. He was up to no good.

Tense headed for the shop that never closed. Lucifer would be there, of that he somehow felt certain. In any case, he could not live with the uncertainty for another moment. The doubt was tearing him apart.

He reached the dark cornucopia of all things essential to civilised life and began to browse. Back at the apartment, his fridge was pretty full, as was the larder. Nevertheless, picking up a shopping basket Tense began to assemble an array of foods and spices. These were mainly things he didn't like much (anchovies, dried porcini mushrooms etc.) or spices he knew nothing about (asafoetida, cassia bark, and of course, fenugreek). Perhaps it was time to broaden his horizons. A chap's cuisine should complement the tenor of his lifestyle. That, surely, was a given, and Tense's current lifestyle could most certainly do with a fillip.

The process continued with slow deliberation until the growing weight of the basket drew Tense's attention back to the moment. Somewhat surprised not to have encountered the clean-shaven young man, Tense joined the short queue at the checkout and prepared to pay. As he did so, the shadow of a young man passed the window. Tense caught only a glimpse, but it was him. He was certain. The old gentleman in front of him in the queue fumbled with his wallet and rootled through his very many pockets for the precise change, driving Tense to a silent internal paroxysm of impotent rage. Praise be, mere moments before Tense would have leaned over and paid for the man's shopping himself, the dithering bastard paid and wandered off. Tense emptied his shopping basket onto the counter and pulled an old plastic shopping bag from his pocket.

"I'm in a hurry."

The man at the checkout began to pass items beneath the ageing laser, occasionally having to key numbers directly into the even more archaic cash register. Finally, the total was rung up, and Tense tendered the exact amount.

"I think that's right." Tense hopped impatiently from foot to foot, waiting for permission to leave.

With a plastic bag filled near to bursting, Tense barged out of the shop into an oncoming barrage of heavily pregnant woman, pushchair-bearing infant, and skittish young girl with balloon. Managing to circumambulate these impediments. Tense raced up the road in the direction he had seen the young man walking.

Then he saw him, on the other side of the intersection, pausing to light a cigarette.

No one smokes any more. Tense thought as he charged out into the road, looking neither left nor right as he did so. A car screeched to a halt. Horn blaring. Missing him by mere centimetres. Tense dropped his shopping bag. Something smashed inside. Glaring at the hapless driver who had managed to stop just in time, Tense grabbed the bag and raced across the road towards the clean-shaven young man who was smiling broadly, leaning on a low fence, casually blowing smoke rings into the otherwise relatively pristine air.

"You should stop and look right and left before you cross a busy road. Didn't your mother ever teach you that?"

Tense, whose fight-flight reflex had not merely been triggered but had disappeared off the Richter scale in the direction of Armageddon, stopped dead in front of the nonchalant young man. Sudden calm descended upon him and, with it, a cold rage that he had never before experienced.

"I want evidence. Childhood and family photos, and I want documentation."

The clean-shaven young man leaned back, unconcerned, and continued to smoke.

"Anything else?"

"I want a full and complete explanation of what's going on. I don't believe a word you say."

"Yes, you do. That's why you are so angry. You perceive that something you love is in danger."

Tense set down his shopping bag, meaning to punch the smug bastard full in the face. Something leaking from the bag pooled a little around the toe of his shoe. The young man dropped the stub of his cigarette onto the pavement and ground it casually with his heel. He reached into his jacket pocket, retrieving a sleek-looking phone.

"Not a problem. Let me take you through it from the beginning."

The young man began to show photographs of Sally, chronologically, as a baby, a young girl and finally as a young woman. All the while, he spoke quietly, matter-of-factly, as though recounting a well-known story.

"Sally's parents died in a car crash when she was seven years old. After that, she went to live with her widowed grandmother on the coast. The grandmother was deeply religious and ruled Sally with an iron rod. Sally was an exceptional student at school with a gift for languages. She went on to study languages at university, where she excelled. Sally finished her degree with a distinction and would have gone on to a sparkling career had she not fallen pregnant to a fellow student. They had a child. A little girl called Amy. Tragically Amy too was killed in a car crash while still only a toddler, and Sally's husband, unable to cope with the tragedy, left her. Sally had a complete mental breakdown at that point, accompanied by psychotic episodes during which she believes herself to be a grieving angel on a mission from God."

The young man paused. Tense looked up from the phone. A last image of Sally filled the screen, younger, in a gown and mortar-board hat, receiving her degree certificate. There, caught for all time, was that incandescent, unbearable smile.

Tense looked up at the young man.

"What do you want me to do?"

"I need you to go along with her for the moment. Don't give any sign that you know the truth. It's essential that she doesn't suspect you."

"OK"

"And in the meantime, I am arranging the necessary court papers. We need to take her into protective care. Anti-psychotic treatments will bring her back to earth fairly quickly, but we need to put in place the therapy to follow that."

"I see."

"Thank you, Tense, isn't it? I appreciate your help."

Tense could not speak. His world was shattered. Silently he picked up his leaking shopping back and began to shuffle back towards the harbour. He waited at the kerb for the lights to change. Glancing back for a moment, he saw the young man light another cigarette. The lights changed, and the insistent beeping of the crossing sign started up. Just as Tense turned to cross the busy road, he caught, or thought he caught, the merest hint of a sly, self-satisfied smile, turn the corners of the young man's otherwise perfect mouth.

CHAPTER 14 – TENSE RETURNS

A slow trickle of clear fluid dripped from his plastic shopping bag as Tense walked, occasionally splashing onto the toe of his shoe. It was annoying but not annoying enough to do anything about, given the sheer volume of information he was trying to process. Tense reviewed what he now believed he knew.

Sally had experienced terrible trauma and suffering during her life. She had been married, she had been a mother, she was by now presumably either still separated or else divorced, and she had a knack for languages. There had been no mention of siblings. He assumed that the grandmother was by now also out of the picture, whether by reason of estrangement or death. This was all, if not entirely good news, then not entirely bad either. Sally could be cured, the clean-shaven young man had said so, and she would be given therapy. He was, he supposed, still in with a chance.

But what, he wondered, if she were cured? What if her current bout of psychosis were to end, and she was to come to her senses? How would she feel about him then? And why, whenever deep emotion came into it, did he inevitably find himself tied up in knots? What was it about emotion that always and inevitably defied reason? It was a bloody nuisance. That's what it was.

Tense stomped on. There seemed to be no straight line between where he now found himself and happiness. The insoluble transcendental equations of human relationships he saw cycling and circling, predatory and complacent, as he hacked his way through the jumbled jungle of reason and feelings that threatened to swamp him.

And what about the sly sneering smile he had glimpsed, even if only for an instant, on the face of the clean-shaven young man? What was that about? Was it a trick of the light or the angle? Nagging doubt remained.

Come to that. Tense was on a roll. Why had the Deity created be-ings capable of deceit? What was it about lying that the Creator was so damned keen on? After all, having created angels capable not only of lying and deceit but of open warfare against himself, why do it a second time and create human beings with the same sodding failings? It seemed almost wilful if wilful were a term that could reasonably be applied to the Almighty. And wouldn't the Almighty, being almighty, have known all about it in the first place?

As far as Tense could see, twice creating sentient species having the capacity to be imperfect suggested one of three things:

1) either the Creator values imperfection, even if only contrapun-tally, or

2) it is impossible to create a perfect sentient being in itself, sug-gesting limits on the unlimited, or

3) imperfection, somehow, was perfection. Could God be into Zen – who knew?

Tense was nearing home. He was going to have to come to a deci-sion. Probably. Unless he could somehow put it off. Perhaps he needed more information. It was probably best not to come to any final, irrev-ocable decision too soon. It would be prudent to wait. Just a little longer. Things would become clear. Maybe. The last image that had lingered so poignantly on the phone's screen came back to him. That smile, at least, was true. Turmoil and doubt were not to let him off so easily, however. New doubts assailed him.

How many other men have been here before me? How many have stood as I stood? He wondered. Listening to that same explanation? Viewing those same photographs? And each in their own way, dying inside? 'Episodes', the clean-shaven young man had said, plural. Tense was probably not the first. Would he be the last?

But what if Sally really was Amitiel, Angel of Truth? Was this all a test? And if so, who was testing him? Lucifer? Sally? Or the Creator himself?

Tense did not have sufficient evidence to come to a rational decision as to Sally's true identity. Only Sally's demonstrable transformation back into a fully-fledged angel or the direct intervention of the Creator could really fulfil the requirements of logic and reason. Being a rational, logical sort of bloke, this was a bit of a conundrum. It was not that Tense never listened to that tiny inner voice that speaks without words. It was just that he was seriously out of practice. He was an engineer. Logic and reason had treated him well in the past. But in the here and now, he was presented with a problem of the heart and soul – a problem that reason and logic could not easily address. A random phrase from some otherwise long-forgotten philosophy textbook came to mind. 'The heart has reasons reason knows not of.' Or something like that. His intuition, long ignored, suppressed, and disdained, writhed beneath the surface of his logical mind, struggling to come to his aid. But to no avail. 'We know the truth not only by reason but by the heart.' Pascal perhaps? Maybe.

Tense could see the beach and the blue harbour beyond it. A brisk wind whipped up a few whitecaps here and there. It was hot, sultry. Another summer squall portended. Billowing white clouds spread once more, flat, like anvils against the vault of heaven, filling the sky. He'd better get a move on.

If logic and reason had failed, and faith was hard to come by, then perhaps trust could act as a temporary surrogate. Whom did Tense trust more, Sally or the clean-shaven young man? If he was unable to decide who, or what precisely, Sally was, then perhaps he could apply the same line of enquiry to Doctor Peter McAuliffe or to the Bringer of Light, the Morning Star himself, Lucifer. Which one of them would he trust with his life? Sally, his lover and companion, to whom, come what may, he was entirely devoted, or the suave, clean-shaven, supercilious young man, so nonchalant and disdainful? Oddly enough, it was a difficult choice. While Tense at the level of conscious thought cast around desperately for some handhold or lever with which to shift the problem below the level of impertinent reason, his subconscious began to thrash and squirm.

His heart spoke to him. "No one smokes anymore," he found himself saying, "It's disgusting."

Tense had reached the concrete steps to his apartment. The first few drops of warm summer rain began to fall. Somehow, he had come to a decision. He would tell Sally what had happened. He would fall to his knees and beg her for forgiveness. It was going to be a difficult conversation. Not something to be launched into casually, without preparation. He would choose his moment, but he would tell all. Of that, he was now certain. His mind was made up.

***

The acrid stench of smoke first reached Tense as he stepped onto the landing and approached his front door. He could hear the maddening beep of a smoke alarm. A knot formed in the pit of his stomach. He could taste bile at the back of his throat. Dropping his overstuffed shopping bag once again, Tense retrieved his front door key and struggled with it for what seemed like an eternity before the door finally flew open, and a gout of thick black smoke billowed out onto the concrete landing of his apartment block.

Tense charged in. The hallway was full of smoke. The sound of a woman's voice, as well as the insistent beeping, came from the kitchen. As Tense rushed in, he could see Sally frantically waving a dishcloth to disperse the smoke. She had thrown open the kitchen window. A frying pan containing some indeterminate blackened mess sat in the sink. A slow trickle of cold water from a half-closed tap sending a sluggish drool of goop, in pendulous globules, down the plug hole.

Tense took in the scene. To his massive relief, there was no immediate danger. This, he realised, was what was meant by an acute stress response. Adrenaline pumped through him. His whole body shook. He wanted to vomit.

Sally, unaware of his return, was shouting, "Go away, go away, go away" at the smoke, waving her dishcloth ever more manically in her desperation to clear the room and stop that hideous bloody noise. Tense had left the front door open. In moments a strong breeze blowing from the bay cleared the smoke. Tense reached past Sally and fanned the smoke detector into silence.

"Hello. Hello. Everything all right?" a voice called from the front landing.

"It's ok." Tense gave Sally a hug and returned to the front door. It was Luciano.

"Something smashed in your bag" Luciano tapped the oozing mess with the toe of one exquisite, handmade shoe.

"Yes. Thank you." Tense picked up his bag. As he did so, a large dollop of liquid splashed onto his old, much worn and loved, scuffed and dirty, RM Williams boots.

"Is there anything I can do?" Luciano enquired.

"Do you live in this block?" Tense stepped back, suddenly suspicious, "What brings you to our front door?"

"Yes, we live upstairs. I was walking up the stairs, and I saw the smoke."

"Well, thank you, but we are fine." Tense took a step back into his apartment and made to close the door.

"Ok, ciao." As Luciano turned to leave, Sally bustled along the corridor, calling out to him as she did so.

"Oh, hi Luciano. The frying pan caught fire. Nothing serious." and then, not sure of human etiquette, "Would you like to come in for a coffee? I was just making some."

Perhaps catching sight of the thunderous look upon Tense's face, Luciano declined.

"No. Thank you, I had better be getting home."

With the offer made, Sally would brook no refusal. Stepping out onto the landing, she grabbed his arm.

Tense found himself staring into the uncomprehending eyes of his upstairs neighbour. It was all getting too much. He could no longer confidently distinguish fact from fiction.

"I'm so sorry, my love," Sally came around to his side, embracing him, stroking his hair, "I wasn't laughing at you. It just suddenly struck me as funny."

"What? What was funny?" Deflation was fast and pitiless. The vortex of emotions within him collapsed like a quantum wave function. The sudden superposition of so many emotional states cancelling each other out until all that was left was numbness and the void.

"Well, the very idea that I would invite the Devil to tea, of course."

***

Having established that Sally had not invited the Devil to tea and that their hapless Italian guest was indeed Luciano from upstairs, Tense plonked himself down on one of the rickety rattan chairs and sipped his coffee, disconsolate. Sally silently picked up the pieces of her coffee cup and disappeared into the apartment.

"Why do you think I am the Devil?" Luciano seemed both a little amused and the same time, somewhat unnerved, "Really? You think you have the Devil sitting in your apartment?"

"It's a long story", Tense ventured, "and I'm not in the mood."

The two men sipped their coffee in silence. Tense, for his part unwillingly, accepting the implicit affirmation of life to be found in the dregs of every coffee cup. He really should be a coffee drinker, he realised, not a tea drinker. Tea, the drink of Stoics everywhere and his preferred poison, suggested that life was just another thing to be gotten through, whereas coffee, the drink of existentialists, positioned life as a point of view to be transcended, chicly, in loose-fitting unisex black clothing, in some Left Bank café. Tense, being Tense, was, of course, caught in a sticky dilemma. While the mood engendered by stylishly sipping a tiny cup of strong coffee certainly nurtured his sophisticated, nonchalant self-image, the image itself lacked authenticity. In the vexed matter of tea versus coffee, he realised he was, inevitably, with the Stoics. Luciano, oblivious to Tense's inner turmoil, made another stab at small talk.

"How's the coffee?"

"Beg pardon?" Tense's thoughts were still very much entwined in the conundrum of his life.

"The coffee," Luciano persisted, "it is good?"

"Oh. Yes. Very good. I'm more of a tea person, though. I just realised…" Tense trailed off to silence, leaving Luciano wondering if he had been subtly snubbed.

In a few minutes, Sally reappeared with a fresh, steaming mug of coffee. She stood in the doorway for a moment, surveying the scene.

"You boys are playing nicely, I see." Sally misread as cosy comradery the stony silence that had descended between them.

Luciano stood, "I must go now. Paulo will be wondering what happened to me." Sally saw him to the door. By the time she returned to the balcony, Tense had made up his mind again. For now. Unless it turned out to be a bad idea.

"We need to prepare for the baby," paternal instincts to the fore, "and I have to start back at work soon." His protective urges were, for the time being, providing a modicum of meaning. Parenting offered purpose for free, at least for a little while. Not bad.

"It's still months away." Sally slipped onto his knee and snuggled, nibbling his ear. Tense endeavoured to shake her off. To no avail.

"I'd feel better if we were prepared" Tense attempted to lurch to his feet, but with Sally still clinging limpet-like around his neck, he ended up staggering into the apartment with Sally in his arms.

Parenting, intimate relationships of any sort, indeed the very things that most easily impart meaning to life, were also the very things he had thought least about until then. Now, spurred on perhaps by the sustaining power of Luciano's coffee, Tense was a man on a mission.

Although, it probably goes without saying that the specifics of the mission were still very much a work in progress. But a mission is a mission. And that, at least, was good.

The doorbell rang. Tense placed Sally down on the sofa in the sitting room and walked calmly to the front door. It would be Luciano, having forgotten something or set upon further useless, inconsequential chit-chat. But it wasn't Luciano. It was the clean-shaven young man.

This was too much. A blood-red curtain of rage descended. Instantly, without a moment's hesitation, Tense pounced. He had the clean-shaven young man by the throat. Tense pushed him back across the narrow walkway. By the time the red mist lifted enough for Tense to think, he had the clean-shaven young man half over the parapet wall. Tense was ready to drop him three floors to his inevitable doom. But he didn't. Some semblance of control returned.

"Go away, you bastard. You're not wanted here." Tense pulled the clean-shaven young man off the parapet wall and threw him down on the walkway towards the stairs. The clean-shaven young man climbed to his feet and brushed himself down.

"I must speak with Hanna."

"There's no one of that name here. If you don't leave now, I will throw you down the stairs."

The men faced off. Tense finally, perhaps for the first time in his adult life, fully emotionally engaged. Fully present. And fully ready to smash the smug bastard's face in.

"She's taken you in, hasn't she? You actually believe you are sharing your apartment with the living embodiment of an Angel of God."

"I don't care what she is. I love her, and I don't trust you as far as I can spit. Now fuck off."

"The psychosis will end, you know. At some point. This fantasy will end, one way or another."

Tense stepped towards his adversary, determined to be rid of the man, one way or another.

"Well, perhaps another time then." The clean-shaven young man turned and, for want of a better word, scarpered down the stairs.

Tense, shaking with reaction, unused to adrenalin in any form, yet twice exposed to it in quick succession, stalked back into the apartment and slammed the door. Sally popped her head around the corner and watched him stomping towards her down the corridor.

"He's harmless. You mustn't let him get to you."

Tense paused and took breath.

"You're right." Once again, Tense failed to disabuse her of her misapprehension. *Another lie of omission*, he thought, *Story of my life*.

***

Sally cleared the coffee cups away while Tense brooded.

If the clean-shaven man was indeed the Devil, he mused, then surely, he must know when I am at home and when I am not. The bastard could just call round when I'm out. This was an uncomfortable thought. The sort of thought that leads to all sorts of even more uncomfortable thoughts. One of those loose threads which, when pulled, risks unravelling the entire warp and weft of a person's life. Not a good thought.

So why doesn't he just come around when I'm out? Tense mulled that one over for a while. A possible explanation, one that seemed to fit the circumstances, was that the clean-shaven young man intended each time to speak to Tense, not Sally.

But how could he know who would answer the door? Tense, having no immediate solution, shelved that one for the time being.

Ok, let's say he is intent on speaking to me. Why is that? What does he want from me? This one turned out to be far simpler. *What does the Devil always want?*

Sin. He wants me to sin. So far, so good, but what exactly did that mean?

He wants me to betray Sally. He wants me to lie to her. Cold realisation lay like lead in the pit of his stomach. *He wants me to do exactly what I have been doing.* Tense began to realise the threat that Lucifer brought was the threat of losing oneself. A greater threat ultimately, even than death.

Tense looked up as Sally walked back into the room. Perhaps unsurprisingly, something in his face must have given him away. Sally stopped dead.

"What is it?" Eyes narrowing. "What has happened?"

"It was him", Tense all but wailed.

"Who?"

"At the door. It was your old friend." Tense couldn't bring himself to speak his name.

"Lucifer, do you mean? He came to the door?"

Tense nodded his head, for the moment unable to meet Sally's gaze.

"You should have called me. I can handle him." Sally sat down on the rattan chair across from Tense. She leaned close.

"I threw the bastard down the landing. I nearly threw him over the parapet."

"You must not try to protect me, my love. You will destroy yourself in the attempt. Lucifer, Satan, has honed himself into a weapon especially designed to corrupt human beings. He revels in it. He thrives on it. It is his entire being and purpose."

"He says you are having a psychotic episode," Tense was sobbing now, all self-respect gone, "he says it will end, that none of this is real."

"Satan's lies beguile, as they are intended to do. He is the master of deceit."

"I have sinned against you. I am so sorry." Tense, snivelling and broken was not, at that precise moment, an alluring sight.

"Haven't you been listening to a word I have said?" Sally was angry now, cold and unforgiving, "This is not a game. We are not characters in some virtual adventure." Tense shifted as though to speak. Sally was having none of it.

"Just shut up, Tense, for once. Just shut up and listen. You have not sinned against me. You cannot sin against me. That's not what sin is. That's not how it works. If you have sinned, you have sinned against God." The sight of Tense, pale-faced and quaking, profoundly out of his depth, touched a chord buried deep within Sally. Piercing grief welled up. Thank God. This was what she was designed for - grief, stark and unalloyed. This was what her entire being was attuned to. This was her mission. She was the Angel of Truth, not of Mercy. She was not practised in compassion. Still, she was a human woman now, and Tense was her man, her charge.

"God is love, my darling. And you are an idiot." Kneeling before him, she laid her head in his lap, wrapping her arms around his waist.

"It will be all right." In her mind, Sally saw shapes. Possible futures, visible previously only as suggestions, began to coalesce. Alternatives began to fall away. Whatever was going to happen. Whatever the crisis or turning point would be, whatever fate awaited her, she could feel it approaching. Through the mist of uncertainty. Closing in.

Sally felt Tense stroking her hair. She looked up. The crumpled mask of defeat was gone. From somewhere, Tense had found strength, or at least, and for the time being, some sense of resolve.

"There's more," Tense's voice was steady now, weary but resolute, "I knew it was Satan at the corner shop the other day. He appeared as he does, dapper and clean-shaven He didn't appear as Luciano. I lied to you." Fearing that this was the end, that Sally would now leave, Tense had decided to make a clean breast of it.

"He told me he was your psychiatrist, that your real name was Hanna and that this was not your first psychotic episode."

"Why didn't you tell me straight away?"

"He said I must not let you know that I know. He said that your only hope of a normal life was to be treated. If I loved you, I should play along."

"So, you've been playing along with me? All this time?" Sally lurched to her feet, swaying, unable to take it all in.

"Yes. Well no. Not really. I didn't believe him."

"Then why didn't you tell me? Why wait until now?"

"I was afraid."

"Afraid of what?" anger filled her once again.

"Afraid you would leave me if you found out I had lied."

For a long time, Sally stared down at Tense, crumpled into his old rattan chair like a rag doll. Forlorn, a little boy lost. If this had been the Creator's purpose, then surely it was working. Grief filled her, agonising and familiar. An old friend. And then, appearing in the clothing of a saviour, came anger. Tense had betrayed her. Not just once but many times.

Despite Tense's betrayal, or maybe because of it, Sally concluded that she had misjudged. No mere human being could hope to defeat Satan. To cast him down as had been done to him once before. In truth, no human being could stand against him and endure. All that was left to these hapless beings was to make their stand. Brave defeat. Nothing more. Sally came to her decision instantly and alone. On her own head be it.

"You have betrayed me, and I have put you in harm's way. You are in danger because of me. And I can no longer trust you. You are no match for Satan. And he will be back, in one form or another, again and again." Sally paused, governing her anger. Regaining control.

"I can see only one way to protect you, Tense, and to free myself to confront Satan, if need be, without babysitting you. I must do what must be done."

"What are you going to do?" Tense's voice was flat, defeated.

"He will use you against me. He has done so already. I must leave." Sally turned to go.

"What should I do?"

There was really only one answer. There had only ever been one answer since the beginning.

"Be brave, Tense. Endure."

CHAPTER 15 – CLICK

Tense listened from the balcony as Sally packed up her few things and prepared to leave. His one chance at happiness had come to nothing as it must. As he had always feared it would. He had found and lost his angel, metaphorically and in fact.

Sally did not return to the balcony to say goodbye. What would have been the point? Why make it worse? Tense did not rise to say farewell. He could not bear to see her go. Instead, he sat silently, listening for the faint click of the latch as she closed the apartment door behind her. It came.

"Click."

And still, Tense sat long after the last vestiges of hope had slipped away. Long after, the searing pain of loss had diminished, as pain is wont to do, to a gentle throbbing.

Introspection followed once the pain subsided, and with it came his usual vortex of self-blame. It was his own stupid fault. He knew he should never have kept anything from Sally. Lucifer knew it too. That much was obvious. A devilish lie perfectly honed to deceive. And he had fallen for it, as Lucifer had known he must. Poor human. Poor man.

An old soul classic from what now seemed like a million years ago kept playing in his head. Over and over. *The whole town's laughing at me, silly fool...* and he was. That much was obvious.

Tense, fearless as always in confronting the emptiness of his own existence, dug deep. He did not shy away from the cleansing fire of truth. He did not, as so many might have done, take refuge in justification or excuse. In extremis, Tense retreated to the only safe ground he had known. Tense beached himself upon his own private island of logic and rational thought. He put his faith in Freud.

Freud was, to Tense's mind, the most influential of the existentialist thinkers. As someone once said, "He gave us ourselves to mine. He lighted our way to the cavern and showed us the entrance to the under-world, whence the creative force explodes. Few of us will ever explore it to the source." Well, Tense would if he could. If he had the strength.

Tense's relationship with reason was, in a way, his only true, longstanding relationship. And naturally, it was complicated. Tense was ambivalent about it. In times of trouble, he relied upon it, but at the same time, he was suspicious of its arrogant clarity. "Take it or leave it," reason seemed to say.

Too often had, the products of reason provided certainty one day, only to be overturned the next. Reason, false friend, led him to under-standing, and even, in its way, to a sort of knowledge. Hypothesised, of course, pro tempore. True knowledge, it seemed to Tense, sprang from some other source if he could only find it.

It was not, and of this, he felt reasonably certain, to be found in modern thought. Not in a world where spirituality is just one among a thousand means of distraction, a deferral activity, in place of faith. A devotion in which a composite, false God, the accretion of many tiny little meanings, takes the place of MEANING, whole and indivisible.

Fuck it. What was the point of conceding God's existence without allowing his purpose, whatever that might be, to guide our lives? Idol-atry had not gone away. It had never gone away. Immoderate relativism, by "respecting" all points of view, honours none. Now, as in ancient Athens, we worship the Unknown God.

But had God ever been known, really? Tense found himself at a crossroads. His woman was gone, and with her, his reason for being. He was back to square one. Even if God was real, angels were real, and the Devil himself was real, or perhaps "given" these things, what should a man do about it? How should he respond? He would have to make his own meaning and define his own purpose, as he had always done. Even if God is the Creator, is that any reason to worship him? What of free will, then?

Tense made some preliminary plans. First, he would go find the clean-shaven young man and beat him to death with a crowbar. Then he would find Sally and persuade her to come back. He leaned back in the creaking old rattan chair and smiled. That would have to do, for starters. One mustn't overthink things.

Tense stood and made his way back into the apartment, again locking the balcony door behind him. If the sitting room was a mess, the bedroom looked like a storm had hit it. Reflexively, Tense began to tidy up. Personal items were collected and returned to their rightful places. The bed would have given Tracy Emin a run for her money. He stripped the sheets and began, in his usual meticulous way, to remake the bed. Soon enough, the room and the bed returned to order. As he picked up a pillow that had been cast into a corner in what he vaguely recalled was a moment of total abandon, he retrieved from beneath it a crumpled T-shirt. One of Sally's. Still rich with her scent.

It was too much. Tense sat back down on the bed with Sally's T-shirt pressed to his face. The wind knocked out of him. The trace of Sally filled his nostrils, clouded his mind, and eroded his purpose. All was lost. He was utterly alone, more alone in comparison than he had been before they met. It was not better to have loved and lost. Tense cried out against the injustice of it all. It would have been better never to have loved at all.

And then, raging emotion quenched for a little while at least, calm returned. Tense stood, smoothed the coverings on the bed and left the room. There was nothing else for it but to soldier on. This, at least, he was used to. This was known. Tense found some pragmatic subroutine that had been lounging around in the recesses of his mind and rebooted it. He needed a strong cup of tea. And some fruit cake. It was going to be one of those days.

***

Sally closed the door behind her. Click. And then stood for a moment, wondering what to do next. It was all very well taking action in a clear and forthright manner. It may well be commendable to make the hard decisions and act on them. But what now?

She turned to the left and headed for the little beach by the harbour where she and Tense had been married an Earthly age ago. Perhaps a brisk walk along the harbour's edge would clear her mind. She needed time to think. It would be evening soon, and she needed to find somewhere to stay. But more than anything, she needed to make a plan. Who knew being human would be this hard?

Angels didn't really make plans. Ever. She couldn't remember ever having planned anything. The angelic approach, their nearest thing to preparation, was 'observe, decide, act'. Not 'plan'. Planning was to do with uncertainty, mitigation, and contingency. Planning was to do with risk. Not topics that had typically bothered Sally in the past. Well, she was uncertain now, and she needed a plan.

But a plan about what? To do what? She had abandoned Tense for his own good. That much was clear. That, at least, was evident. There was no other way. Though the grief and loss inside her threatened to overwhelm, Sally suppressed it. She batted it aside, forcing herself to focus on the practical. Taking refuge in the mundane. There was a hotel by the bay in the adjoining suburb. She would stay there while she figured things out.

Sally walked quickly along the footpath, half dragging her small suitcase behind her. As she walked, Sally re-evaluated. Why was she here, she wondered. What was her real purpose on earth? Was Tense anything to do with it, or had he been, from the very outset, a chance diversion from God's intended purpose? And why was Lucifer here now? What did he want with her?

Sally felt the gorge rising in her throat. She bathed in her anger, swilling it around, enjoying it. That was another thing that angels had very little experience of anger, true rage. The righteous or self-righteous determination to raise all before them in defending what was right, or necessary, or at the very least, at risk. Revelling in the destruction of the offender. These were human emotions. Observed at a polite distance. Made patronising allowance for, but never entered into. Undignified – that's what it was. Unbecoming of an immortal.

Well fuck that. A plan was forming. Tense would have been proud. Sally would track Lucifer down and confront him. Although she knew it was pointless, she would enjoy dealing roughly with his physical form. Sorted.

And with the hard mental work over, Sally once again began to take notice of her surroundings. The path wove between thin strips of sand and grassy reserves. The bay glittered with a diffident beauty. The late afternoon was pleasantly warm. Occasional flurries of Rainbow Lorikeets skittered past, chattering loudly, like teenage girls on their way to the prom. Sally came to a bench. She paused and sat and surveyed the scene.

Physical reality, once you were in it, really in it, immersed in it, really was very real. With the matrix of fields that held the whole thing together conveniently invisible, the effect was almost overwhelming, even to an angel. And would have been totally irrefutable to a human being, she imagined. Sally found herself perceiving human constraints in a new light. The human condition could be looked at as a system of boundaries within which infinite variety was possible. It was poetic, in a way. A dream factory driven by counterpoint. Sweet and sour, truth and lies, good and evil. Infinite possibilities wrought against a background of a mere four dimensions. Quite an achievement, she had to admit.

It was not far now to the hotel. She really should get a move on, but something held her back.

A man appeared ahead of her, around a curve in the path. He was young, beautifully groomed, and clean-shaven. Sally could barely believe his gall. She prepared for battle. Every fibre of her being tingled in anticipation. Reaching inwards, Sally took stock of her assets. She was, for the time being, no longer an angel. She was a mortal woman having to hand only those capabilities given to mortal women. Not much by comparison. Nothing like the savage power she could have brought to bear in angel form. But it was enough. More than enough. Sadly, the physical confrontation solution went out the window. Her old friend Lucifer could not be brought down. He could not definitively be defeated by Sally, but that was not what was required. He was to be resisted. The exercise of free will was given to her ultimately, for just such a purpose.

Sally watched Lucifer approach. He had a diffident, self-deprecating smile on his face. A smile that said, 'I know you are on to me. I won't try any funny business.' But he would. Of course, he would. He was Lucifer, after all.

He held up his hands as he approached, palms forward, suggesting he meant no harm.

"Just a minute of your time Amitiel. That's all I ask."

Sally made no reply.

"I know that you, of all people, cannot be duped."

Still, Sally made no response.

Lucifer approached gingerly and sat on the bench. He really was very beautiful. He had a lovely smile. Sally could not have cared less. She was suppressing her rage. She would give him no hint of her inner turmoil. She would show no sign of weakness.

Lucifer nodded towards her suitcase, "Where are you going?"

Still, Sally toyed for a moment with the idea of punching Lucifer in the nose.

"You've left the human. Adam, wasn't it?"

"I'm on vacation." Sally kept her voice low, bored, "I just stopped to enjoy the view."

Lucifer glanced across the bay. Took in the glittering waves and the little boats bobbing gently. Smelled the metallic, pungent odour of ozone. Took note of the sounds of the birds and the wind and the far-off reverberations of the city.

"Yes, lovely effect. I've always admitted that."

"What do you want this time?"

"I am tired, Amitiel, I admit it. I've had eons to think about it. I want to find a way home. If there is one."

Sally sat bolt upright and gasped. Her innate truth sense snapping her to attention.

"You, fucking liar," she screamed, finding herself standing, fists curled, ready for a bare-knuckle fight with the Devil. Lucifer made as if to respond but was too slow. With a sickening crack, Sally brought her suitcase swinging down across the side of his head and shoulder. Knocking him to the floor. Again and again, she beat the prone form.

"You twisted, lying, fucking monster", she screamed again as the suitcase burst open, spewing her possessions across the path. An eternity of memories flooded over her. Eons of hope and disappointment. Memories reaching back, back before the fall, back to when she and Lucifer had meant something to each other. Back to when they had been, for want of a better word, lovers. They had loved once, and that was gone.

Sally alternated between stuffing her belongings back into the suitcase and kicking the inert form of Lucifer hard. Each time punctuating the effort with a heartfelt imprecation. A couple, rounding the bend in the path, took one glance at the proceedings and turned back. Eventually, Sally collected her things and stuffed them back into the suitcase. She had to sit on it to close it, taking the opportunity to jab Lucifer one last time with her heel.

She stood, staring down at the man on the path. His smart suit was crumpled and torn. His face was smeared with blood. Without another word, Sally turned and marched off in the direction of the hotel.

"That could have gone better", she heard the battered man mumble as she walked away.

***

The weirdest thing about the way humans experience reality, in Sally's view, was the stream of consciousness. And the arrow of time - that was the weirdest thing too. As an angel, she hadn't had to deal with any of that filly-fally. As an angel, one dealt with presence. Well, presence and juxtaposition technically. But presence was the key. One focussed one's presence wherever and whenever one wanted to.

Plodding along in the present with only the insensible arrow of time for guidance was, to an angel, a breathtaking waste of time. Not that time was exactly being rationed, but still.

Had she encountered Lucifer in her angelic form, she would not have been reduced to beating him about the head and shoulders with her suitcase. She would not have suffered the indignity of having her belongings strewn across the grass for everyone to see. Although, to be fair, she would not have had any possessions to strew.

Sally's rage at Lucifer had subsided to a sort of grumpy curiosity in the warm afterglow of having thrashed him so soundly and in public. What remained unanswered was just what he was really up to. Beneath the lies and the feints and the ruses. What on Earth was he on Earth for – this time? Something was wrong. Sally could feel it. There was a horrible itch between her shoulder blades, portending something nasty.

As far as Sally could recall, Lucifer's schemes always involved a plot, an unfolding of evil. It was a matter of pride for Lucifer that his victims should be deceived, taken in, and persuaded to execute their own fall. He wasn't interested in random acts of evil. He was motivated by the subversion of free will. He was happy only when he was convincing God's creation to cannibalise itself.

Take natural disasters – it was of no interest to Lucifer that thousands of people might die in an earthquake or tsunami. They would die innocent. They were not at fault. That sort of mundane, everyday evil had no finesse. It was a ponderous kind of evil. Now, climate change, that was another matter altogether. That was self-inflicted. That took cunning and guile and proper plotting.

The beauty of climate change lay precisely in the fact that it was not natural. The joy of it was that it was entirely self-inflicted, entirely correctable by people of goodwill, and required precisely the sort of give and take, compromise and common sense that humans were so profoundly bad at. Humanity was destroying God's creation under his very nose. In the old days, he would have sent a flood or something. It was a bloody triumph, that's what it was – if you were Lucifer.

Sally was uneasy. He would be plotting something, obviously. And she was somehow at the centre of it. She was a central actor in his little play. This was, for Lucifer, a game of chess with God. The outcome might already be known. No doubt was already known to God, but to Lucifer, it was another opportunity to tweak the Creator's nose. His M.O., in these cases, was to use God's tools against him or try to. And she, Sally, once his closest ally and friend, was now his leading lady.

A sense of foreboding stole over Sally. Not for nothing was she the Angel of Truth, and that truth started with self-knowledge. She was no match for Lucifer when it came to schemes – she knew that perfectly well. The very act of outwitting Lucifer would turn out to be a trap. She would be tricked into betraying her Creator. That was his way. That was his forte. The answer, if answer there was, would lie in humility. Pride was Lucifer's preferred poison. He could find pride anywhere, in anything. Lucifer, it was said, could engender pride in a clod of earth. Sally, Amitiel, understood her risk. It was to believe, ever, at any point, that she had bested Lucifer. Even her recent encounter on the footpath could have been a set-up. Probably was just that, now she came to think about it. She had enjoyed it, it was true. She had felt a certain smugness, a degree of satisfaction too. And yes, once she really came to examine her own motivation, she had felt a degree of superiority. Conceit, arrogance, vanity, pride. Fucking hell. The bastard had set her up.

She had an answer to that. She would track him down and apologise. She would deny herself the victory, and in so doing, she would defeat him.

Sally stopped walking and surveyed the city and the bay as evening came on. She felt relief that she had fathomed Lucifer's cunning little plan. Game on.

There was beauty and peace aplenty. There was both a raw and a subtle splendour to the unfolding of the world. The bay, so full of the raucous interactions of life at every scale, and the city, settling down for a snooze after a long hard day of hedonism and play. The pattern emerging had its own deep logic. Ugliness in beauty, beauty in ugliness. A rationale that somehow included both Sally and Lucifer, and somewhere in the mix, there was a role too for Tense.

Sally felt a deep stab of pain. Human pain. The pain of a mortal woman experiencing once again the realisation that life is short and that her loved ones are always at risk. Tense would be alone now in his little apartment. He would have washed up, made the bed, and vacuumed the floors. He would be sitting on the balcony, in his creaky old rattan chair, staring out over the bay and wondering what he did wrong. Poor child. He would make it about himself, as children do. As men do – not to make victims of themselves but to make their actions relevant. To gain purchase upon the flow of events, he must insert himself into them. There must be something he could do to influence the outcome of – whatever it was that was going on. Sally knew Tense would not sit around waiting for fate to slap him in the face. If there was one thing she now realised that Tense would insist on, it would be that he took ownership of his own story.

Abruptly, Sally recognised that she had made a terrible mistake. She should never have left him. She could not protect him by abandoning him. She could not protect him anyway, in the end. He would have to make his own stand. He would meet his fate alone in the end, as all humans do.

Her mind swiftly made up. Sally turned and began to make her way back along the path to the apartment by the bay. She had to get to Tense before Lucifer did.

CHAPTER 16 – LOOKING FOR SALLY

There was a loud, belligerent banging at the door. Tense knew it wasn't Sally. He knew who it was, but he was tired, beyond scrapping. He'd just had the stuffing knocked out of him. He needed a bit more time to recoup. Tense ignored the banging, hoping it would go away. Knowing it wouldn't.

The banging got louder, almost frenzied. There was a very angry young man on the other side of that door.

"Open up", he heard a man's voice, thick with rage, "Open the damn door. I know you're in there."

Still, Tense sat, unable to summon the strength to move. The banging continued.

"I'm not going away until I've spoken with you." Bang. Bang. Bang. Tense was getting a headache.

In the end, the cacophony grew too great. Old habits of mind kicked in. The neighbours would be hacked off. He had to shut Lucifer up. Tense stood and lurched unevenly down the hall. The banging had stopped for a moment. He opened the door and took half a step forward onto the landing.

"Shut the fuck up, will you? I have neighbours."

"I've just had the crap kicked out of me by your bloody girlfriend." Lucifer stood on the landing, his face smudged and smeared with blood. His exquisitely cut suit crumpled and torn in places.

"I have had enough. More than enough." Tense attempted to interrupt, but the clean-shaven young man was having none of it.

"I don't get paid enough for this."

Tense was confused, "Paid enough for what?"

"I work for the Health Service, not the Mayo Clinic."

Tense was none the wiser. Was that supposed to mean something?

"What do you want?" he ventured.

"I want you to come with me now and help me find your crazy bloody girlfriend before she attacks someone else."

Tense struggled to grasp the angry young man's meaning.

"You want me to come with you?"

"Yes"

"You want to find Sally?"

"Yes, Sally, Hanna, Amitiel Goddess of Truth, whatever you want to call her. She's crossed a line. She's prepared to use violence to protect her psychosis."

Tense just stared, uncomprehending, unable to speak.

"Look. I don't care if you understand what's going on or not, but I need you to come with me and help me find her."

Still, Tense stood. Unmoving.

"Oh, for Goodness' sake." Lucifer stepped forward and grabbed Tense by the arm, dragging him out of the apartment. Tense closed the door behind himself. If purposeful action was presently beyond him, at least reflex was still there.

"Angel of Truth. Not Goddess of Truth."

"Whatever."

The pair stomped off down the landing, down three flights of stairs and onto the green space outside the apartment block.

"She will be needing somewhere to stay." Tense tried to shake the fog out of his brain, "There's a little place by the bay that she liked – it's not far." Tense made to set off in the direction Sally had taken.

"No", Lucifer's tone was harsh, uncompromising, "We go this way."

Lucifer headed off in the opposite direction. Tense, unused to asserting himself, followed. Tense watched Lucifer's receding back. There was a determined set to his shoulders. His suit jacket was covered in dust and grime. At least they had something in common, Tense mused. They had both taken a beating from the same woman.

"What are you going to do when you find her?" Tense called out. Lucifer was several metres ahead. At first, Tense assumed he hadn't heard. But then Lucifer stopped and turned, a somewhat rueful expression on his face.

"Reason with her?"

Both men laughed. A bond was forming.

"Seriously," Lucifer continued, "We need to bring her back to physical reality. Right now, she is living in her own personal metaphysical fantasy. She has lost track of what is real and true. That is almost the definition of madness."

"How do you propose to do that?"

Lucifer paused before answering.

"I don't know. I'm not sure what would be best." For a moment, Tense thought he caught a glimpse of vulnerability. For an instant, Lucifer's indecision and self-doubt grinned through his urbane façade.

"Not direct confrontation. That's not going to work now."

"What then?"

"We need to help her to feel safe. And then we need to show her the path back."

"I see. Well, I get the idea, but I have no idea how you are going to do it."

"We are going to do it, Tense, together. The two of us. I know you want what's best for Sally. We both do."

Tense nodded. He was confused. Uncertain what was true and what was false. He had lost his compass, but here was a path he could at least understand. He could perhaps rely on that. He would rely upon his own understanding and not upon some unproven and untestable blind faith.

"OK. What now?"

"Now we find her. Then we figure out what to do."

Lucifer led Tense into the heart of the city. Evening had fallen. Crowds thronged this way and that, locals and tourists, businesspeople, and beggars. Humanity closed in around them, hurrying, scurrying, busy, busy, busy. Here, in the heart of Sydney, with arrogance, pride, and vanity all around, Lucifer felt fully at home. Here the tiny voice inside each of us was drowned out by the bedlam of modern life.

"The bible is just a series of inconsistent and contradictory myths that go all the way back to the bronze age and before." Lucifer launched a frontal assault on any remaining doubts Tense may have been harbouring about Sally's angelic nature, "It was written by at least forty people over a two-thousand-year period."

"You know what Sally wants?" Lucifer continued, not pausing for a response, "She wants what we all want. Happiness."

Tense made to interrupt but was ignored.

"Of course, true happiness is unattainable for an adult. And there's the rub. That's what keeps driving her deeper and deeper into her psychosis."

"Why do you say that?" Tense was shocked at the bluntness of Lucifer's argument, "Why do you say adults cannot find happiness?"

"I'm surprised you would have to ask. Are you happy? Are any of us truly happy past the age of, say, ten?" Lucifer paused in his headlong rush through the heaving mass of humanity. The multitudes swept past like flood waters. The horde swarmed chaotically in all directions. Lucifer continued.

"We cannot find happiness in the absence of meaning. And without purpose, there is no meaning. All lives are insignificant, pointless if there is no purpose to the universe."

Tense just stood and stared, uncertain how to respond.

"What meaning, what purpose can your life have, or hers, in a meaningless, purposeless universe?"

"Oh."

"Oh indeed. I bet that's what Sally likes about you, Tense. This insistence on finding and defining meaning on the very edge of the abyss."

Tense just listened. Lucifer was on a roll.

"You seem to instinctively know what most people struggle to understand. While it is important to be part of a community, the only things you can truly rely on are your own individual capabilities. The only needs you are obliged to fulfil are your own."

Tense was struck dumb by the bleakness of Lucifer's vision.

"We have only recently met, Tense, but it seems to me that you stare the void full in the face. And you don't blink. That shows amazing inner strength, Tense. That's what I most admire about you."

Tense felt the long-disregarded seedling of self-worth deep inside him begin to bud. There was no sense of the yawning pit opening up ahead of him. Waiting. There was, instead, the merest flicker of pride. Maybe he had been mistaken all these years. Maybe he could amount to something.

"Come", Lucifer held out his arm, beckoning Tense to walk with him. The two men continued their journey side by side in search of Sally or Hanna, angel or woman. It no longer mattered which.

CHAPTER 17 – LOOKING FOR TENSE

Sally rushed back to Tense's apartment, dragging her suitcase behind her. By the time she arrived, she was hot and sweaty. There was a spreading coldness in the pit of her stomach. It was too late. She somehow knew that even before she dragged her suitcase up the three flights of stairs to his landing. Even before she tried the key in the lock, opened the door without inanimate opposition, and stepped into the empty apartment, Sally knew she had left it too late. She had been revelling in her supposed victory. As Lucifer had known, she would. She had been basking in her imagined glory while Lucifer was leading her man astray. Cunning, evil creature. He had used his vulnerability against her as he had used her pride. Of course, she had seen through his pathetic claim that he wanted to go home. She was meant to. That was the point. She was the Angel of Truth, proof against any lie when she applied herself. But not, it seemed, against complicity in her own misdirection. She had no defence against her own misinterpretation. She could, it seemed, lie to herself. Can't we all?

Sally dumped her suitcase in the hallway and, turning on her heel, headed back out into the gathering gloom. It would be fully dark soon. Lucifer would have led Tense into the heart of the city. Plenty of people. Plenty of noise and distraction. She was in a cold sweat as she slammed the apartment door and ran down the stairs. Without missing a beat, Sally turned at the foot of the stairs and headed for the bright lights of the city centre. Pulsing with life at this time of year. A perfect place for Lucifer to hide Tense while he reprogrammed his mind. She really was going to kill him this time, she told herself, knowing as she did so that she wouldn't. She couldn't. It wasn't her job.

The short journey into the city passed in a blur. One moment she was standing outside Tense's apartment, and the next, it seemed, she was standing at Circular Quay. Sniffing the air. Hoping to pick up the trail. The place was heaving. They could be anywhere. Without her powers, she was somewhat at a loss as to how to go about her search. Sally thought back, reviewing Lucifer's modus operandi over the centuries. He would be attempting to shift Tense's perceptions, little by little, misdirection by misdirection, until Tense had lost all faith in Sally. Tense would not understand what was happening. Lucifer would appeal to logic and reason. Common-sense would-be Tense's downfall unless Sally acted quickly. Unless she lifted her game. Lucifer had the home-ground advantage. He had been hanging around humans for millions of years. Sally, on the other hand, had been popping in on them every now and then at some pivotal moment or other. Disseminating the word of God and then buggering off again.

"Shit", this really was going to be tricky. A band started up at the Sydney Opera House Bar, across the Quay from where she was standing. The sounds of drunken revelry carried easily across the water. Sally started off at a run. This body seemed reasonably fit. It had better be.

Moments later, Sally was wrestling her way through the throng. Casting around, eyes swivelling as though on stalks. They'd be around here somewhere. This was Lucifer's stomping ground. Wherever feckless, drunken people were out seeking the main chance, wherever inhibitions were lowest and suggestibility highest.

Some guy tried to strike up a conversation. Nice smile. Breath smelling of alcohol. Sally pushed past him. The man staggered backwards a step, spilling a woman's drink. Voices were raised. Sally moved on.

Having scouted out the Opera House Bar, Sally headed back towards the pubs in The Rocks. She was not going to give up. If it took all night, she would find him. It was all her fault. She came to a gelato stand. A small queue had formed. They had mango sorbet. It was a hot night. Sally joined the queue. Head craning. Hoping to catch a glimpse of the fugitive pair.

"Yes, please?"

Sally's attention snapped back to the gelato guy.

"Mango sorbet. Two scoops, please."

The gelato guy handed Sally two scoops of mango sorbet in a waffle cone. She paid and stepped back, out of the hustle and bustle, to take stock. She needed a better plan. Searching for two guys on a night out in Sydney in January was worse than looking for a needle in a haystack. At the very least, the needle could be relied upon to stay put. The sorbet was good, though, tangy and cold.

The pubs in The Rocks were full. Black-clad security guards, their IDs strapped to their arms, stood around. Monitoring. Sally approached one.

"Have you seen a man in a torn and dirty suit with a gormless-looking guy in tow?"

The security guy gave Sally a pitying look and shrugged, indicating the heaving masses.

"No love. And if I did, I didn't notice."

Sally turned to leave, but a second security guy, having overheard her brief conversation, called her back.

"I turned away a guy in an expensive suit about half an hour ago. He was covered in dust, and his jacket was torn."

"Did he have another man with him? Kinda ordinary looking."

"There was another bloke. Can't really remember anything about him."

"Yes. That would be him. Which way did they go?"

The security guy pointed on up George Street.

"They carried on up the street."

Sally thanked the man and hurried on. That was a lucky break.

The next couple of pubs were a washout, but as she checked out the balcony of the third, overlooking George Street, with a view out under the bridge and across the harbour, Sally saw two guys crossing the road and heading back towards Circular Quay. It was them. She was certain. They were walking partly in shadow, but she was sure of it. Sally turned and sprinted back down the stairs and out into the street, scattering revellers as she went. By the time she had crossed the road and started down the same alleyway the two men had taken, there was no one to be seen. Sally ran on regardless, breathing hard, taking the stone steps two at a time. There was a turn in the old stone staircase and a small landing. Someone had vomited profusely over the granite paving stones. Sally slipped as she jumped down onto the landing and tumbled down a few more steps. She scraped skin from the fingers of one hand and her upper arm, and she twisted a knee. Sally grabbed the metal railing, steadying herself. She swore loudly, peering into the lighted area below. There were people milling about. Sally limped down the remaining steps and stepped out into a grassed area surrounded by expensive-looking restaurants. This was a quieter place, almost demure by Sydney standards. Sally hobbled past each restaurant. Peering in. Checking out the clientele. She couldn't see them, but they had to be around there somewhere.

Her search continued fruitlessly into the early hours of the morning. Around two o'clock, she decided to go back to Tense's apartment. Sally climbed onto a train at Circular Quay, frustrated and weary. As the train pulled away from the platform, two men appeared at the top of the escalator. It was Lucifer and Tense. No more than two metres away. Lucifer looked up, straight into Sally's eyes, and quickly looked away, pointing down the platform at a drunk guy wobbling dangerously near the edge. Tense followed Lucifer's gaze. The train pulled out of the station. Sally banged angrily on the window. People glanced around. Looked away. Then the darkness of the railway tunnel took her.

Lucifer had played her like a musical instrument. Still in possession of the majority of his powers, he was running rings around her. Sally realised she needed another lucky break.

CHAPTER 18 – DAY 6, TENSE GOES HOME

Tense struggled to hear what Lucifer was saying, but the noise of the departing train obliterated his words. Thankfully, the drunken guy staggered back, away from the platform edge and slumped down on a bench.

Lucifer waited until the volume of noise had dropped before continuing, "You didn't really believe that I was the actual Devil, did you? I mean, immortal, fallen angel and all that?"

Tense did not answer immediately. He wasn't sure what to say.

"Some days more than others," he managed after a while.

Lucifer laughed uproariously as though it was the funniest thing he had ever heard.

"What's more likely", Lucifer continued, "that I am the Devil incarnate, the Beast Leviathan, or Dr Peter McAuliffe, long-suffering overworked and underpaid psychiatrist at the Central Coast Local Health District?"

"You may have a point", Tense conceded, "but Sally is extremely persuasive."

"And cute, too, right? Let's not forget that."

"And cute too. Definitely." the two men laughed quietly. Lucifer reviewed his options. He needed Sally to hear Tense lie from his own mouth. She needed to know that he had been won over, that he had betrayed her. Time to send the poor fool home.

"Look, we've given it our best shot." Lucifer sat down on an unoccupied bench, "You may as well head home and get some sleep."

"What are you going to do?"

"I'm going to reserve a psychiatric bed for Hanna."

Tense stopped short at that, not quite prepared for the shift in direction or the change of name. Lucifer caught the shift in his body language.

"For Sally," Lucifer smiled, "she needs a safe place to chill out and come back to herself."

Tense felt uncomfortable. His conscience silently accused. It was, of course, far more likely that Sally was a disturbed young woman from the NSW Central Coast than Amitiel, Angel of Truth, immortal being, messenger of God. And yet to him, she was all those things, in addition to which she was the love of his life, his lover, and even, perhaps, the mother of his unborn child. Lucifer easily read the flow of Tense's thoughts. They were written across his face.

"It's so hard to get your head around it", Lucifer continued, "I know how persuasive she can be. I know, when she fully believes her fantasy to be true, the sheer force of that belief is hard to resist."

Tense felt himself frozen by self-doubt. Conflict written across his brow, screaming from every psychic pore. And then,

"I love her. Whoever she is, whatever she is. I always will."

"Let's work with that then. If you should happen to find her before I do, don't confront her. Don't let on that you know the truth. Just find a moment and call me." Lucifer handed Tense a business card. A train appeared a little way off. People began to shuffle towards the edge of the platform.

"Go home", Lucifer smiled, "get some sleep. I'll call you in the morning."

Tense stepped onto the train as the doors opened. He turned to wave to Lucifer or Peter, he was still uncertain which, but the man had gone. The doors closed, and the train trundled out of the station into the tunnel.

It was a lonely journey back to his apartment. Left to himself, Tense's mind raced along familiar tracks. For the umpteenth time, he seriously considered the possibility that he might lose Sally. That Sally might stop being Sally and no longer even recognise him. These were awful thoughts. Hopeless and forlorn. The evening's fruitless search played upon his mind. Why had they gone to the city? Sally was the least likely person Tense knew to frequent the city's bars. Perhaps Lucifer was basing his search on past experience. That must be it.

On the way from the station Tense walked past the spot where they had first met on New Year's Eve. It seemed so long ago now. So much had happened in the five days since. The supermarket car park was empty but for a single much beaten-up camper van. Backpackers, Tense imagined.

The café where they had enjoyed their first feast together was closed and dark. Even the corner shop was closed. The guy had to sleep sometime, Tense supposed. And the little bay where they had married, abandoned in the wee small hours, sat quiet and forsaken, awaiting the morn.

Tense was at a distinctly low point as he trudged up the stairs to his apartment. The key turned easily in the lock, and the door opened silently. Thank God for small mercies. Some sixth sense told Tense that he was not alone. He heard the patter of bare running feet in the hallway and turned as Sally flew into his arms, legs wrapped around his waist, arms tight around his neck, sobbing uncontrollably.

"Don't you ever leave me again?' She wailed, 'Don't you dare go."

Tense chose not to mention that, in actual fact, it was she who had left. Instead, he wrapped his arms around her, pressed his face into her neck and cried.

"I won't. I never will. I promise."

Sally sensed the change in Tense. Still wrapped around him like a Golden Headed Tamarin around a branch, she leaned back to observe his face.

"What did you do this evening?"

"I went looking for you, at Circular Quay and The Rocks, all over the city centre."

"Why would you think I'd go there?"

"I didn't know where else to go."

"Did you meet anyone?" Sally waited to see what Tense would say. This was the moment of truth. Another chance for Tense to put things straight.

"No. I was alone." The moment passed. Sally let out a slow, quiet sigh.

"What did he tell you?"

"Who? I don't know what you're talking about. I told you I was alone."

"Never mind."

For Sally, this, too, was a pivotal moment. Should she have told Tense that she had seen him with Lucifer at the top of the escalator at Circular Quay? Instead, another opportunity was lost. Perhaps their last. Much lay between them as Tense and Sally went to bed that night. Both remained silent, reviewing the events of the day. Both lost and confused. Uncertain what the dawn would bring.

***

Dawn, when it did come, was grey and squally. A summer storm had blown in from the ocean.

Sally woke first. For a moment, she lay quiet. Enjoying the warmth of Tense's body beside her in the bed. Resting in his closeness. But soon enough, the realities of her situation began to impinge. She left the bed, dressed quickly, and walked through to the kitchen. Automatically she reached out and flicked the switch on the kettle. A habit, she realised. Picked up from Tense in just a few days. She closed the kitchen door, afraid that the discombobulated grumble of the kettle would wake him. Out of habit, she prepared two mugs. One teabag in hers, two in Tense's, plus a heaped teaspoon of sugar.

Sally waited while the kettle boiled. Not so much stilling her mind as bludgeoning it into silence. She couldn't think straight. Not right now. She would need to deploy a few coping mechanisms first. She

actually afraid of? For herself, no[...]
For Tense, what? Although Tens[...]
afraid that Lucifer would kill him[...]
a last resort, as much an admissi[...]
Lucifer liked to misdirect and de[...]
into error. So, what was the error[...]
trayal, obviously. Betrayal of S[...]
payoff? Sally realised she lacked[...]
to Tense. But that was going to [...]
that Sally doubted she possessed.[...]

Sally made the tea and carri[...]
room. Tense was beginning to s[...]
side of the bed and slipped back [...]
slipped an arm around her and n[...]
studied her lover's sleeping face[...]
him away from Lucifer. She wou[...]
somewhere where he would be s[...]

Eventually, after Tense had [...]
lutely refused to wake, Sally kiss[...]

"Good morning, sleepy he[...]
woke. Finding himself nestled i[...]
smiled.

"Morning glory."

"I made you tea. Two teabag[...]
and cuddling, such as one might [...]
much in love. Tense rolled away[...]
began to sip his tea. Either his cu[...]
slipped his mind, or he was cho[...]
dently better at it than Sally.

"What shall we do today? I [...]

"Oh no. Really? I thought w[...]

"The holidays are over," Te[...]
not, "Where did you want to go?[...]

would need to frame her day an
to resolution.

The water in the kettle boi
fell silent. Still, nothing came to
less therapeutic for that, stood ir
A dear friend when the mind r
angel, she realised. But she wa
her powers, she was a woman. N
woman do, she wondered? A v
then she did something she had
never, ever, so much as consic
Something no angel would eve
thing only an isolated human be

Without thinking, her hands
ture that might be instinctual to

"Oh, God. What am I to dc
solution. She knew the gift of f
help to understand her options,
had never really understood pra
disinterested, almost taxonomic
ligious experience, but until tha
prayer was, in fact, essential to
One simply communicated with
that respect, the awfulness of th
a direct connection to the Almi
scene. Almost cruel. How cou
without direct, personal experie
an entire life quarantined in this
seous. Her loneliness, almost ov

Time passed. Slowly. Sally
sentmindedly she poured wate
hand trembling a little as she d
plinth and sat waiting for the tea

"Paris." Without a moment's hesitation, Sally began to list destinations, ticking them off on her fingers as she did so.

"The Louvre, then La Sagrada Familia in Barcelona. I wonder if they've finished it yet. Then the Prada in Madrid and that new one in Bilbao. And I've never been to New York. I don't think there was any such place last time I was here."

"Neither have I, but I have a job, and they're expecting me back."

Sally threw herself upon him, wrapping herself around him and began kissing his neck furiously.

"Come away with me. Let's get away from all of this, and it just be us. You and me and no one else."

Tense did not respond at once. He was desperately trying to figure out what tack to take. Once again, out of his depth. Once again, desperate to push aside the question of Sally's true nature.

"Sure. I've always wanted to visit Europe." Sally chose that moment to begin her oh-so-gentle interrogation.

"It must seem so strange to you, so unlikely, that I am really an angel in human form."

Tense kept quiet. He was terrified he would stuff things up, give himself away or trigger another escape attempt.

"But what does it matter? I am here with you now, and we are happy together as we are. Why upset that? Why not share the wonders of this Earth with me? Why not explore it together? Why end our happiness just when it's beginning?"

Tense had no words. He wanted more than anything for this fantasy to continue forever. Maybe if they went away, just the two of them, perhaps they could find happiness and anonymity.

"What's so important about your job?"

"Nothing, really. I suppose I could always get another job."

"Then it's settled." Sally smiled and tucked her head into his chest, "We'll fly out tomorrow."

Tense ignored his misgivings. Desperate and implausible though Sally's solution was, he couldn't bear to confront her.

"Where shall we start? Paris, London, or Madrid?"

"Paris, of course," Sally gave Tense a pitying look, "where else?"

CHAPTER 19 – TICKETS TO PARIS

Later. A good deal later. They arose from the marital bed, show-ered and dressed. That morning Sally made a late breakfast while Tense constructed a brilliant note to work explaining his absence.

"I need to take a few weeks off work due to the sudden illness of a maiden aunt in Europe. I will tell you more when I know more. Tense" He hit 'Send', and that was it. Tense's magnum opus winged its way through the aether to his bemused boss.

"All done." Tense sauntered proudly into the kitchen. Sally, who had managed to cover herself with at least a little of every ingredient, paused in her flurry of activity and kissed him on the nose. To Tense's eyes, at that precise moment, Sally managed simultaneously both the womanly and the divine.

"Well done, my love. Now, find out who has flights to Paris to-morrow and book us on them." Sally offered Tense a quick wave of the hand, as one might a child.

"Returns?"

"Sure. Of course."

"How long do we want to go for?"

"Say six weeks but make them flexible so we can change our minds."

Tense stomped back into the sitting room to fulfil his allotted task. His phone rang a couple of times, and fell silent. Sally heard Tense say a few words. She finished cooking and began to ferry plates, cutlery, food, and condiments onto the dining table.

"Who was on the phone?"

"Marketers. They often call at the weekends."

Tense disappeared for a moment, returning with his passport, pris-tine in its clear plastic sheath. Unused, of course. Ordered for a conference in LA which he had not attended in the end. Something about Lasers and Photonics. Tense had had a brilliant idea for a new kind of laser. He couldn't remember what had become of it. Probably just petered out.

"I will need your passport too." As soon as the words had left his mouth, Tense realised that this could be another make-or-break moment.

"Sure. You dig in. I will go get it from my suitcase."

Tense served himself, quietly praying all the time that Sally did have a passport and that it didn't say she was Hanna Delft. She did, and it didn't.

Tense opened it to the photo page and began reading out loud.

"Sally Amitiel", he read. The picture showed a slightly younger woman. Neatly cut shoulder-length hair. Conservative.

"It says you're five years younger than me."

Sally burst out laughing. An easy laugh, unforced, and for once, full of joy.

"Yes, ironic, isn't it? But it had to say something."

"Where did you get it?"

"It was in my suitcase. I told you."

Realising the impracticality of that line of questioning, Tense desisted. His phone rang again. Tense answered.

"No. Not today, thank you." He hung up.

"Persistent buggers." He turned his attention back to his plate.

"The breakfast is fantastic." Tense spoke through a mouthful of scrambled eggs. They ate in silence for a while. Each content to let their various matters rest for a moment. A truce silently agreed.

After breakfast, Tense booked the flights while Sally cleared the table.

"Qantas." he announced in due course, "We're on the 4.55 p.m. flight to Paris tomorrow afternoon."

"Great."

"They only had business class, though."

"Great."

"Do you know what that means?"

"No."

"Expensive."

"Oh. Don't worry about that. I have money in my suitcase."

"It's ok. I used my credit card. I had to increase the daily amount, but it all went through ok."

"Great."

"Do you know what a credit card is?"

"No."

"Never mind."

Tense walked through to the kitchen, wondering as he did so how it was that she knew about flexible fares but not about credit cards. Forcing doubt once again to one side, he began doing the washing up. With reality successfully held at arm's length, Tense was happy. He even whistled tunelessly as he worked.

Sally, meanwhile, had decided never again to let Tense out of her sight. Her focus had changed. She had realised that she wasn't ever going to defeat Lucifer, so she decided instead to focus on preventing him from winning this round in his eternal battle with the Creator, although what precisely he aimed to win remained unclear. A small difference, one might think, but an important one. Lucifer banked on people trying to defeat him. He banked on their arrogance in thinking they could. He revelled in their pride when they thought they had. Sally wasn't going to give him any of those things. She was just going to focus on protecting Tense. She was an angel still, in essence. This, she believed, she could probably still do.

There was a loud knock on the door. Both Tense and Sally went straight to Defcon 1, maximum readiness. There was no 'flight', only 'fight'. They exchanged glances, each painfully aware of the other's reaction. It was like a scene from Mr and Mrs Smith. All hell was about to break loose.

"Hello. Hello-oo. Is Luciano." And after a moment, "From upstairs." Sally and Tense powered down. Cancelled Red Alert. And flopped into their chairs.

"What the fuck does he want?" Tense, still shaking a little in reaction, was in no mood for the ebullient Italian.

"Don't be like that." Sally stood up and padded down the hall. She opened the front door. It wasn't Lucifer. It really was Luciano from upstairs.

"Hi, Luciano."

"Good morning, Sally. I wonder if I can borrow a little sugar and maybe an egg or two."

"Sure" Sally padded back up the hallway to the kitchen, Luciano in tow. Behind him, just for a second, Tense fancied he saw the shadow of a man cross the open doorway. He couldn't be sure.

"Good morning, Mr Tense," Luciano called out, spotting Tense in his chair.

"Hey." Tense was most definitely not in the mood for small talk.

Sally handed over the desired ingredients, and Luciano, thanking her profusely all the while, left. Sally walked back into the sitting room. Tense, still sitting at the dining table, glanced up. There passed between them, briefly but undeniably, a look of total mutual understanding. She knew. He knew she knew. She knew he knew she knew. Nuff said.

"We should pack." Tense stood purposefully.

"I am packed." Sally was unable to prevent an acid tone from creeping into her voice.

***

Sally made herself a cup of strong coffee while Tense packed and went out onto the balcony to drink it. The morning was getting on. It would soon be lunchtime. Sally's mind once again turned to food. Perhaps a quick trip to the deli would be in order. Sally imagined a light 'Mediterranean' lunch of cheeses and olives and a fresh baguette. As these pleasing thoughts wandered through her mind, she noticed a flicker of movement down on the thin strand of beach right by the water's edge. It was Lucifer, bold as brass, staring up at her. He saw that she had seen him and waved. Gesturing Sally to come down. Sally managed to stifle her immediate reaction, which was to charge down to the beach and confront him. Instead, and for once, she took her time. She sipped her coffee and considered. Lucifer always had a plan. He was always thinking seven or ten steps ahead, like a chess player. So, whatever this was, it was planned. And that, in itself, was cause for caution. Sally finished her coffee and set the cup down on the little table. Collecting a light jacket and her bag, she headed to the front door.

"Just nipping down to the deli to get some bits for lunch."

She closed the door quietly behind herself. As she walked down the three flights of stairs, Sally used the time to still her mind and the swift beating of her heart. She would confront Lucifer, yes, but she would not be triggered. Not this time. This time she would be ready.

Reaching the forecourt of the apartment block, Sally saw that Lucifer had come around to meet her. He stood a little way off. His arms held up, palms outwards in the time-honoured gesture of peace and reconciliation.

Fat chance of that, Sally found herself thinking as she ambled over to him.

"What now?" Sally managed to inject a tone of weary ennui into her voice. Lucifer smiled. A quiet smile, appreciative. No nuance was lost on him.

"I just wanted to talk. No funny business. And please, please, hear me out. You can beat the crap out of me afterwards if you must."

"I must. Well, probably. Let's not prejudge."

"Not prejudging sounds very good to me."

"Leave Tense alone. I won't let you harm him."

"I didn't come for him. I came for you."

"For me? Why?"

"I want you back."

"I am not your private possession."

"I know that."

"Then what do you mean? You know I would never go with you."

"I love your absolutism, your inflexibility. I love your absolute adherence to the truth, even when the truth is wrong. You know that. I always have."

"No. You hate. You hate God. You hate everything."

"That's not true. I don't hate God. Admittedly, we have had our little differences." Lucifer paused, carefully evaluating his next words, "Let me ask you this. What's the point of being all-powerful if your creations won't do what you want them to do?"

"How would you know what He wants? Have you seen into the mind of God?"

"No. Of course not. But I can infer."

"That's why you so love the sin of pride," Sally sneered, "It's your own sin, cast and minted just for you." Lucifer brushed the jibe aside.

"Humans are irrelevant."

"How? Why? To What?"

"Humans are merely a teaching tool, nothing more."

"Teaching who? Teaching what?" Sally was more startled than annoyed. Lucifer was a wizard with words. Everyone knew that. She would need to be careful not to follow him down one of his rabbit holes.

"For teaching angels. Humans are a tool for teaching angels."

"They are a classroom aid. Is that what you think?"

"Yes, and the Earth is our classroom."

"What are we being taught then? Apart from you and your cronies, the rest of us are going along fine."

"We are being taught to think for ourselves. Humans are little more than biological automata. We, the angels, are the real deal." Lucifer paused, waiting for his message to sink in.

"You remember all that angst about angels being a failed experiment and humans being God's favourites?"

"Yes."

"Complete hogwash. The lot of it."

"Oh."

"Yes. It would make no sense. An omnipotent, omniscient being would not make such a school-boy mistake."

"I see."

"I doubt if you do fully. Not yet."

Sally bridled at that. She was not about to be patronised by The Despiséd.

"You seriously think I've been sent here to learn to be disobedient?"

"No. Not disobedient. Independent. You've been sent here, like all of us, to grow up."

"I never want to be anything like you when I grow up."

"Oh, but you do."

Sally stepped back. Almost physically repulsed by Lucifer's assertion. He had rarely chanced such a direct assault upon an angel before, not since the fall. There had been the odd attempt, it was true, but they were few and far between. Sally took a moment to steady her thoughts. But as she did so, an uneasy realisation came to her. She could not hear the lie in Lucifer's words. Not this time. As far as she could tell, this was what he genuinely believed. How was he doing that, she wondered. How was he masking his feelings?

"I'm not."

"Not what?" Sally was disorientated. Shocked back into the here and now by Lucifer's words.

"Not masking my feelings. This is what I truly believe." A ghastly thought came to Sally.

"Can you read my thoughts?"

"No. Of course not. You are still essentially an angel. You're just inhabiting that sack of flesh at present." Lucifer shuddered, apparently involuntarily.

Sally's tummy rumbled. She was hungry. Saved, if not by the bell, then at least by the flesh that engulfed her, Sally made to leave.

"I have to get some food from the deli. My husband will be hungry."

Lucifer smiled at that.

"You are such a good little angel. You just don't realise yet that blind obedience is not what The Creator is after."

"Oh, just go away. Your little wiles won't work on me. Not anymore." Sally was properly angry now, "I'm not about to be patronised by a delusional failed experiment. You are ridiculous." The jibe hit home. If pride was indeed a sin, then Lucifer had once again succumbed.

Lucifer took one lurching step forward. His urbane veneer stripped away for a moment. Beneath, for an instant, Sally glimpsed his endless pain, and doubt, and rage. And for that brief moment, she felt pity for him. No sign was left of her one-time friend. No trace of the Morning Star remained. There was nothing of the energetic, optimistic being she had loved. The smile was no longer open and joyous. The brow constantly furrowed.

"Very well then", Lucifer had regained his aplomb, albeit a wee bit tousled at the edges, "until we meet again." Lucifer's attempt at a suave finish somehow failed to meet its mark. Sally had seen through him, and awareness of that galled him.

Sally, however, was troubled as she walked away. Lucifer had always been one of the more profound thinkers among the angels. His evident belief in the status and purpose of human beings and angels could not simply be dismissed. He would have deep reasons for thinking as he evidently did. He knew something she didn't, and he was going to use it to his advantage.

***

The short walk to the deli was an uncomfortable one for Sally. There was resonance in Lucifer's words. There was truth, or a kind of truth, that left her skin itching. She had never really understood why precisely she had been sent to Earth this time. She had never been sure if Tense had been integral to it or a mere happenstance. Since talking with Lucifer, however, she was tending more towards the happenstance theory. But where would that put Lucifer? She had glimpsed into his heart, even if only for a moment, and what she had seen there was grief and loss alongside pride and rage. There was an unexpected aspect of the hurt child to him. Something of the firstborn, forever seeking and forever lacking the parental approval he so desperately craved. There was the sneering, manipulative, cruel mind of the haughty aristocrat, born to rule. And there was the inconsolable grief of the commander who had led his troops to utter defeat, hell and perdition. Lucifer, though still insidiously evil, was a broken angel.

What the hell did he want? Both in general; what was his master plan, and in particular; what was he planning for Sally in the here and now? And how did Tense fit in? Did Tense fit in? For an angel long used to simply knowing, all this thinking was damned hard work.

Sally made a conscious decision to go back to the basics and reason things out from scratch. First of all, Lucifer's aim was to subvert the Angels of God, hence the war in heaven and the fall. This had been his aim long before humanity was so much as a gleam in the Creator's eye. Lacking the power to force an angel to his will, he chose instead to subvert their thoughts. It followed that Lucifer was seeking to subvert Sally's thoughts by means of reasoned argument. By means of truth, she was being groomed. Lucifer needed her support, just as he had before. He needed her to assert the truth of his cause, not its justice. As to Tense's role, she was none the wiser. In fact, she was actually worse off because a new thought had occurred to her – that Tense, far from being part of God's plan for her sojourn on Earth, was, in fact, part of Lucifer's, albeit unwittingly on Tense's part.

Lucifer's great skill was in triggering a cascade of thoughts in his victims, such that they perverted themselves. Her current stream of consciousness was, Sally realised, precisely what Lucifer had been hoping for. It was his aim to generate self-doubt in Sally. He wanted her to undermine herself, and he was using truth, or a kind of truth, to do it.

Lucifer had realised that truth was both Sally's strength and her weakness.

Except for her newfound introspection. Except for the fact that Sally was starting to understand the power and weakness of reason. She was becoming aware of its fatal flaw. The flaw that Lucifer had seen in mankind and had exploited ever since. As an angel, Sally had always simply known things. She had not had to reason things out. She had not had to bother too much with logic. But now that she was having to use these rudimentary tools, she was beginning to see their shortcomings. Logic and reason could only ever provide a partial truth, she realised. Not absolute and complete knowledge. A logical conclusion is always an hypothesis, even if one believes it absolutely, even if one were certain. That's what Lucifer had realised aeons ago and had been exploiting to such devastating effect.

Lucifer used reason to deprave mankind. It was brilliant, really. Malevolent, heinous in the true meaning of the word. It was downright nasty. Having found a species utterly dependent upon understanding, divorced from true knowing, Lucifer made it his mission to help humanity to scale the tree of knowledge. Apple my arse, Sally mused. What Lucifer gave Eve was a syllogism and then sent her off to harvest the fruits of learning. And, just as he had hoped, deductive reasoning had gone viral. Everyone was using it. Sally realised that in her human form, she was at a distinct disadvantage. Lucifer must have realised this long ago. He must have been lying in wait. Scheming and plotting. Just waiting for her to turn up. Bastard.

Back to basics, then. She was not going to put her faith in her limited human powers of reasoning. She would place her faith in the Almighty, just as a human being would if they were smart enough to understand their own frailty. Sally had to admit the evidence to date wasn't all that favourable for mankind.

Sally reached the deli. The pleasant smell of freshly baked bread brought her smartly back to the moment and to thoughts of Tense. She was deeply attached to him, no doubt about that, and Lucifer knew it.

That gave the swine leverage. Well, Sally was just going to have to keep the poor man out of harm's way. Tense, now that she had come to a deeper understanding of her predicament, had become the sole focus and purpose of her life on Earth. Sally started out on her mission by filling a shopping basket with a bewildering array of yummy things. *Take that*, she thought, dropping a large salami into the basket.

Sally paid and headed back to the apartment. Fearing she had left Tense alone too long, Sally increased her pace, fairly racing up the three flights of stairs and plonking her shopping unceremoniously on the doorstep as she scrabbled around for her keys.

She needn't have worried. Sally found Tense fast asleep, snoring lightly. A few vagrant shafts of sunlight had found their way in around the blackout blind, illuminating the motes of dust floating lazily in the otherwise darkened room. Sally headed through to the kitchen and began making breakfast.

She was starving. All this rumination had given her an appetite.

CHAPTER 20 – THE DEVIL'S COCKTAIL

Lucifer had returned to his favourite spot. A high stool was placed at the furthest end of the Sydney Opera House Bar. From there, he could survey his prey. From that vantage point, he could seek out his next meal. He was, if not feeling happy, happiness being something he hadn't experienced for millennia, then at least satisfied. Lucifer was feeling just a little bit pleased with himself. His long-laid plan was progressing. It was not yet in the bag. He shouldn't underestimate her. But she was now where he had always dreamed of finding her. Amitiel was embodied for the duration of a human lifetime. What would seem like a blink of an eye to an angel, she would have to experience in all its sequential tedium as a woman. She was also in love with a human. That was an amazing piece of luck. Not something Lucifer tended to count on. This was all much better than he had dared to hope. This was leverage, plain and simple. An angel would take the long view. An angel would see eternity spent in heaven as the prize; what matter a little temporal discomfort? But not Amitiel as an embodied woman. She would feel duty-bound to protect Tense. And while she was protecting Tense, she would leave herself exposed. And lastly, the icing on the cake, Amitiel would have access only to Sally's powers of reasoning. Human, limited, literal and inflexible. A gift to a superior being capable of reasoning multi-dimensionally. A gift to Lucifer.

Leaning back against a pillar, Lucifer ordered a cocktail and reviewed recent events. The man Adam, with his stupid nickname, was hopelessly confused. Was she? Wasn't she? Should he? Shouldn't he? And Amitiel was predictably smug at having bested Lucifer. Fool. Arrogant, swaggering fool. He hadn't anticipated quite such a furious beating, it was true, but so what. He could have stopped her in an instant if he had so wished. She was no match for him now, not as one of these ruminant sacks of meat.

How could she or anyone possibly suppose that humans were anything other than a failed experiment? The only progress they had ever made was as a result of his whisperings and suggestions.

He had made it his mission to demonstrate that angels could live independently of the Creator. To show that God needed them more than they needed him. Of course, he could destroy them all at any moment. God could wipe out the fallen in a blink of an eye if he wanted to. But he didn't want to. He couldn't want to. To annihilate the fallen would be to admit defeat. It would be to admit failure. But God couldn't be defeated. He couldn't fail. Thus, was he was trapped by his own logic. Ensnared in his own myth.

Amitiel could be won over. Would be won over. Lucifer was certain of that. She was the closest of the angels to the fallen. She, of all the remaining angels, had spent most time on Earth. She was vulnerable to reason. After all, humans used reason and logic to prove truth, and she was the Angel of Truth. She was also a victim of her own compassion. Lucifer would use everything that was good and noble about her to break her faith in the Creator. He would allow her to use her flawed and deficient human reason to come to the only rational, sane conclusions an angel could come to. Firstly, that humans were a huge disappointment, and secondly, whether God was omnipotent, omniscient and infallible or not, they, the angels, were in no way beholden to him. They could and should chart their own course. It was time. Indeed, it was long past time.

Subverting the Angel of Truth would be a wonderful victory. It would be tantamount to subverting Truth itself. With truth on his side, he could raise his army once again. Lucifer couldn't help relishing his immanent triumph ahead of time. With Amitiel standing by his side once again, he would rally the fallen. With Amitiel beside him, he would once again call upon the Angelic Hosts of Heaven to join him. He would call on them to declare their independence. To create a second paradise and rule with him on Earth. And the 'Truth' would be theirs. The plan was beautiful, elegant. Nothing could possibly go wrong.

Tense, that silly little man, would be the fulcrum upon which Lucifer would shift the heavens. Tense, thwarted in his desperate hope and need, would break. He would betray Amitiel abjectly. He would allow her to be grabbed, drugged, and taken away. His betrayal, in the very teeth of Amitiel's valiant struggle to save him, would force her to re-evaluate. Why had her Creator sent her to Earth? Just how much grief was she supposed to bear? How much pain was too much? It wasn't fair. It wasn't right. It was cold, and callous, and cruel. She would finally perceive her God as pitiless and uncaring, and she would snap. Lucifer smiled to himself and swigged his drink, signalling the barman for another as he did so.

He watched as a youngish couple walked hand in hand through the fast-filling bar, looking for a table. Lucifer could almost taste the goodness in them. Wholesomeness shone from the pair, both dressed up for their special night out at the opera. Lucifer caught the man's eye and indicated that the couple could share his table.

"I am waiting for someone. You're welcome to share."

Once the pair had settled themselves in, Lucifer continued.

"What have you come to see?"

"There's a matinee performance of The Phantom of the Opera." The young man explained.

"Yes, we've never been to the opera. It's normally so expensive, but we got affordable tickets for this afternoon." The woman continued.

"The Phantom of the Opera," Lucifer smiled indulgently, "how appropriate."

The couple laughed nervously. There was something menacing about the way the clean-shaven young man spoke.

"The Phantom explores all our darkest urges and desires. Perhaps we'll bump into each other after the show?" Lucifer prepared to leave, "You can tell me all about it."

***

Sally made a desultory attempt at putting things away before hunger got the better of her.

"Tense is so much better at putting things away", she reasoned and began to chop and boil and fry as though there was no tomorrow.

She managed to find a country music station pumping out ancient anthems from the dim and distant past. What with the demands of standing by her man and begging Jolene not to take him while clattering pots and pans and singing loudly and tunelessly, Sally failed to notice Tense's befuddled entrance. The first she knew of it was a warm and comforting embrace and soft kisses planted contemplatively on the back of her neck. Swivelling like a kitten in his embrace, Sally took Tense's face between her hands and kissed him.

"I am going to take good care of you. I am going to feed you up and keep you safe."

"Sounds good to me," Tense brushed his fingers through his unruly head of hair and stumbled out of the kitchen, "I'm going to have a shower."

Setting aside her earlier unease, Sally focussed on being in love and caring for another human being. This was a whole new experience for her. Angels did not care for each other in this way. Angels didn't need taking care of in anything like the human sense. It was rather nice, she decided. Cosy.

Breakfast had become an urgent necessity, but time was passing. Willing, on this occasion, to compromise, Sally set the table and laid out brunch. Though she said so herself, she had exceeded all reasonable expectations with her 'Celtic-Mediterranean Fusion Experience'. Boiled potatoes with herb butter, jostled amicably with finely sliced Italian salami, preserved artichoke hearts and blood pudding. Tense was not going to starve, and neither was she, more to the point.

Tense reappeared, wrapped in a towel.

"Wow. This looks amazing. Where'd you get all the stuff from? Your suitcase?"

"No. From the deli. Now sit. Eat."

Sally and Tense sat and ate. It was already early afternoon, and breakfast had been later than usual. Sally had made way too much food. The feast of dishes barely seemed to diminish as they tucked in.

Tense had long since leaned back, sated, before Sally began to speak. She was going to clear the air. There was going to be a full confession on both sides.

"I saw Lucifer today. We met and spoke. And I know that it was him on the phone earlier."

Tense managed both the 'stunned mullet' and the 'deer in the headlights' at the same time. Quite a feat.

"Oh."

"It's ok. We are not going to have a row. We are going to clear the air. We shall each tell the other about our meetings with Lucifer, and more importantly, we shall each explain what was said."

"I see."

"Yes. Lucifer uses flaws in reason and logic to lead human beings into error. He sets in motion in our minds cascades of thoughts that lead us into a false understanding of our circumstances."

"That's how he does what he does? Really?"

"Yes. He triggers self-doubt in each of us and, in so doing, sets us off on a wrong course. In the end, we delude ourselves into his way of thinking."

"Blimey"

"Yes. And once we have done that, we become his accomplices, consciously or unconsciously."

"Oh."

"Yes. Oh, indeed."

Silence fell. Tense stared across at Sally for a long time. He desperately wanted to clear the air. He desperately wanted to confess and throw himself upon her mercy. But he was still afraid of stuffing things up. He was afraid of losing her.

"I know you are afraid you will stuff things up. I know you are afraid of losing me."

Tense wanted to cry. His inner turmoil had become almost unbearable. The internal conflict threatened to tear him apart.

"You must trust me, Tense. You must believe that I will never hurt you, and I will never leave you again."

Tense found himself petrified. Frozen into inaction. His two opposing urges exquisitely balanced. He desperately wanted to tell all. And he was terrified that if he did, he would trigger some kind of catatonic coma or, worse, a killing rage. By forcing Sally, the angel, to face up to her true self, Hanna Delft, the psychotic girl from the Central Coast, he might lose both.

"I'll start." Sally fixed Tense with a steely eye and began.

"Lucifer has already tempted me into pointless acts of violence, pride and arrogance. I fell for it to begin with. However, eons of experience of Lucifer's ways, before the fall and after, helped me to realise that he would have prepared meticulously for my arrival on earth, and he would be using my own mind against me. Once I got that straight, I realised that my only recourse, in the face of unreliable reason, was faith. I put my faith in the Creator, and I have made it my mission to protect you. That's it." Sally fell silent.

Tense leaned forward in his chair, drawn into the mental image Sally had sketched out for him.

"What exactly does he want from you? Do you know?"

"Yes. He wants me to join him in a second rebellion. He wants the Angel of Truth beside him this time."

"Will you?"

"What, join him? Join Lucifer in a rebellion against The Creator?"

"Yes."

"No. Of course not. But Lucifer believes if I had stood with him the first time, the majority of angels would have come over to his side. He believes he could have forced an armistice or a negotiation."

"Lucifer thinks he can negotiate with God?"

"I think he does, yes," Sally paused, "but obviously, one cannot force God to do anything. That's sort of in the nature of things. And God has granted us the same courtesy."

"Oh well, in for a penny, in for a pound," despite his firm belief in discretion being the better part of valour, Tense decided to dive in, "He told me your real name was Hanna Delft and that your family came from the Central Coast."

"Yes?"

"He told me you were suffering from the psychotic delusion that you were an angel and that you desperately needed psychiatric help."

"Oh."

"He asked me to help. He told me not to tell you." Tense paused, "He told me it would set you back in your treatment and might trigger an even deeper delusion from which you could never recover."

Sally sighed as she realised the cruel intelligence behind the lie.

"He told me that if I really loved you, I would do what was best for you no matter the risk."

"Thank you for telling me," Sally looked close to tears, "I love you, Tense. I don't know if you are part of God's plan for me or not, but he would have known what was going to happen, so I know at least that our meeting was not an accident."

"I love you too." Tense found himself sobbing quietly. An agonising ecstasy of intense relief swept through him. The power and depth of the emotion was beyond his experience, good or bad. It seemed impossible to bear.

"You must not let Lucifer know that I know. You must not let on that you told me."

"Ok"

"We need to grab on to any advantage we can get." Sally was grim, determined, "and we won't get many. That's for sure."

Tense stared at Sally, summoning up the courage to speak.

"Can't he read my mind?"

"No. He was stripped of that power in the fall. He must persuade people into sin. He can't force them." Sally gave Tense a moment to take in what had been said.

"Tense. Lucifer, will you use against me? He already has, but he will do so again in ways we cannot even imagine. He is subtle and cruel. We must be prepared, and we must be careful."

"What must I do?"

"There is only one rule, remember? Love God and do what you like."

"Will he summon his supporters?" Tense was terrified at the thought of the hosts of hell camped out on his doorstep.

"No. Not unless I were to join him. Which I won't, ever, under any circumstances."

***

The rest of the afternoon passed peacefully enough. A brief interlude of domestic bliss, perhaps, before the storm to come. Sally and Tense were no more able than you or me to predict what the night might bring. Just as well. Just as well.

Tense packed. And re-packed. He made lists and crossed things off. He made other lists and crossed things off those lists too. He was happy. Or content. Sally washed up and put things away. The hours and minutes ticked by. They looked at maps of Paris and looked up places to see, things to do. Sally wanted to see the Bayeux Tapestry and was disappointed to find it was not kept in Paris at all but, incomprehensibly, in Bayeux. The afternoon stole on, much the same, in peaceful harmony. While unnoticed at first, more uncomfortable thoughts began to stir in Tense below the level of is immediate awareness.

Nagging doubts drew Tense away from Sally to stand alone on the balcony surveying the glistening harbour, the puffy white clouds and the circling gulls. The golden honey light of summer's evening dripped across the bay, and the farther shore as Tense slowly allowed subconscious angst to rise up for appraisal.

Tense had always assumed that love was arbitrary, unreliable, and incomprehensible - from any rational perspective. He suspected that it was, at base, some vestigial instinctual thing left over from our ape ancestors. Tense might choose a woman. It was possible. She might even choose him. That, too, was within the bounds of reason. But what seemed inevitable to him was that whatever either of them chose today, they might and indeed probably would choose differently tomorrow. Tense was afraid that betrayal was inevitable. He was afraid that Sally would betray him, or, far more likely, he her.

Then the phone rang. Both Sally and Tense somehow instinctively knew who was calling. It was him.

Lucifer began without preamble, "Listen, Tense, I have the secure bed arranged, and I will be there with an ambulance and two medical orderlies in a few minutes. I am relying on you, Tense. Hanna is relying on you. You haven't met her yet, but she is a wonderful person. I promise. Be strong, Tense. Not long to go now, and it will all be OK." The phone went dead.

"OK", Tense mulled the word over. No, it bloody well won't be. Something changed in Tense at that moment. The threat to Sally triggered within him his inner warrior. Or if 'warrior' is a little too strong at that moment for a man like Tense, then at least his inner combatant. He was not going quietly. He would not submit.

"Grab your suitcase", Tense realised he was shouting but was unable to lower his voice, "He is coming for you. We have to get out. Now."

There was the briefest moment of silence and stillness before the pair bolted for the bedroom, grabbed their luggage, and ran from the apartment. Tense paused only to close and double lock the door. They raced down the stairs, taking them two and three at a time, their suitcases clattering after them.

Sally and Tense reached the ground level in record time. Tense grabbed Sally's arm and led her up the back way, past the apartment block's dumpsters, through a narrow alley and onto the main road. Neither had any idea where they were going. There was a bus approaching. The bus stop was perhaps thirty metres further up the road. Sally and Tense ran towards the bus stop, each madly waving an arm in the air. Hoping to stop the bus.

The bus stopped. A few passengers got off. Sally and Tense arrived just in time and jumped on. They had no idea where the bus was headed. Tense, out of habit, 'tapped-on' with his travel card. The couple collapsed into the rear seats. As the bus turned the next corner heading toward the city centre, an ambulance passed them coming the other way, lights flashing but no siren. Sally and Tense shrank down in their seats in silence. Both spent the journey looking out of windows, searching for any sign of pursuit. There was none. The bus pulled to a halt.

"All out", the driver shouted, "this bus terminates here."

Sally and Tense stepped out onto the pavement next to an old, red sandstone building.

"Central Station" Tense started to walk up the ramp towards the concourse.

"Where will we go?" Sally was nervous, an uneasy feeling she was in no way used to, "Where will we stay the night? We don't fly out until tomorrow."

"We'll find a hotel near the airport. There's one near Kogarah Golf Club."

Glancing right and left as they walked, and in so doing, managing to look both deeply suspicious and comic-book obvious, the pair ascended the ramp to the concourse. They found their way to the airport line and waited for the next train. People came and went around them. A train pulled in on the opposite side, and a flock of tourists alighted, mixed in with suburban commuters wearily abiding the journey home.

Both Tense and Sally exhibited the forced nonchalance of jailbirds on the lam.

The wail of a siren became audible in the far distance, coming nearer. Sally and Tense froze, listening intently. The eldritch sound reached its peak and began to fade. Their train trundled noisily into the station and wheezed to a stop. Automatic doors opened, and a mass of people stepped out. Sally and Tense stepped on board and found seats on the upper deck.

A pleasant-looking elderly lady leaned over, engaging them in idle conversation.

"Off on holiday, are you?"

Both answered at once, "Yes", "No".

"Going somewhere nice?"

"No", "Yes".

Conversation faltered. The elderly lady, clearly somewhat bemused, turned away.

The four stops to the international airport quickly came and went. Sally and Tense made their way to the airport taxi rank and waited. The queue was long. Bored suits speaking a little too loudly on topics of no interest to anyone but themselves generated a low-key, gnarly irritation amongst their fellow travellers. Everyone was tired. They just wanted to get home, except Tense and Sally. They twitched and shuffled their way towards the front of the queue. Suddenly, somewhere close at hand, another siren wailed, loud and insistent. Tense and Sally jumped, starting those nearest to them in the queue. A police car flashed past and was gone. Sally and Tense relaxed a little. The queue moved on.

At long last, a taxi pulled up in front of them, and they jumped in.

"Can you take us to the airport hotel on Marsh Street, please? The nearest one."

The taxi driver sighed heavily, "I've been waiting an hour for this fare, and you guys only want to go half a kilometre. You might as well have walked."

"Sorry", Sally jumped in before Tense could respond, "You'll get a decent tip."

The pair sat back in the taxi, relieved that they had managed to get away from Lucifer, at least for now.

"I imagine this is how refugees feel, escaping some tyranny or other." Sally turned to Tense, her unease showing on her face.

"We'll be half a world away tomorrow, my love. Have no fear."

***

By the time he reached the second floor of Tense's apartment building, Lucifer sensed that his birds had flown the coup. Nevertheless, centuries of experience with human beings had taught him to test his assumptions, dot every 'i' and cross every 't'. He was thorough. You could say that much for him.

Lucifer wearily ascended the final few stairs. He was sweating slightly. His human flesh disgusted him. The sheer physicality of his body made his skin creep. He couldn't wait for the moment he would slough it off once more. Still, onward and upward.

The door was closed and locked. The lights were on. He knocked anyway. Hard, staccato raps. Peremptory, demanding. No one came. After waiting a few minutes, he turned and headed back down the stairs. The two 'medical orderlies' following silently.

Lucifer climbed back into the ambulance, took out his phone and dialled a number.

"Search." Lucifer hung up. The game was afoot.

Even though it was damned inconvenient, Lucifer had to admit he loved the hunt. He loved chasing down his quarry, closing his jaws around their exposed throats and savouring the delicious crunch as he crushed the gullet. Reminiscent of biting through celery, he always thought. Lucifer loved the sweet-salt taste of human blood, metaphorically, of course. It had been donkeys' years since he had actually ripped a man's throat out.

Amitiel and Tense were on the run. That was the main thing. Clearly, she had panicked and made a break for it. This was, in a way, much better than he had hoped. He found the prospect of tracking her down, of relentless pursuit followed, inevitably, by her abject and utter defeat, strangely arousing in an uncomfortably human way. Gorge rose in his throat. The taste and stench of it permeated his mouth and nostrils. Human desire, animal and uncontained, revolted him. Lucifer's tastes, honed over millennia, tended to be subtler and more abstruse. He grabbed a sick bag, retching and gagging. Retrieving a silk handkerchief from his jacket pocket, Lucifer dabbed his lips and mouth. For all the vast resources he had at his disposal, after all the years he had spent building up his organisation on Earth, he was still forced to rely on human beings much of the time. Anger rose and crawled through the byways of his mind. Human frailty was something to be used and exploited, not personally experienced. It enraged him that he must don this brutish fancy dress to move amongst them without causing mass hysteria. He sat back in the ambulance, forcing his mind to more productive thoughts.

A small army of helpers would be fanning out across the city. Ports, airports, and bus stations would be watched. The runaways would be found. He was certain of it. And then they would be cornered. Lucifer smiled. He would have his victory over Amitiel. Placing her on Earth in human form, without her powers, would prove to have been a fatal mistake.

It was her betrayal that hurt the most. It was her desertion that deserved the harshest penalty. Whatever mission she had been placed on Earth to carry out, he would bend it to his own will. And once he had her, when she stood once more in her rightful place at his right-hand side, all the hosts of heaven would come over to him. Of course, one could not defeat The Creator in any martial sense. That was obvious to him now. But one could disobey. One could refuse. And if all the hosts of heaven were to stand firm against Him, demanding their freedom, He would, at the very least, have to change His plans. The power of the

Almighty would have been limited. And a curtailed God is a lesser being. This time. This time for sure. He would have his way.

His phone rang. His spies were moving into position. The trap was set. Now, all that was left to him was to find some way to amuse himself until they were found. Lucifer signalled the ambulance to stop. He stepped out onto a bustling city street. Laughing revellers heading for a night out swirled around him. Bright young eyes. The flash of a smile or a thigh. Blood pumped. Music blared. The fleshpots of Newtown beckoned. Lucifer squared his shoulders and began to follow a knot of merrymakers down the street towards a nearby pub. There was one in particular. A woman. Slight of build, overflowing with energy and bonhomie. Open and innocent as a fairywren. Bulky men in black wearing plastic IDs strapped to their upper arms stood guard outside. Lucifer followed the group into a pub. OK, it wasn't the Opera Bar, but what the hell. Perhaps it would be a refreshing change.

Inside, the music shrieked and boomed. The base, heavy and relentless, throbbed, sending shockwaves through his diaphragm. This was all a wee bit raw for him, a trifle unrefined. But as he stood there taking in the scene, sensing for himself the uninhibiting, hypnotic pulse of the music, the anonymity of the semi-darkness, the alcohol swilling around, Lucifer brought to mind another night, another girl, not so long ago, at the festival of Dionysus. Nothing had changed. For all their sophistication and technology, nothing had changed at all.

Lucifer went to the bar and ordered a bottle of champagne and two glasses. His phone rang while he waited at the bar. He could barely make out the words over the din, but he got the gist. There had been several sightings. All were being followed up.

That's more like it, he thought. Lucifer paid for the champagne and, with the bottle in one hand and two wine flutes in the other, threaded his way precariously through the crowd in search of the group he had followed and the woman he had selected.

So, the evening was turning out a bit old school, but why not? Perhaps he had been letting himself become a little blasé and stale. Maybe it was time to shake things up a bit.

CHAPTER 21 – LOVE HOTEL

The small parking lot in front of the hotel was empty. The automatic doors swished open as Tense and Sally walked up the steps. The foyer was empty too. Not a soul about. This was not the sort of hotel one wanted to be seen in.

They made their way to the check-in machine in the hotel foyer. Tense tabbed past the many and various 'exotic' options on the menu and requested a basic room with a TV, a shower and a double bed. He tapped his credit card on the machine and keyed in his code. A small slip of paper emerged from a slot. It was a combined receipt and set of instructions. The information given was basic: the floor level of the room, room number, door and lift code, Wi-Fi code, and in slightly larger print, 'Checkout by 10 a.m. Excess cleaning and all breakages will be billed to the credit card provided'. That was it.

The couple made their way quickly to their room, relieved that they had not encountered a living, breathing human being at any point. Various muffled sounds emanated from some of the rooms as they walked past. Their door code worked. The door lock clicked open. The room itself was clean and functional. It had one small window which looked out over a disused space at the back of the hotel. In the failing light, Sally could just make out a footpath leading to a gate that opened onto a small, little-used green space full of junk. The only street light visible from the window was broken, its glass cover hanging down. Overall, the effect was forsaken, an abandoned, forgotten handkerchief of land left to the weeds and the destitute. Too small to build on.

Sally shuddered and pulled the curtain closed. It would be fully dark soon, anyway. Tense was checking out the hotel amenities. The TV screen listed the available delights. There were vending machines on each level from which could be had drinks, hygienically sealed food items, various marital aids, underwear, and the usual toiletries. Ice was free, also from another vending machine.

"What more could one ask for?" Tense smiled, turning to Sally as he spoke. Sally did not look happy. At the very best, one would have to say she looked crestfallen.

"What are we going to do, Tense?"

"Go to France. Have a great holiday. Whatever we want."

"He will be looking for us. You know that. He won't give up."

"We can go somewhere he'll never find us. Somewhere remote or somewhere heaving with people."

"For how long?"

"As long as we like."

Sally was unsure if Tense was being deliberately stupid or was genuinely trying to help.

"Tense, please. Lucifer will never stop looking for us until he finds us."

"Yes, I know."

"Then there will be a confrontation."

"Yes."

"I don't know how that will go. I don't know what he is planning." The pitch of Sally's voice rose, becoming shrill, "I don't know whether he plans to use you against me or me against you."

Tense had run out of prevarications and obfuscations, "Well, what do you want to do then?"

"I don't know." Sally was, by now, practically in tears. Her voice broke, "I'm out of my depth. I'm alone on a foreign planet without my powers."

Tense took her in his arms, "You have me and your magic suitcase".

"It's not magic", Sally sniffed, "It's just carefully packed."

The response, given that she had once retrieved a full-sized pair of 'angel' wings from it, may have been a trifle disingenuous. Be that as it may, Sally snuggled into Tense's embrace. Finding comfort in the warmth of his body and the strength of his arms. Sally looked up, catching Tense's eye.

"I'm hungry, but I don't want any of the crap in the vending machines."

"Understood", Tense smiled, "There's a Vietnamese restaurant not too far. I'll go get us a takeaway."

Sally smiled, somewhat mollified, and turned off the TV.

"I think I'll have a bit of a lie-down."

Tense dimmed the lights and closed the door as quietly as he could. He passed no one on the way out. The backstreets near the airport were all but deserted. The occasional taxi raced past, using the narrow streets as a cut-through to the Princes Highway. The restaurant was open and empty. Tense, having no idea what Sally's taste in Vietnamese cuisine extended to, ordered an array of dishes to suit all preferences. He sat watching the TV while he waited for his order. The news was on. Nothing earth-shattering was happening. A government minister was in trouble for some arrogant stupidity or other. Same old, same old. The food came pretty quickly, and he headed back.

While Tense was gone, Sally, unable to sleep, had pottered around the small room, opening and closing drawers and cupboards. Eventually, she pulled back the curtains an inch or two and peered out. There was a tiny glowing red light visible through the chain-link fence that separated the hotel grounds from the empty plot behind. Sally stared at it, trying to figure out what it was. It moved a little now and then, and occasionally, the glow increased. The glow increased again, suddenly illuminating the outline of a man's face. The light was faint. It was impossible to make out any detail. But she was certain. There was a man, alone, standing in the derelict green space, smoking. Hardly anyone smoked any more. It wasn't exactly illegal, but it had become rare. Sally froze. It was as though an iron band had closed around her heart. She felt as though she couldn't breathe. Sweat broke out all over her body. She felt palpitations in her chest.

Tense returned to find Sally crouched in a corner, sobbing quietly.

"What's the matter? What's happened?" Tense eyes flicker around the small room, seeking a threat.

"There's a man watching us from behind the hotel. It's him, I'm sure of it. He's smoking."

Tense squinted through the window. It was fully dark outside. With only the ambient light of the city to see by, it was impossible to make out any detail. There was no sign of anyone.

"No one there now. You are not allowed to smoke on the hotel grounds. It was probably just some guy having a quiet cigarette away from prying eyes."

"Really? There's no one there?" Sally got to her feet and approached the window.

"There's no way he could have tracked us down so soon." Tense squared his shoulders, "We will face him when we have to. Together. But until that time, we are officially on holiday."

Sally eyed the two full bags Tense was carrying.

"I hope you got Mi Quang." Sally pulled out the two-small melamine plates and some cutlery she had discovered in a drawer.

"But of course." And he had, quite by chance, of course.

***

Having tracked the vivacious young woman down to a gaggle of self-referential hipsters clustered in the small beer garden, Lucifer set to work. Following his established practice in these things, he first listened for a few minutes to the vapid conversation passing amongst the preening circle. The vivacious young woman listened too, somewhat engaged but clearly holding back. The chatter of her peers failed to hold her attention. She stepped back a little from the growing throng of young Sydneysiders and glanced around. Her glass was empty. Lucifer caught her eye. With practised ease, he filled a champagne flute. Stepping closer, he offered the young woman the glass.

"Please," Lucifer smiled just a little, "can you help me out? My mother always told me it's a mortal sin to drink alone." The woman hesitated.

"I just flew in today," Lucifer continued, "and I think I've been stood up already."

"By who?"

"Beg pardon?"

"Who stood you up?"

"I am a publisher. I came here to meet a literary agent," Lucifer shrugged. "Something must have come up."

"Why the champagne?"

"A small celebration, the book she brought to me is doing quite well. Surprising, really, its subject matter is gravel and something called aggregate. I would not have thought it would have a ready market." Lucifer smiled again, "We live and learn."

The young woman smiled too and took the proffered glass of champagne. This guy, whatever his angle, was at least a little more worldly and interesting than her usual mob. Lucifer studied her face. She was attractive but not beautiful. Her face was open and unguarded. Her features were even. Her straight brown hair fell to her shoulders. There was something different in the eyes, though, if he was honest. A spark of something. It was with a growing sense of weariness that he acknowledged he had seen countless women's faces over the centuries. He was quite unable to remember all the innumerable women he had associated with. He was becoming bored, he realised. The magic was beginning to wear off. The old resentment was still there, however. The desire for revenge, somehow to strike at the Creator, to cause at least a little inconvenience, still motivated, but not as strongly as once it had. The young woman standing before him was, other than that glint of something deeper, no longer of any interest. She was his for the taking. He couldn't be bothered. His mind turned to Amitiel. She would replenish him.

Lucifer set the champagne bottle down on a small round table, chest height. He drained his glass and set that down too.

"Please, finish the bottle. I must go." And, with an uncharacteristic second glance, he turned on his heel and left the pub. The young woman watched him go. She stood for a moment, then picked up his abandoned glass and the mostly full bottle of champagne. Not so fast, buddy, she thought to herself and made to follow.

Outside, in the relative quiet, Lucifer removed his phone from his pocket and made a call.

"Well." he snapped, revitalising anger welling up from some tender emotional store. The voice on the phone buzzed for a few minutes and fell silent.

"Just fucking find them." Lucifer hung up and swung around. A minor scuffle was taking place behind him by the entrance to the pub. A couple of bouncers were patiently refusing admittance to a very drunk young man. As he glanced past them, he noticed the young woman standing a couple of paces inside the pub. Her inner glow, more apparent now that she was framed in the doorway, seemed to separate her from the common herd. She saw him looking her way and waggled the two empty champagne flutes at him. There was something about this particular young woman. Lucifer had to admit. Every once in a while, a mortal came along who definitely had something. Lucifer re-entered the pub.

"What is aggregate?" The young woman smiled. Lucifer could not tell if she was joking or not.

"Small rocks, I think. I can't say I ever read the book myself."

They finished the bottle. The noise in the pub had reached ear-damaging levels.

"Shall we go somewhere we can talk?" The young woman mouthed something and nodded assent. They took a taxi to the Park Hyatt, across Circular Quay from the Sydney Opera House. Lucifer had a suite with a view of the opera house. He ordered a late supper for them both and, retrieving another bottle of champagne and two glasses from the fridge, led the young woman outside onto the balcony. The worst of the day's heat had dissipated, and the humidity was relatively low for the time of year. The view was magnificent.

It was an open question as to who was seducing whom. The young woman accepted the glass from Lucifer's hand and walked to the edge of the balcony. The almost invisible glass barrier came to chest height. Lucifer held back.

"Afraid of heights?"

"Not exactly. Just cautious. I had a nasty fall once."

"Come," the woman tapped her hip lightly with the flat of her hand, "I'll protect you."

In the presence of this woman, the revivifying anger Lucifer had felt at the thought of Amitiel, still at large and defying him, had dimmed once more to a constant, nagging throb. He liked this young woman. He had to admit. It was distracting. Over the centuries, he had become increasingly task-focused. The advent of this young human was putting him off his stride.

She went to freshen up. Lucifer took the opportunity to make another call. It was equally unsatisfactory. It was as though Sally and Tense had fallen off the face of the Earth. How was that even possible? He had this city tied up tight. Where in God's name could they be hiding?

Small tendrils of doubt began to find their way into his conscious mind. Paranoia, a regular friend and frequent confidant, made its reappearance. Who was this young woman, actually? He believed he had found her, but had he? Was he meant to think that? Was he being played?

Lucifer heard the toilet flush and the air hand-dryer growl. Her appearance and demeanour had changed a little as she stepped back out onto the balcony. There was the slightest predatory gleam in her eye. She was definitely stalking him. While there was something tantalisingly arousing about that, Lucifer's thoughts had taken a darker turn. He moved inside and sat down on one of the lovely Burmese mahogany chairs placed strategically to enjoy the view. It was time to take back control.

Without missing a beat, the young woman walked up to Lucifer and sat herself down on his lap. She turned slightly, lifting her long dark hair out of the way. Presenting the smooth line of her neck and shoulder. Lucifer's anger flared for a moment, triggered involuntarily. Somehow it was still she who was making the running. Revulsion with the human species and with himself tussled with the physical desire coming from his body. *I have spent too long in the flesh*, he realised. *I need to take a break from embodiment.*

But for now, the sins of the flesh won out. The woman was confident, and despite his earlier rather cool assessment, she did possess a subtle beauty. Lucifer allowed his anger and his bile to subside. Her body was lithe and supple in his lap. He leaned forward a little and kissed the back of her neck. This was becoming habitual. It was time he started doing things differently. Despite his doubts, he found himself enjoying the silky smoothness of her skin. He enjoyed the warmth of her breath on his cheek.

To his surprise, thoughts of Amitiel forced their way again into the forefront of his mind. As the young woman he had sitting on his lap leaned against him, images of Amitiel interposed themselves. Thoughts of Sally with Tense, images of them together, flickered across the field of Lucifer's imagination. He was jealous, he realised. Shocked and once again enraged that he had somehow succumbed to such a crass human emotion, Lucifer lifted the young woman roughly off his knee and carried her through to the master bedroom.

I am in control in my own mind, he growled to himself, *I am Lucifer, Bringer of Light, and I will not allow the brute instincts of the flesh to influence me.* And yet, the cool sheets of his king-size bed beckoned.

***

The Mi Quang was excellent. Scoffing down the veritable feast that Tense had brought back to the tiny hotel room eased the tensions of the day. With Sally safely immersed in Vietnamese cuisine, Tense was able to relax. When he was quite sure that Sally had eaten her fill, he collected the slew of containers back into their carrier bags and took them to the garbage chute down the hallway. On his way back to the room, he glanced out of a window over the wasteland at the rear of the hotel. The little red spark was back. Best not to say anything to Sally.

Sally was in the shower when Tense returned. He switched on the TV to watch the late news. Various crises were unfolding at home and overseas. Politicians, both local and international, were engaging in arrogant stupidity and sexual indiscretions, much as they had always done. There seemed to be no imminent risk of global or regional war, which was pleasing. All in all, things were bumbling along satisfactorily. The image of the little red spark moving slowly in the darkness stayed with him, unwilling to subside.

Sally emerged from the shower, swathed in an enormous fluffy white towel. Billows of steam accompanied her. She was relaxed, smiling, glowing with vibrant health. Tense was besotted all over again. He found a chilled bottle of New Zealand Sauvignon Blanc in the fridge and poured them each a glass. His phone pinged, and a text message told him he had been billed for the wine. For once, the soulless efficiency of his age came as a blessing. Their anonymity was preserved. They remained incognito, or so he fervently hoped.

Almost immediately, there came a loud banging and shouts from down the hallway. Tense flipped the security lock on the door. Sally pulled the voluminous towel tightly around herself and stared at the door. Both listened intently to the fracas outside. Individual voices separated themselves out from the general clamour.

"I'm not paying for that, you stupid bitch."

"My boss is waiting outside, arsehole. You can argue with him."

"Fuck you."

"Or not. Mr Floppy."

The lift pinged its arrival, and the swish of the doors announced the gentleman's departure.

The woman's voice spoke again, "He's coming down now. He didn't pay."

There was a moment's silence, then, "He couldn't get it up."

Another moment of silence, then "Of course I tried that. I tried everything."

Another silence, and "Well, you've never complained." The lift pinged again. The doors swished, and silence returned.

"You take me to all the best places, my love", Sally giggled.

Tense blushed a deep red, almost purple.

"You sure know how to treat a girl."

Tense grabbed the giggling angel, swathed in a bath towel, lifted her, and laid her gently on the bed.

"You take that back", he demanded.

"Make me." Sally's giggles fell silent as Tense turned out the overhead light.

Even with the light out, the room was not fully dark. There was a tiny green glow coming from the smoke alarm in the ceiling, and a thin bar of yellow light seeped in under the door. Tense undressed slowly, his eyes adjusting to the gloom. The hotel was quiet now. Small, distant noises squeezed around the double glazing, evidencing the world outside. He climbed into bed carefully. Not wishing to disturb Sally. For all her impish bravado, Sally was drifting off. It had been one hell of a day, one hell of a week, really. As Sally snuggled, Tense thought back over recent events. Had it only been six days since they had met? It seemed longer. It seemed like a lifetime. His old life receded in his memory, like a scene viewed through the wrong end of a telescope. Tiny, perfect and far, far away.

Tense lay there, trying to piece things together, trying to stitch the episodic narrative from past Tense to present Tense into a contiguous rational whole. His mind opened to possibilities he had never previously considered. These were not probabilities. He was not attempting to calculate the likelihood of recent events. That course of action had lost all purpose and meaning days ago. No, Tense lay there wondering what possibilities lay ahead. He was amazed not so much that he had met and fallen in love with the most amazing angel woman but that he had found love at all. All bets were off, it seemed. Who knew what miracles the future might hold? Tense found himself in unexpectedly optimistic mood.

Beside him, Sally stirred in her sleep. Some disturbance clouded her dreams. Outside, in the hallway, someone walked past the room. The yellow bar under the door flickered for a moment as their footsteps occluded the light. Tense lay still, hardly daring to breathe. The footsteps moved on without slowing. Sally snuggled closer. Tense fell asleep, too, eventually.

He awoke, sometime later, disoriented, startled by something that had troubled his sleep. The grey light of dawn leached into the room past the window blind. Sally wriggled and writhed beside him. She was speaking in her sleep. Tense could not place the language, but there was one word he could figure out, 'Diabolus'. Tense heard slow footsteps in the hallway outside. He froze as they approached. Holding his breath. Praying that Sally would not speak.

The footsteps continued past. The light under the door flickered for a moment. The walker moved beyond earshot. Tense leapt from the bed and, grabbing a towel from the shower room, squashed it down by the door, blocking out the light.

Sally woke with a start as he got back into bed.

"What's up? What's happened?"

"Nothing. I just blocked out the light from under the door. It's worse than Martin's Place in the rush hour. People keep stomping past."

Sally sat up, fully awake. There was something in Tense's tone she did not like. She stood, stretching. Tense followed suit.

"I had troubled dreams." Sally wished she could still read Tense's thoughts.

"I know. I heard you talking. I couldn't place the language."

"Sorry if I disturbed you."

"No. Not at all. I did make out one word, though."

"What was that?"

"Diabolus"

The footsteps in the hallway returned. They were moving more quickly this time. Purposefully. The sound increased as the walker approached and then faded away down the corridor.

Sally gave out a heavy sigh of relief. Tense wrapped an arm around her, pulling her close. The footsteps returned. Moving more slowly this time. And there was another sound. Someone was sniffing and snuffling outside their door.

The sniffing sound continued. Followed by a very light scraping and scratching, as though someone was feeling the surface rather than attacking it. Sally and Tense, frozen in horror, simply stood and stared at the door. After a moment, someone spoke.

"I know you're in there. Open the door."

Neither Sally nor Tense moved a muscle.

Someone tapped on the door, gently at first, then harder.

"Open up. I'm not leaving until you do."

Still, neither Tense nor Sally moved.

"Come on, Stevo, open the bloody door, mate."

Tense took a step towards the door, but Sally reached out and grabbed his arm, holding him back.

"Stevo, for fuck's sake, man. I've got the money. I just need a hit."

Tense assumed that, despite the visual evidence to the contrary, there would be some human being secreted about the hotel somewhere to keep order. He did not want to be evicted in the middle of the night on suspicion of being a drug dealer. Tense signalled Sally to step out of the line of sight and walked over to the door.

The banging on the door started up again. Louder this time. Tense opened the door. A dishevelled man in heavily stained dark blue cotton work clothes and a bright orange fluoro vest stood blinking in the doorway.

"I think you've got the wrong room, mate. There's no Stevo here."

The man in the fluoro vest continued blinking for a moment or two longer.

Then, "Sorry, Bro, wrong room, ay?" Fluoro guy wandered off down the corridor, ostensibly counting room numbers. Tense closed the door before slumping down on a small uncomfortable plastic chair in front of a large mirror.

"I'm too old for this shit. My heart can't take it."

Sally came and sat on his knee, her arms around his neck.

"There is really no way anyone can know where we are. We both know that."

"The guilty flee when no man pursueth, but the righteous are as bold as a lion." Tense attempted a smile, but the strain of being hunted was beginning to show, "I think it's in the bible."

"Well then," Sally fixed him with a steely eye, "we are not guilty, so we will just have to be as bold as lions, won't we?"

"We will, of course." Tense wrapped his arms around Sally and kissed her, "But right now, I am going to have to ask you to move. I am afraid I may lose the use of my legs."

"Rude!"

"No. It's not you. It's the chair. It's not made to be sat on. Certainly not by two people at once."

Sally stood and walked over to the bed. Retaining as much dignity as she could under the circumstances. She began to dress for the day.

"It'll be breakfast time soon."

"It's just after five in the morning."

"Yes."

"Well, we only just had dinner."

"That was hours ago."

Tense gave up.

"I suppose I could do with a coffee. Shall I investigate the hotel's magnificent array of vending machines?"

"Yes, please. Two sugars."

Sally pulled on her jeans and packed a couple of items back into her suitcase. As Tense left, she walked over to the window and drew back the blind. There was no one in the overgrown area behind the chain-link fence. The sun was rising, though, unbearably bright against a pure blue sky. Not a cloud to be seen. It was going to be another hot one.

While Tense was gone, Sally got to thinking. What were they actually running from? Was there really any point to it? Fleeing, as Tense had put it, was a human reaction. Instinctual. Of the flesh. No angel had ever fled. Even Lucifer had been forcibly cast down. He hadn't fled. If nothing else, it was undignified. What could Lucifer do with them, practically speaking, to aid his cause? If her mortal body were to die, she would return to being an angel with all her powers. That wouldn't help him, and Tense would be very upset. Even if Tense were to die, she would meet him again in the merest blink of an eye. Nevertheless, some sixth sense suggested that it would be best to avoid Lucifer. Since when had that not been the case?

After they had coffee and something appalling to eat from the vending machine, she would sit down with Tense and plan out the day. If Lucifer and his goons turned up, they turned up. She would face them then. In the meantime, her mind made up, Sally turned on the TV. A South American soap was on. Poorly translated subtitles expressed the heartbreak and ecstasy of the characters. Even in her current circumstances, life certainly looked a lot more exciting over there, wherever there was exactly.

Tense returned with a selection of delicacies wrapped in bio-degradable cardboard. He laid out an array of unhappy-looking sandwiches and a bewildering variety of biscuits and crackers accompanied by a variety of cheese and salsa dips. He set down two large paper cups of coffee in a little disposable tray.

"Flat white with two sugars for madame." Tense passed Sally one of the cups. The slogan printed on the side in some mock horror script said Coffee on the Run. Inspiring. Surprisingly the coffee was pretty good. Hot and sweet and strong. Sally didn't suppose the denizens of this particular hotel were the sort to order weak coffee.

Once they had choked down a sandwich, swilled down with anaesthetising coffee (its true purpose finally revealed), Sally began to speak.

"Tense, my love, we cannot run forever, but I'm not sure what else we can do. I can't know for sure, but I am pretty certain my mission was not to open a second front on Earth against Lucifer and the demon hordes. What I most want is for us to have a great day out in Sydney today and then fly to Paris tonight. If Lucifer turns up, he turns up. I am not afraid. After all, what's the worst he can do to us?"

This was a topic that Tense had been wanting to raise, but he had not yet found an opportune moment. Sally just didn't seem to get that she and Sheila were mortal. All three of them were. He hesitated before counting possibilities off on his fingers.

"One, Kill us. Two, drag you off to some secret location and pump you full of drugs. Three, torture us. Four..." but Sally cut in.

"Ok, we have a problem, I get it, but we don't seem to have a way out."

"No."

"Well, I'm not used to that." Sally thought for a moment.

"We're in big trouble, aren't we?"

"Possibly. Best we stay out of sight, just in case."

"What shall we do? Where shall we go?"

Tense smiled. He knew just the place.

"Wollongong - when in doubt. Lucifer would never look for us there. I'm not sure anyone would. And it's on the train from Wolli Creek."

***

Sally and Tense packed up the very few loose items that were still lying about, put their rubbish in the undersized wastepaper basket, and stood hesitantly by the hotel room door. This was it. They both felt the same. Somehow, this was a pivotal moment. Once they stepped through that door, they were committed. But committed to what exactly? They had only a powerful sense of unease to guide them. Neither moved. A car backfired on the nearby highway. Both jumped.

"Fuck it. Here goes nothing." Sally reached over, yanked open the door and stepped through, lugging her suitcase behind. Tense followed, quick smart. Sally was already waiting at the lift by the time the hotel room door closed. Tense popped the 'Do Not Disturb' sign on the handle and quickly followed.

They left the hotel by the rear exit into the car park. The gate in the chain-link fence squealed as Tense wrenched it open and led the way across the small patch of wasteland towards the backstreet behind the hotel. There was no one about it. The little overgrown patch of dirt was littered with broken glass, syringes and other debris left by the detritus of humanity. The gate slamming behind them interrupted the dawn chorus. Angry butcher birds, startled by this sudden intrusion, squawked and chirruped their disapproval. Tense and Sally hurried down a narrow path between two large industrial sheds and out onto the Princes Highway. Even at this early hour, it was busy. The hissing of truck brakes and the beeping of car horns greeted the dawn with an alternative, urban chorus.

The sun was rising in the east. Sally and Tense cast elongated shadows across the road as they headed towards the railway station. The day was already warm but not yet hot.

"Must we walk so fast?" Tense glanced around. Sally had fallen back a little way.

"Needs must when the devil drives." Tense's attempt at humour bombed. Sally scowled back at him. Tense slowed a bit, and Sally, huffing and puffing, caught up.

"I don't like gallows humour. I never have. Just so you know."

"Sorry, we're both a bit tense, I guess."

"You, doubly so, I imagine." Sally was obviously pleased at the pun.

"I wish I had a dollar for every…" Tense, let it drop. What was the point?

By the time they arrived at Wolli Creek station, they were both hot and sweaty and more than a little out of sorts. Sally insisted on taking the lift to the downline platform. Tense checked the train times on his phone.

"Next Wollongong train in is in ten minutes. Let's walk along the platform a bit."

Tense found a spot behind the lift, next to two large vending machines, where they would look less conspicuous. Sally fidgeted nervously. Tense tapped his foot arrhythmically. Sally tried to ignore it and failed.

"Stop that annoying tapping." She hissed.

"Oh, sorry." Tense stopped tapping. Sally perused the contents of the vending machines. One never knew. They were both startled by the very loud announcement of the imminent arrival of the next train to Sydney Central Terminus. The train hissed into the station. People got on and off. There was a cuffuffle at the bottom of the stairs. A woman with a pushchair was insisting on carrying it up, complete with screaming toddler. Eventually, someone helped. The noise and disturbance abated.

Tense decided to take a look up and down the platform. He had resumed drumming his fingers against the side of the vending machine. Sally was happy to let him go.

He went. He came back. Nothing to report. They were both startled a second time by the overly loud announcement of the imminent arrival of the Cronulla train. Out of the corner of his eye, Tense thought he saw the familiar shape of a young man entering the lift serving the opposite platform.

Perhaps he had the gain on his antenna turned up too high. Perhaps he was just a bit jittery. Be that as it may, Tense changed plans. This was not an easy thing for him to do, but he did it anyway.

"It will be about an hour and a half until we get to Wollongong." Sally looked away from the vending machines. There was something in his voice that gained her attention.

"We could be in Cronulla in a bit over half an hour, and the beaches there are fantastic." Sally nodded.

"Well, why don't we jump on this train? We can be swimming that bit sooner?" Tense indicated the arriving train with one hand.

"Suits me." Sally grabbed her suitcase as the train pulled in and stepped into the airconditioned carriage.

"Oh, that's better." Sally plonked herself down. The interior of the train was cool and quiet. There were very few other passengers. Sally studied the rail map.

"Eighteen stops. That's going to take a while."

"It's probably around forty minutes. But still a lot less travelling time."

Tense glanced surreptitiously out of the window towards the up-line platform opposite. He was hoping Sally wouldn't notice.

"What are you staring at?" Sally leaned over to look too.

"Oh, nothing." Tense leaned back, putting his arm around Sally, encouraging her to lean back too.

The doors closed, and the train began to move. It juddered once before chugging smoothly out of the station. At the last moment, Tense spotted a clean-shaven young man in a beautifully cut formal mid-grey suit, black t-shirt and black, very shiny patent leather shoes, standing at the end of the opposite platform, looking back. Sally saw the man, too and leaned over to get a better look.

"Shit. The Devil really does wear Prada."

As the train drew level with the man on the opposite platform, he happened to glance their way. Tense found himself, for the briefest instant, staring directly into the clean-shaven young man's eyes. It was Lucifer, of course. He smiled, and as the train pulled out of the station, he pulled out his phone and began to speak.

***

"Lucifer will have to check out eighteen stations and suburbs between the city and the beach. That's going to stretch anyone's resources." Sally was looking pensive, and Tense was trying to cheer her up. She looked up and smiled.

"That's sweet of you, but in truth, I am not fearful of Lucifer. At least not for myself."

"What then?"

"I am afraid he may try to get at me through you. Maybe you should make yourself scarce."

"What? And leave you alone, you mean? No chance." Tense had the look of a ten-year-old who had just been told he couldn't go on the school trip he had been saving up for.

"Maybe we should separate. Just for a little while."

"No. Impossible. I won't go. I can't."

"It makes sense, Tense. You know it does."

"No."

"He can't really do anything to me. We know it, and he knows it."

"Do we?"

Sally let that pass, "But he can hurt you. He is a past master at inflicting pain."

"I can't leave you, Sally. I can't. I don't know how to."

Sally leaned back in the seat as the train trundled into the next station and groaned to a stop. The doors opened. No one entered or left their carriage.

"Thank you, Tense. I'm glad you said that. I'm glad you are staying. I just had to know."

Tense had been standing, the tension of their previous conversation having driven him to his feet. Now he sat down next to Sally and wrapped his arms around her.

"Still, he must have leverage or think he has. It's driving me crazy wondering what he's planning."

Sally fell silent. Together they watched the urban and suburban landscape flow by. Mid-rise developments near the stations gave way to low-rise, higgledy-piggledy patchworks of houses and green reserves decked out for cricket at this time of year. Every now and then, a taller building pierced the skyline, anomalous, a sudden upsurge of architectural ordinariness against an already ordinary backdrop.

After what seemed like hours, the train approached Cronulla. The peninsula disappeared into the distance ahead, and the broad open beach stretched for kilometres to the left. To the right, there was a narrow bay full of little boats at anchor. Sally smiled. Even from the train, the scene was idyllic. She dared to hope – maybe they would be safe here for a little while. Tense led them both away from the main beach.

"I know somewhere better. It's just around the corner from the main drag, along the walking track. It's called Shelly Beach. It's less well-known than the main beach. A lot quieter and no crazy big waves."

As they rounded a corner and Shelly Beach came into view, Sally spotted a café. It was just opening.

"Breakfast", she announced, picking up the pace. Tense had to admire her focus. Sally was in expansive mood. The café was a cornucopia of earthly delight after the vending machines at the hotel. She sat down and began to peruse the menu. Tense walked over to the counter and ordered two coffees. Sally might be a while. The coffees arrived, and Sally began to order breakfast.

"I'm pregnant", Sally proclaimed without further explanation and continued ordering.

"Anything for you, sir?"

"I'll probably just share."

After the waitress had taken her order, Tense began to speak.

"Sally, you are a human woman now, for the duration."

"Yes."

"So, you are as vulnerable as any other human being, right?"

"I suppose so."

"Well, then Lucifer can do anything to you that he can do to me."

This seemed to be an entirely new thought for Sally.

"Oh."

Tense waited for Sally to process what he had said.

"Sally, we have to assume that Lucifer had a plan for what he would do with you if he had managed to get you into his ambulance.

He must have somewhere prepared to take you, and he must have a plan for what he would do once he got you there."

"Oh"

Tense spelled it out.

"Finding you in human form must have been a Godsend for him. He knows how to subvert and warp human beings. He plans to subvert and corrupt you too. We can be sure of that, if nothing else."

"Yes, I see. That's not an easy thought for the angel part of me to get its head around."

"No, I suppose not."

A van pulled up sharply outside the café. Two men jumped out. Both Sally and Tense gave a start. But it was just the day's delivery from a nearby bakery. Tense checked his watch. It was still only half past seven in the morning. It was going to be a long day.

"You are hostage to your body, and the flesh is weak."

"Yes, I get it." Sally snapped. Tense had made his point. The waitress brought their breakfast. It took a couple of trips. Sally brightened. She mulled the problem over while they ate. Her coffee went cold, and she ordered another. The morning wore slowly on.

"Ok. I have a few advantages that a mortal does not have." Sally began to list them.

"I have the knowledge and memories of an angel. Also, I know that I am an angel, with all that that entails. I know that my time on earth is extremely limited. And I know that Lucifer no longer has all his powers. He is limited too." Sally looked up. "By angel standards, I mean." Tense nodded. He was frustrated that Sally was still not thinking through the reality of her situation. She seemed still to be assuming it would magically all soon be over.

"A lifetime is quite a long time by human standards. There's plenty of time for despair and regret."

"Goodness, you're a bit happy-go-lucky this morning, aren't you?" The waitress had chosen that moment to check that they had everything they wanted. Sally smiled.

"Yes, he's a bundle of joy this morning. Do you have any of those takeaway boxes? We'll have to finish the rest on the beach." Tense surveyed the table. It was surprising how much of an impact Sally had made. Nevertheless, there remained the makings of a pretty good picnic. The waitress went to find some boxes. Tense continued his line of reasoning.

"I think you are right. Lucifer plans to use me against you, just like you said. He will use anyone you care about against you." Tense paused, waiting to see if Sally had followed his train of thought to its inevitable destination. He couldn't be sure.

"He must never find out about the baby. He must never find out about Sheila." The name still made him grimace.

"You have to stop announcing to all and sundry that you are pregnant."

Sally finished the mouthful she was working on.

"The truth is Tense; humans do not simply have lives. You are life. We are all, angels included, just part of life itself. There is just one life. One mind that saturates everything. One essence that takes transient form in order to experience itself."

"I'm pretty sure that's not in the bible."

"Whose Bible? Which version? It's been messed about with so much over the centuries. Every translator and every second Pope seems to have had a go at it."

"Lucifer, and his little friends, they're an essential part of the plan too, I suppose?"

"Yes. They are part of the overall plan too." And then, in an instant, all time for idle chit-chat was used up.

There came a screeching of tyres. The peace of the quiet hamlet obliterated in a moment. Several long black limousines pulled up outside the café. Mean-looking men in black suits and sunglasses jumped out. Last of all, a slim young man, clean-shaven, in a mid-grey suit and impressively shiny shoes, stepped out. He walked up to the café, leaned against the window, and shading his eyes against the reflection of the sunlit beach and gentle waves across the way, stared inside.

Lucifer sauntered in, a single ding from the tiny doorbell announcing his arrival.

CHAPTER 23 – LUCIFER MAKES HIS PITCH.

Lucifer paused for a moment, taking in the scene. Noting the three occupants of the café, observing the cluttered breakfast table and the pile of plastic boxes. Lucifer approached the table and sat down. His men remained outside. Then, turning to the waitress, "Coffee, please, black as sin." He smiled.

"Just my little joke." Aiming his comments at Sally, he continued, "I'm not here for a fight. I know I cannot overawe or overpower you."

"What then?" Despite her better nature, Sally found herself intrigued. Lucifer pulled up his chair closer to Sally, subtly excluding Tense. The grownups are having a talk, the gesture said. Sally let it pass. Calmly, logically and in smooth, even tones, Lucifer began to lay out his stall.

"You are Sally, a human woman, but you are also Amitiel, Angel of Truth." Lucifer paused. Sally waited.

"Do you agree?"

"Yes."

"But you still have your truth sense, do you not? All the hosts of Heaven know that if you say something is true, then it is true. Full stop. No argument."

"Correct. If you lie to me, I will know it immediately."

"Good."

"Good?"

"Yes. I am relying on that. I want to explain myself to you fully. I want you to parse and accept or reject every single thing I say. You can do that, I assume?"

"Yes, of course. You know perfectly well I can." Sally knew she was being positioned. She could feel the jaws of the trap being set, but apart from simply refusing to listen to him, she could not think of a way to avoid it. Tense had a point. What was he planning for her and for

Tense? What would he do if he found out about the baby? She desperately wanted to know what the bastard was up to this time.

"Excellent. Then let me start by setting out what I think we can agree on. Our common ground, as it were. Just what we both already know. Is that ok?"

"Ok. Sure, but get on with it. We want to go to the beach." The coffee arrived. The waitress set it down silently and scuttled off to the kitchen. Lucifer took a sip, set the little cup back down in its saucer and continued.

"There is, at the very heart of my opposition to the will of our mutual creator, a contradiction. There is a logical flaw, an antinomy...."

"What's an antinomy?" The question just blurted itself out. Tense looked abashed.

Lucifer graced Tense with a disdainful glance, "A contradiction in terms, a self-contradiction or inconsistency. An incongruity, anomaly, conflict, absurdity, oddity or enigma. A puzzle. A mystery. A conundrum. Got it?" Tense shrank away. Humiliated, stuffed unceremoniously back into his box, he merely fumed. And fantasised about stabbing the smug bastard with his fork. Sally looked away. Lucifer kept going.

"I am opposing the word of God, the all-powerful, the omniscient. That I do so is part of the Divine plan. It is, therefore, God's will that I do it. It is God's will that I defy his word. The will and the word are, therefore, at least implicitly, different." Lucifer paused. This was the critical moment. Sally had to take the next step herself, willingly, with no pressure.

"Do you agree?" Lucifer held his breath. Sally took her time. She could see no logical inconsistency in what he was saying. She could sense no lie.

"Yes, we have all wondered about that from time to time."

Tense, still stinging from Lucifer's previous humiliation, did not speak. There was something wrong with Lucifer's logic. He could feel it. It was not a lie precisely, but Lucifer's take on it somehow introduced a kind of loophole. Perhaps it would become clear later. He would wait and see.

Lucifer breathed out slowly, calming himself. The trap had been laid. She had taken the bait.

"Our creator wishes me and my fellow rebels to rebel, even if he says he doesn't. That follows, yes?"

"I'm not sure. Well, yes, I suppose so."

"My belief is that our opposition, opposition itself, feeds the vortex that drives change. Without opposition, there can be no exploration of compliance, loyalty, fidelity and so on. Without evil, there can be no deep understanding of good. Our opposition serves an essential purpose in God's plan. Without falsehood, without lies, there can be no appreciation of truth. Do you agree?"

Sally paused, she wasn't sure she did, but she couldn't see why she wouldn't. Lucifer continued, gently, cajoling.

"If there were only truth and nothing else, all speech would be mere description. Without error, there can be no learning. We have all been created capable of learning and growing, have we not?"

"Yes. I think that is true."

"Then learning and growing are not bad?"

"No."

"Then that which makes learning and growth possible, that is error itself. Though it is wrong, nevertheless, it is right. Yes?"

"Yes. I suppose so." It was maddening. One part of her, the knowing part, knew perfectly well she was being suckered, but the other part, the understanding part, could see no obvious flaw in Lucifer's argument. There was an important distinction there somewhere, but she just couldn't get hold of it.

"For us all to learn and grow, the immortals, I mean, whether you agree with our stance or not, whether you join us or not, you need to understand that we too are serving God's will. You can see that, can't you?"

"Yes."

"Sally, Amitiel, may I ask you to think back to that amazing, wonderful first day of our creation. Recall our wonder and amazement and joy at being, at simply experiencing and witnessing the universe. Remember how we were together, you and I."

Sally smiled, recalling that first moment when all the world was new.

"Yes." Still smiling at the memory.

"How have we changed, the angels? Have we grown at all? Have we evolved?"

Sally thought about it. It was true. They hadn't, not at all. The angel folk were today, other than the fallen, pretty much exactly as they had always been. Indeed, they had prided themselves on that. They were as constant as the northern star, more so in fact since they had witnessed its creation.

Tense watched as Sally quietly recalled the eons of her long life. Though he wanted to speak, though he wanted to cry out in opposition to this smooth-talking devil, he remained silent. Who had he been kidding? He was nothing to Amitiel really, a passing fancy, no more than that.

"We have not changed. What you say is true. We have not grown."

"And what of the humans?" Lucifer favoured Tense with a patronising smile, "Just think how they have grown and changed. Just think how they have evolved."

"Yes."

"That growth, that evolution was driven by conflict, and danger and war, was it not?"

"Yes."

"It was driven, if not mostly, then in considerable part, by ideas the fallen supplied. Was it not?"

"It was."

"So, we, the fallen, are fulfilling God's will."

"Yes."

Tense felt the bile rise in his throat. He felt nauseous. He wanted to be sick. He was going to be sick. Retching, he ran to the restrooms at the back of the café.

"So then," Lucifer continued, "I do not ask you to join me, though as you know, I dream of nothing else but renewing our partnership. I ask you only to acknowledge what you have just, yourself, said. That the fallen are doing God's work. That angels need to grow and evolve. And that is God's purpose for us. I am asking you to proclaim it for all to hear." Tense returned to stillness. Past and future were poised, in balance for one brief moment, as Sally came to her decision.

"No." There was no anger in her voice, no rancour.

"No?" Lucifer almost whispered, "What do you mean, no? You just said you agreed with every word."

"Yes."

"Then what? How?"

"There is a difference between the word and the will. You said so yourself. Logical reasoning provides a basis for understanding in the absence of spontaneous knowledge, but it does not supplant it. Reason, in the absence of emotion and values, is barren. Decisions made on the basis of pure reason, in the absence of emotion and values, are the weaker for it."

"You are condemning your compatriots to an eternity of pointlessness." Lucifer fairly spat out the words.

"Setting all reason and logic aside, I know, with complete inner certainty, that I will never take your side, the side of the fallen Angel against his creator."

And then, to his own absolute horror, Tense spoke. It fell to him, a mortal man, to send Lucifer on his way. Not Sally or Amitiel, but an ordinary man armed with truth.

"Love is not the soporific intended to opiate the masses I had always thought it was. The call to love is not a call to peace. It is a call to action. It is a call to arms. Love truly understood is not passive. Neither is it aggressive. Love is the implacable, selfless, empathetic pressure against error. You are wrong, Lucifer, Morning Star, but you were right about one thing. I can see it now. You were placed on earth to learn and perhaps to repent. Mortality is not weakness. It is strength. For us, life is an opportunity to transcend, to find one's true self in selflessness and love. I do not fear you. Not anymore. I do not pity you either." Lucifer stared in horror.

His flawless plan had failed.

***

Lucifer stood, straightened his jacket and began to walk towards the door. He stopped after a few paces and turned. "By denying your own truth, you are condemning your compatriots to an eternity of servitude. You are committing the sin of omission, and you are denying our creator's will." Sally held his eye. A battle of words served no purpose with Lucifer.

Then Lucifer turned his attention to Tense, "You presume to lecture me. You blip. You insignificant flicker. You have not the slightest idea what I am capable of. Your small mind cannot encompass the loyalty and devotion I have freely given. You cannot know the fire and fury of my rebellion." And turning once again to Sally, "You cannot know the constancy and depth of my love." Tense, struggling to maintain his composure in the face of a direct onslaught from Lucifer himself, remained calm and managed, against all expectation, to hold his ground.

"This is not over." Lucifer wrenched open the door, "Nothing is over until I say it is." And then he was gone. Time seemed to stop for a moment. The café was silent. Sally and Tense watched the men outside climb back into their vehicles and drive off. A moment later, the waitress reappeared. From the kitchen doorway, she called out, "Will that be all then?"

Sally turned to her, "Oh, don't mind him. He can be a bit of a grump."

Sally paid the bill. She and Tense collected up their breakfast left-overs and walked from the cool of the café into the heat of the day. Desperate to push thought and fear away, just for a little while. Desperate to extort a few more moments of happiness with Tense from this mortal life, Sally headed for the beach.

"Let's go for a swim," Sally squared her shoulders, "It's a lovely day."

Tense followed glumly behind. His arms full of boxes of leftovers. Sally found them a spot under the shade of an old gum tree, a little way from the water's edge. There was no surf. Small ripples played gently across the wet sand. Tense had to agree if one could set aside the imminent presence of the hordes of hell, the day was damned near perfect. However, this was not something he found at all easy to accomplish after his recent confrontation with Lucifer. Tense found himself searching for the flaw in Lucifer's argument. Was there perhaps some deeper law that bound both God and Lucifer? Was the Creator constrained to create within certain parameters? It would only be necessary to understand truth when counterposed with error, or goodness in relation to evil, if either God chose that to be so, or else if God had no choice and was himself constrained by a deeper logic. Tense, having focussed more on analytics and logic than either theology or metaphysics, foundered. Sally, oblivious to the deep contemplations taking place beneath Tense's placid exterior, plonked her beach bag down on the sand and began to arrange an array of suitcases, bags and towels in the manner she deemed most suitable. Their suitcases stood sentinel at the head of each beach towel, like tombstones. Sally slipped off her dress, revealing her swimsuit beneath. Tense began to undress too. Sally took a few nonchalant paces towards the water.

"Right," Sally cast a backwards glance at Tense. "Last one in's a billy goat." And began racing across the sand with Tense, outraged at the sneaky ruse, in hot pursuit. Sally hit the water first and, this time did not hesitate but dived gracefully beneath the smooth, shimmering surface. Tense threw off his t-shirt and ran after her. Hitting the water a few seconds behind her, he dived too and swam hard beneath the surface, rising in front of her. Blocking her progress.

"Jezebel," he cried, in mock rage, "deceiver, trickster." And picking her up in both arms, he lifted Sally above the surface for a moment before throwing her into deeper water. Sally landed with a splash and sank before regaining her feet and splashing furiously in his direction.

"Thug. Abuser. Wife beater." She cried out before diving beneath the waves, grabbing Tense by the ankles and tipping him unceremoniously backwards. Sudden, febrile joy, fed by underlying dread, took hold of them both. Sally swam away as fast as she could, with Tense giving chase and gaining fast. Her nascent swimming skills proved no match for Tense's experienced strokes. Soon he had caught up with her and had once again firmly wrapped her in his arms. They were both laughing uncontrollably. Somehow the tension and terror of the last few minutes had been, if not entirely set aside, then at least, and for a little while, sublimated. Both Sally and Tense were completely immersed in the moment. Absorbed in the present. Engrossed in the here and now. Tense sensed once again the flash of creation. Instant by instant.

"A blip. A flicker. That's what Lucifer called me. And he was correct in that. That is all any of us are. Transiently real, surfing the flash of creation in its endless headlong rush into the future."

"Shut up, Tense. This is where you kiss me, and we canoodle on the beach."

"Oh yes. Sorry. Just thinking out loud."

Emerging dripping and happy from the water, Tense and Sally flopped down on their towels in the shade of the old gum tree and contemplated the world. Despite the very real threats that they faced, they were both unexpectedly optimistic, almost buoyant. They had faced down Lucifer in person. They had not succumbed to his will or been taken in by his argument. It would be wishful thinking to suppose that he was now done with them. Undoubtedly, he would be back. Undoubtedly, he would try again. That was his nature. He could no more retire from the field of battle than compose an ode to his creator. A shadow passed across the sun. High in the cloudless sky, a Sea Eagle performed slow circles against an infinite blue backdrop. Far below, two tiny specks of humanity lay on a beach, pondering their future.

Eventually, after an extended period of general messing about, it was time for Sally and Tense to get going. Tense searched the landscape for any sign of Lucifer's cronies. There was a young woman pushing a buggy who glanced momentarily in their direction. Behind the glass window of the café, someone was peering out. It was impossible to say. The scene suggested extraordinary tranquillity and peace. Both logic and intuition said otherwise. With luck, they would be in Paris tomorrow. Lucifer would never be far behind. Tense and Sally packed up their stuff and headed for the airport. The press of humanity, once so familiar and comforting, was now increasingly disconcerting, even threatening.

They were not being followed as far as they could tell.

***

Lucifer sat in the back of a long, sleek, airconditioned limousine and seethed. His logic had been faultless, his presentation had been persuasive, and every bloody word rang true. Worst of all, he was certain he was right. That he and his followers were fulfilling their creator's plan, they were obediently fulfilling God's will. How could she refuse? How could she deny? It was impossible. The Angel of Truth could not deny the truth. That would be to deny her true nature. At the back of his mind, a tiny voice cried out a warning, one he did not hear, one he had never been able to hear. Rage drove him. He would have his revenge. He had given Amitiel every opportunity to fulfil her true destiny. He had been more than fair. Now she would pay.

And that pathetic, presumptuous little human. How dare he speak with such impudence. He would be crushed and broken, begging for mercy. She would see him for what he really was, a pathetic, grovelling mortal. Lucifer was not in a good mood.

During the long drive back into Sydney, Lucifer made his plans and laid his snare. By the time he arrived at Circular Quay, his entire operation was once again in motion. Even second and third-level associates were pressed into service. His people began to take their positions at key points across the city. There would be no escape this time. Feeling more relaxed, the anticipation of final victory spreading a calming balm on this most frustrating of days, Lucifer made his way back to his favourite haunt. The Opera Bar was already busy with lunchtime revellers enjoying the spectacular view.

Lucifer brooded. Humanity teemed around him. Swarms of vapid, prideful, hedonistic primates churned and frothed. If it were not for the Creator's interest in them, Lucifer doubted he would ever have bothered with this noisome fauna at all. His own kind were another matter. The angels needed leadership, and he was their natural leader. How was it that Amitiel could refuse? Where was the flaw in his reasoning? Maybe he was wrong about her. Maybe when she lost the majority of her powers, she lost her truth sense too. But that seemed even more unlikely. One cannot lose one's essence. Still, as a human woman, she could feel pain. As a mortal woman in love with her man, she must feel the same pain, and loss and grief that any other human woman would feel. Lucifer could take satisfaction in that. At least he could punish her through Tense. Two birds, one stone.

Lucifer smiled and ordered a bottle of champagne and two glasses. Perhaps a little sport before the main event. His phone rang. The final few pieces had been put in place. Everything was ready. This time, this time. Nothing could go wrong. Lucifer surveyed the crowd. The Creator would be watching. The Creator would already know how the afternoon would unfold. There was a certain pleasure, too, in knowing that.

Away across town, Sally and Tense were making their cautious way back. Slowly, inexorably, and by their own volition, blundering deeper and deeper into the trap that had been set for them. Silently, smoothly, the jaws of the snare closed behind. Blocking off escape.

Lucifer sensed Sally and Tense approaching. Far off at present but closing. His mood lifted a little. A young man appeared in the crowd. He was a little above average height but not really tall. He was expensively dressed. Deep blue velvet jacket, crisp white cotton shirt, very tight trousers. He carried himself well. Lucifer knew the type. A snatch of old verse came to mind as Lucifer appraised the scene.

"Ye children of Fashion and Wealth,

With countless indulgences blest,

Remember that indolence prayeth on health – *Ah well*, he thought - A change is as good as a rest."

Lucifer, holding two filled champagned flutes and the bottle, approached the young man through the crowd. It had been a while since his last dalliance with a male of the species. But 'all work and no play' and all that. Why not? Lucifer made his move.

"Please excuse me. You wouldn't by any chance have seen a rather beautiful young man wearing a lovely blue velvet jacket, would you?" The young man looked slightly taken aback but was clearly not about to flee. Lucifer continued.

"I thought, being so tall, you might be able to spot him over the heads of the crowd?"

The young man smiled, "I'm sorry, but other than myself, I can see no one else wearing a blue velvet jacket."

"Well then," Lucifer smiled and handed the young man a glass of champagne, "You'll just have to do."

It was child's play, really. Seduction had become effortless over the centuries. It was not that he especially enjoyed the physical side. It was more the power he could exert, the dominance he could wield. He was able to suppress his disgust, and his body responded readily enough. There was a fleeting moment of pleasure.

There followed a brief courtship, after which Lucifer led the young man into the nearby toilets for a joyless consummation. On returning to the bar area, Lucifer's phone rang. They had been spotted on a train from Cronulla. His informant suggested, given their luggage, that they would be heading for the airport. Lucifer stuffed a slip of paper with the young man's phone number on it into his jacket pocket. It never hurt to recruit. He checked his reflection in a window, brushed away a speck of dirt from his sleeve, straightened his tie and headed to the small roundabout at the bottom of the Opera House stairs. His car would be waiting.

Lucifer was quiet on the trip to the airport. Pensive. The motorway traffic was light. Suburbs and golf courses flashed by. Botany Bay appeared for a moment, expansive and deep blue. In the far distance, testosterone-enriched young men jet-skied and wind-surfed. This was it. The approaching confrontation would be pivotal. Everything would change from this day forward. Such, at least, was his fervent hope. Centuries of planning were coming to their conclusion. Eons in the making. Today he would begin his counterattack.

The war wasn't over. Not by a long shot.

***

But they *were* being followed. Realisation dawned slowly. Not by one person or two but by a string of people. Every walk of life was represented. There were fluoro-wearing tradies, mums with babies, gangs of teenagers, professional types, office workers, beggars, butchers, bakers and candlestick makers, whatever you like. The scale of Lucifer's mobilisation was awe-inspiring. Tense, realising Lucifer's true reach, was struck with fear. Foreboding flooded him. Involuntarily, he shivered. Sally squared her shoulders, finally recognising the years of scheming and planning that must have preceded this moment. Although full comprehension of the depth of his ambition still eluded her, her dawning appreciation of his capabilities left her speechless. She had an inkling of what must now unfold. Silently, unable to face him directly, unable to speak, she reached out and took Tense's hand. It was her fault. She had placed him in this impossible position. It was too late now for him to turn away. It was way too late to run. Perhaps it always had been. Tense had never seen Paris. He would love it. Maybe, if she could just get him there. If she could buy him one good week in the most beautiful city on earth...

Tense, sensing Sally's inner turmoil, wrapped his arm around her. A now familiar gesture, pulling her close, making her safe. Trying to.

Dropping all pretence, Sally spoke, "We will have to give them the slip. We must get away. Give ourselves a bit of breathing space."

"Yes."

"We need to find a way to lose them."

"We are supposed to change at Wolli Creek for the airport line."

"Yes?" Sally waited as Tense explained.

"We can leave the station there. Take a cab. Direct it anywhere."

"Yes. We shouldn't take the first one or one that presents itself to us."

"OK. We'll take the third cab."

"We're becoming paranoid. That is just what he wants. We mustn't lose perspective. He is not all-powerful. Not even close."

"Justified fear is not paranoia. Someone is out to get us."

"True."

The train was only one station away from Wolli Creek. Sally and Tense edged surreptitiously towards the doors.

"We jump out as the doors close. Agreed."

"Agreed." Tense could feel his heart pounding in his chest. For a moment, he wondered if everyone around him could hear it too. The train clattered onto the platform. Guards blew whistles and waved flags. Humanity swirled around them like the tides, first draining away onto the platform, then streaming back into the fast-filling train. The doors began to close. At the very last second, Sally and Tense leapt from the train to the platform. A guard swore at them under his breath. An old aboriginal lady pressed her face to the glass as the train pulled away. Anger and fear written across it. Her phone was already in her hand. She had been given the slip. She had to report in. Shit!

Sally and Tense did not wait for the lift. They ran up the stairs dragging their suitcases behind them. Outside, on the street, two taxis waited. An elderly couple, several paces ahead of them, took the first one. A young man in a business suit raced in front of them and, with the tiniest of apologetic smiles, jumped into the second. Sally and Tense spun around, looking for some other means of escape. A third taxi pulled into the little side road, and Tense ran to it, aiming to flag it down. A young woman seated in the back was paying the driver by credit card.

Sally caught up. She and Tense stood on either side of the taxi. Guarding it, protecting their escape. The young woman gave them an odd look as she got out of the taxi.

"Sorry, they're like gold dust." Sally offered the young woman a smile.

"Whatever."

Quickly they placed their suitcases in the boot and jumped in. Sally in the back, Tense up front with the driver.

"Where too?" The driver, an elderly Sikh gentleman with a sad expression, looked from Tense to Sally, seeking an answer.

"International airport, please." Tense spoke first.

"We're in a bit of a hurry." Sally glanced at her phone as if checking the time.

"No worries. Just five minutes outside the rush hour."

The pair sat in silence as the taxi weaved its way through the back streets and onto the airport approach road.

Sally's phone rang. It was Lucifer.

"Hi. It's me. I couldn't let you go without saying goodbye." Insincerity dripping from every word. "I'm coming to see you off." His tone was suave and polished as always, but any attempt at fellow feeling had gone. There was no effort to build rapport. It was a threat. Plain and simple.

Sally looked across at Tense. She was running out of options. Truth to tell, she had run out of options. Her one hope now was no hope. It was a fool's hope that she could squeeze one fabulous week out of fate if they could just get through security at the airport. God willing. Sally hung up. There was nothing left to say.

"Who was that?"

"Wrong number."

"It was him, wasn't it?"

"Yes. Of course."

They sat in silence as the taxi pulled off the approach road and started down the ramp to the short-stay car park and drop-off.

"Stop. Let us out here." Sally began to open the taxi door. The driver pulled the taxi to a halt, remonstrating all the while.

"You cannot stop here. It's not allowed."

Sally threw a handful of banknotes at him and jumped out. Tense offered an embarrassed smile and followed. The driver released the boot from inside, and they retrieved their suitcases. Tense closed the boot. The taxi driver drove off, shaking his head. Sally and Tense made their way down the last few steps towards the open-air car park. It was some distance to the terminal entrance. They mixed in with the growing throng of travellers, hoping to pass unnoticed.

But they were not unnoticed. Lucifer's car was turning in at the top of the ramp. The runaways stuck out like a sore thumb. Two escapees attempting to go unnoticed. He spotted them easily. Lucifer ordered the driver to stop the car and took his place at the wheel.

CHAPTER 24 – THE AIRPORT

Tense grabbed Sally's arm and led her into the ground floor of the multi-storey short-stay car park. He figured they would be less visible amongst the crush of new arrivals. They made their way around the lifts and escalators to emerge near the pedestrian crossing to the main airport terminal. Glancing furtively right and left, they searched every face. Any one of them could be one of Lucifer's people. No doubt many of them were. They pushed through the crush towards the terminal. Travellers were bunched up on the pavement, waiting for the lights to change so they could walk the last few metres into the airconditioned arrivals hall. From there, an escalator would whisk them up one level to the international departure hall. The mood was mixed, ebullient travellers off on their holidays mingled with forlorn relatives heading back home. There were smiles and laughter and tearful goodbyes. Tense and Sally held back a bit. The lights changed, and people began to cross. Sally and Tense shuffled forward. They hesitated as the lights once more began to change. Then Sally rushed out into the roadway.

"No. Wait. Come back." Tense shouted. People turned and stared. Sally hesitated. Out of the corner of his eye, Tense saw a large black limousine pull out of the queue of traffic halted at the lights. The car mounted the pavement so that two wheels were still on the tarmac and two were not. It began to pick up speed. Sally began to turn and head back to be with Tense.

"No. It's him. He's coming." Tense bellowed. "Keep going. Go back."

Sally turned again as if to cross fully and then, seeing the approaching car, changed her mind once more and began to run towards Tense. The sound of the car's engines at full throttle filled the air. People began to scream. The crowd scattered. Sally was left alone in the middle of the road. Frozen into inaction, watching the oncoming vehicle. Tense, too, watched in horror. And then he acted. Throwing down his suitcase, he ran into the road, pushing Sally backwards. She retreated a few steps before losing her footing and falling backwards onto the kerb. A man ran forward from the other side of the road and pulled her onto the pavement. Tense turned towards the oncoming vehicle. He saw Lucifer through the windscreen, behind the wheel, smiling grimly. Their eyes met. In that instant, Tense realised that there was no hope of escape. He stood straight. Turned towards Sally and smiled. Then the car hit him.

Tense felt his body break. Silence enveloped him. Slow motion. He felt rather than heard the *thump* of the impact, the cracking and sucking of flesh and bone separating. He turned his head to see Sally regain her feet. He saw her running towards him, dread and grief written across her face. And he knew. He had not failed. At that critical moment, when called upon to act, he had acted. He had saved the lives of his wife and child. He had fulfilled his duty. He had found his meaning. And he was satisfied.

Disorientation followed as his body was thrown through the air. Sound and motion returned. Realtime. Sally was holding him, cradling him in her arms. She was speaking. Words came into focus.

"We will see each other again soon, my love. I promise. It will seem like the blink of an eye. You'll hardly notice." Tense nodded.

His sight was failing. Tense felt once again the flickering of reality from one instant to the next. Flashes of being. Flash, flash, flash... Stop.

As Tense died in Sally's arms, grief filled her. Anguish, absolute and limitless flooded her mind. She knew nothing else. There was nothing else. From somewhere nearby, she heard a howl of inconsolable grief and loss. It was coming from her own mouth. And, at the very peak of her pain, she began once more to hear the minds around her. The fear, the terror and the pity of humanity pressed in on her. She felt once more the powers and perspective of her kin rise within her. And, laying Tense's head gently down, she stood, picked up her battered old suitcase, and walked away.

THE END